BASEMENT LEVEL 5:
NEVER SCARED

L R WRIGHT

Basement Level 5: Never Scared

L. R. Wright

Basement Level 5: Never Scared
Copyright @ 2012, 2014, 2020 by L. R. Wright

ISBN: 978-0-9994213-3-8

Elle Writes Boooks, LLC
Ypsilanti, Michigan
www.ElleWright.com

Cover Design:
Sherelle Green

✿ Created with Vellum

Alexa Martinez was raised to believe that murder, deceit, and lies were a part of life. A trained killer, she follows in her father's footsteps, specializing in political assassinations for Martinez Security—contracted through the CIA. She thrives on the power, money, respect, and—most of all—the adrenaline rush. Despite the danger associated with her profession, Alexa strives to give her children a normal life.

But when her past catches up with her, they become pawns in a deadly game of revenge. Operating from a secret base five levels below ground, Alexa struggles to unravel the puzzle, uncovering secrets that will their alter lives forever. Now she must make a choice—is she willing to die to give her children a life outside the bullet proof glass?

To my Friends and Family, I dedicate this to you and thank you for your unwavering support. I appreciate your time, your prayers, and your positive thoughts from the beginning—after I had the "dream".

I dedicate this story to my mother, who taught me the importance of reading and always encouraged me to follow my dreams. You are missed.

To Jason, thank you for loving me and inspiring me to reach for the stars. Thank you for believing in me.

To "the boss", my muse, you've inspired me in more ways than you can imagine!

Acknowledgments

I'm thankful to God, first and foremost. I would be nothing without Him.

To my husband and children, thanks for supporting me through every low point, every success. I love you so much.

To my sista friend, Sheryl Lister, you already know!!!

To Sherelle Green, you rock!

Nicole Falls!!!! Thanks so much for providing a listening ear. I can't even begin to repay you for everything.

To my "Secret Project" squad, thank you so much. You know who you are!

A special shout-out to the amazing readers and awesome writers that I've met on this journey. There would be no "Elle Wright" without your love and encouragement, your enthusiasm and understanding.

Dear Reader

———————

Oh boy, where do I begin.

Basement Level 5 started with a dream. As cliche as it sounds, it did. I dreamed of a cast of characters running from a dangerous situation. I dreamed a mother determined to protect her children at all costs. I dreamed this book.

It's not a romance, it's not an "Elle Wright" book, even though there is a love story within the book. It explores to love between a husband and wife, the love between siblings, the love between a parent and child. It is about the love of family.

At its core, this is the story of a woman who is at a crossroads in her life, a woman who wants to give her children the life she didn't have.

I hope you enjoy the ride!

Love,

Me

www.ellewright.com

Chapter One

NOVEMBER 3, 2011:

THE RAGING storm increased in intensity as the hours crawled slowly by. Violent gusts of wind howled and rocked the huge mansion. Flashes of lightning filtered through the closed blinds, followed closely by loud, crashing thunder. Tree branches scratched against the roof as the pounding rain battered the house.

Alexa had just started to relax when she heard a distinctly different sound outside. *Gunshot?* She bolted upright on the sofa and listened intently. Standing up, she walked to the window to investigate. Suddenly, there was a loud knock at the door. She started for the door then hesitated. Another knock sounded a few minutes later. Slowly continuing to the door, she peered through the peephole. The man looked familiar, similar in height and build to one of the newer guards, but she couldn't be sure. Alexa paused before finally opening the door. A cold chill ran up her spine.

The stranger smiled at her, but it didn't reach his eyes. "Are you Alexa Martinez?"

Sweeping her gaze over him, she catalogued every detail about his face, his haircut, and his attire in case she needed to remember it later. She scanned the immediate area behind him, then nodded.

He held up a wallet sporting a gold badge. "I need to speak with you."

In the middle of a severe storm? She frowned. "About?"

A flash of irritation swept across his face, but disappeared quickly. "Can I come in? I have some questions for you."

Her grip on the doorknob tightened, turning her knuckles white. "I'm sure my lawyer would like to be present for any questions you have for me. Come back tomorrow morning and I'll make sure he's here."

She tried to push the door closed, but he stopped it with the toe of his boot. "Mrs. Martinez, this is official business. You need to open the door."

Without warning, she kicked him in the shin. When he jerked his foot back, she shoved the door closed with her hip and slammed the deadbolt. He pounded on the door, yelling at her to open it. She fled to the back of the house and rushed into her daughter Kyleigh's bedroom.

"Come on, Ky," she whispered, shaking her shoulder. "Let's go. We have to get out of here."

The sound of something heavy ramming against the front door caused the nine-year-old to jump. Alexa's four-year-old son, Alex, raced into the room. "What's going on, Mommy? Somebody hit the door."

Alexa pressed her finger to her lips. The children nodded and followed her into the long hallway. She darted over to a family picture hanging on the wall and shoved it aside. When she pushed a button, a panel in the wall opened, revealing a secret door and a hidden set of stairs.

The children held tightly on to her arms. "Mama, I don't want to go down there. It's too dark," Ky whispered.

Alexa bent down to eye level with the children. "Babies, you need to go downstairs. I am right behind you."

They all jumped at the sound of glass breaking and wood cracking. She gently nudged the children toward the stairs.

Grabbing for her cell phone, she found her pocket empty. *Shit!* She urged them down the stairs. "Go now! *Rapidamente!*"

The children hurried down the stairway like they were told. Waiting until they were halfway down, Alexa raced back to the couch.

The stranger, along with a few more men, barged into the living room, taking the front door off its hinges as they pushed their way inside. They spotted her and shouted.

She grabbed her cell phone, dashed into the hallway, and scanned the dark staircase. Alex was still there, but no Ky.

"Ky," she shouted. "Come now!"

Ky ran from her bedroom, with a little pink bag in her hand just as the men rounded the corner.

Fear ran through Alexa's veins as one of the men tried to grab her daughter. Ky was quick, though, and jumped into the stairwell...

———

ALEXA WOKE from the nightmare with sweat running down her face. She patted her front pants pocket for her

3

cell phone and found it there, snug and safe. Both children were asleep, tired and worn out from playing all day.

Running a hand through her long hair, she sighed. After the recent threats to her life, they'd taken extreme precautions to ensure her safety. The safe house was secluded, the location a secret even to her closest family. *Everything's fine.*

The TV was still turned to her favorite soap opera. She glanced around the room, making sure the house was calm. The only sound was coming from the TV and the wind howling outside. She pressed the power button on the remote, pitching the room into silence and darkness, and then wandered to the window to check outside. *That's strange. Where is the guard normally assigned to the front of the house?*

The storm had gotten worse since she dozed off, hurtling leaves and branches across the yard. Her eyes searched for the guard, but the weather prevented her from seeing anything clearly. She leaned her forehead against the window, closed her eyes, and sighed. *Calm down, Alexa. He's probably checking the grounds.* When she opened her eyes, she noticed a sudden flash of light in the yard.

She stood there for a minute and waited for the security guard to appear. There was no sign of him. Worried, she peered out into the darkness, hoping to see where the light was coming from. A figure, all in black, raced past the window. It wasn't her guard.

Oh Hell! She dropped the blinds and jumped into action, charging to the front door to make sure the deadbolt was locked. It was. The house was dark, but she knew every inch of it and was able to move quickly. Running to the side door, she secured the bolt on that one as well. That was when she heard the first knock.

Leaving all the lights out, she woke both children and

urged them not to make a sound. As they followed her into the long hallway, shouting erupted from outside the house.

Turning to Ky, Alexa struggled to keep her voice calm. "Ky, this is serious. Someone is trying to get in the house. I need you to look out for your little brother."

Her heart broke at the look of terror on the young girl's face. "It's okay, baby." She squeezed Ky's hand. "It's going to be okay."

Ky grabbed Alex's hand. Alexa turned to her son. "Baby, I need you to listen to me. Don't let go of your sister's hand. You hear me?"

He nodded.

With a surreal sense of déjà vu, Alexa shoved the family picture aside, uncovering a padlock. She punched in a secret code and opened the hidden panel, revealing a small elevator. The sound of wood and glass breaking echoed through the house.

Sara, the nanny, was upstairs in the attic, studying for her exams. Alexa had to get to her, but first she needed to get to Nicholas in the basement. She pushed "B" on the elevator wall. The doors closed, trapping them inside.

As they descended to the basement, she thought about Chase. He was one of her closest friends, her family. If something happened to him... *Where is he? He should have been here by now.* Once the door opened, she nudged the children out.

"Nicholas!" she shouted, heading toward the security room.

Asleep at his computer, Nicholas jerked awake. "What's going on?"

She rolled her eyes. He was supposed to be monitoring the grounds. She eyed the security cameras, noticed at least four men coming into the house, and sighed. "There are strangers in the house. We need to get out of here. Chase

5

should've been here by now. I don't know why he isn't, but we need to warn him. I don't want him to get ambushed."

Nicholas glanced at the children. "We'll call him," he said softly as he grabbed a cell phone. "What about Sara?"

"We have to get to her."

"Did you take the stairs down here?" he asked.

"I didn't want to take the chance. I was closer to the elevator, so I took that."

"Okay, let's go up in the elevator." He grabbed his gun off of the desk and placed it in his back holster.

Thunder roared in the sky. The kids jumped. Alexa bent down to their level. "It's going to be okay! Come on."

She hated that her children had to go through this, but she knew Ky was a strong, capable girl. She would protect Alex to the death if she had to, and Alex would protect her as much as he could.

They all raced back to the elevator and rushed inside, pressing the "A" button. Nicholas dialed his phone then shook his head. Apparently, Chase wasn't answering.

Sara was lying across her bed with her iPod on when they got to the attic. She jolted when Nicholas touched her arm. "Oh my God! You scared me." She scanned the faces of the group. "What's wrong?"

"Intruders," Alexa whispered. She was afraid she wouldn't be heard above the rumble of the thunder, but she didn't dare speak any louder. Out of the corner of her eye, she saw Nicholas with the phone to his ear again. "We won't be able to get out of the house," she continued. "We have to go to B5."

Sara's eyes widened, but she grabbed her backpack and followed Alexa and Nicholas to where the children waited, huddled by the door.

Nicholas yanked out a silver key, hurried to an old curtain on the far side of the wall, and unlocked the door hidden behind it. "We have to take the back stairs," he said softly, then glancing at Alexa, he added, "I still haven't been able to reach Chase."

Alexa closed her eyes. The last thing she needed was to be worried about Chase. He would walk right into the trap if they couldn't get in touch with him. The sudden ringing of her phone pierced the silence. She yanked it out of her pocket. "Hello."

"Alexa?" Chase demanded.

"Thank God!" She let out a sigh of relief. "Where are you?"

"I'm on my way," he replied, but the static made him hard to hear. "I saw that Nicholas had called me. Is everything okay?"

"No. We have uninvited guests and they're not friendly. I didn't see much, but there are at least four of them. There may be more. I don't know. They're all over the house, though. We're up in the attic and heading down to B5."

Chase cursed. "Hurry down there. I'll be there in a few."

"Dro's flight doesn't land for a few minutes." She swallowed past a lump in her throat, imagining how her husband would react once he learned what had occurred. "I—"

"Don't worry. I'll make all the necessary calls. Concentrate on the kids right now."

She hung up the phone, setting it on vibrate only. "Let's go."

"Is he going to call?" Nicholas asked.

"Yes. We need to hurry."

He opened the door. The walls of the staircase behind it were still unfinished, the steps uncarpeted. Once they were all on the landing, he pulled the curtain

7

closed, shut the door behind him, and locked it with the key.

"Don't touch anything," Alexa told the children. "And stay close. Ky, remember to hold Alex's hand."

They scrambled down the staircase as fast as the children could go. Sara held on to Ky's hand while Nicholas brought up the rear. As they made their way down several flights of stairs, shouts could be heard in other parts of the house. Apparently, the men wouldn't stop until they had searched every inch of it.

Chapter Two

ALEJANDRO WAS SPEEDING down Interstate 81 when the phone rang. His flight had landed early and he was ready to get home. The rain had slowed down, so he was making good time. "What?" he answered, his eyes on the stretch of road ahead.

Chase's voice filtered through the Bluetooth speaker. "Dro, it's me."

Dro noted the edge to his friend's voice. "What's up?"

"There's a problem at the house."

Dro's stomach rolled as dozens of possible scenarios came to mind, each one worse than the other. Clenching his jaw, he asked, "What kind of problem?" He switched lanes and picked up speed.

"Unwanted guests," Chase said.

"Shit." Dro slammed his fist against the steering wheel. "Is she...?" He couldn't finish the thought.

"She's fine. I talked to her myself."

"The kids?"

"They're good. Alexa doesn't know the exact number, but she saw four men enter the house."

Dro let out a ragged breath, as relief washed over him. "Where are you?"

"I'm headed there now," Chase replied. "I'll go down through the garage."

"Is Nicholas there?"

"Yes, he's with them. We need to contact everyone." Chase sighed heavily. "There's no way anyone should have known the safe house's location, let alone get close enough to break in."

Dro met his sister Ariana's worried gaze. Then he glanced at his twelve-year-old niece, Alana, asleep in the backseat. "Call Kendrick and I'll call Lei. Get there now and make sure no one sees you."

"I'm right around the corner. Hurry."

KENDRICK YANKED his ringing phone out of his pocket. It was his brother, Chase. "What?" His frantic wife and children were screaming, making it hard for him to hear.

"Kendrick, what's going on? Is that gunfire?"

"We have a problem—unwanted guests with big guns. I'm trying to get Kara and the kids out of here." He paused to shoot at their attackers. "Shit! Come on, Kara, grab the kids and let's go." He put the phone back to his ear. "We're headed out to the garage. I hit one of them, but there are more. Where are you?"

"I'm on my way to the safe—"

"Kara, try to calm the kids down," Kendrick shouted. "I can't hear."

"I'm headed to the safe house," Chase continued. "Alexa has her own share of these bastards. They are headed to B5. Come quickly. Dro will meet you there."

"Okay," Kendrick yelled as he unloaded a few more

rounds. He didn't bother hanging up as he started the engine of his Lincoln Navigator and backed out of the driveway.

"Get down!" He glanced at his terrified wife and kids and took a moment to reload before returning fire on the relentless strangers. Bullets whizzed by the truck and bounced off the glass. Thank God, he'd invested in the special bullet proof glass. Unrolling the window slightly, he fired his semi-automatic pistol through the opening.

Then he screeched around the corner on two wheels and sped away, watching his rearview mirrors to make sure he didn't have any followers.

LEI LOUNGED ON THE COUCH, drinking a glass of scotch and watching a movie with his wife, Makayla, who was lying next to him.

His cell phone rang. "What's up?"

"We have problems." Dro's voice was eerily calm. "Some men broke into the safe house."

Lei jolted in surprise, dropping his glass to the floor and startling his wife. "Is Alexa okay?"

"Chase talked to her. She and the children are heading to B5. I have Ari and Alana with me. Chase is on his way there. I need you to call Pop and then get there as soon as possible. Meet me at the garage."

Lei hung up the phone and turned to a wide-eyed Makayla. "You need to get up. We have to get out of here."

"What's going on?"

"I'll tell you in the car. We have to go. Now."

She rushed to the bedroom and came back with her purse.

Lei dialed his mother, Veronica. While the phone rang, he packed his laptop into a briefcase. "Ma, I'm coming over," he said when she answered. "Pack a bag and be ready when I get there. Call Pop and tell him we have a problem at the safe house."

"Is Alexa okay?"

"She's fine, Ma, but we don't know what's going on. I'm on my way, be ready." He snapped the phone shut and hurried to the garage.

The car was already running when he charged out of the house. Makayla had started it. He jumped in, backed out of the driveway, and sped down the street. After a few minutes, he looked at Makayla. "It's going to be okay."

She stared into the night. "Is it ever going to be okay? What happened to Alexa?"

"Someone learned the safe house's location and broke in. She had to take the children to B5. But she'll be all right."

"You always say that, Lei. But what if she's not? The fact is no one should have known where she was. She didn't even tell *me* when I talked to her the other day. Obviously, someone is hell-bent on getting to her. First, someone attempts to snatch her from the grocery store. Now, she's getting ambushed at a location very few people knew about? And you're telling me everything's okay?"

"She's fine, Makayla. Alexa can take care of herself." He tried to stay calm, but it was harder as time passed. He hoped he was right. Although he knew she could indeed take care of herself, she was still his baby sister.

Makayla didn't say anything else, and they rode the rest of the way in silence. When they pulled up in front of his mother's house, Veronica barreled out the front door with a black bag on her shoulder.

"I called your father," she said as she slid into her seat.

"He's going to catch a plane home as soon as possible. He's worried about Alexa."

Lei looked at his mother in the rearview mirror. "Pop shouldn't worry. He knows Alexa can take care of herself. She's fine."

Veronica's dark eyes welled with tears as she sputtered, "But—the children—she hasn't—"

"Ma, don't. She's fine."

———

DRO'S DEATH-GRIP on the steering wheel had turned his knuckles white. What was happening at the safe house? If any harm had come to Alexa and the children...

He couldn't stop thinking about his family. He was farther away from the safe house than anyone else. What if he didn't get there in time?

Ari had been watching him without comment. She placed a hand on Dro's arm. "*Hermano, todo estara bien.*"

"You don't *know* that it's going to be all right," Dro growled. He kept his eyes on the road, and willed himself not to think of worse-case scenarios.

"B5 is secure," Ari said. "And we'll figure the rest out when we get there."

"I hope so, Ari. Because if she's not okay..." He couldn't finish the thought. Alexa had to be all right. If she wasn't, there would be hell to pay.

Chapter Three

HER HEART THUNDERING in her ears, Alexa herded everyone down the dusty, narrow staircase. Who could have known where they were? Only a handful of people knew the location of this safe house, which meant someone close to them had betrayed them.

The children were silent. Sounds from above told her the men were still in the house. They were obviously searching—probably destroying everything of value—and wouldn't stop until they got what they came for. Fortunately, Chase had thought of all that when he designed the elaborate tunnel system and hidden stairways.

Once they reached the landing at the bottom of the stairwell, she peered down the long, narrow hallway on her left then turned and headed that way. "Are you okay?" she asked, glancing back at the kids.

They answered her with nods, but didn't speak.

When she came to a dead end, Alexa pulled a brass key out of her pocket. Smoothing her hand across the wall, she hunted for the ridge Chase had told her about. Once she found it, she lifted it, revealing a keyhole. She inserted the key and turned it.

The wall slid open.

Alexa walked through the opening then looked for another keyhole. Once everyone was on this side, she used the key again and the wall closed.

What a difference from the dungeon-like hallway! The freshly painted walls and the plush carpet seemed strangely out of place, considering they were in an underground bunker.

Alex tugged on her shirt. "Mama, where are we going?"

"We're going on an adventure and we're almost there." She picked him up and headed down another corridor then down two more short flights of stairs.

A steel door blocked their way. Using the same key, she unlocked this door and heard a short beep. The lights flickered on and fresh cool air flowed from an overhead vent.

They stepped inside. Nicholas pushed the door closed. It locked automatically with a loud clang.

Turning around, Alexa sighed deeply. The foyer was decorated like their house—ceramic tile, coat hanger, and a half bath off to the side.

"Wow," Ky whispered as she took in her surroundings.

"It's nice, huh? Uncle Chase did well, didn't he?" Alexa shifted her weight because Alex was squirming in her arms, wide-eyed and eager to explore. She lowered him to the floor.

Chase had thought of everything when he designed this place. Alexa wasn't surprised, though. He'd always been a calm and dependable friend. Over to the left, there was a hallway leading to a great room. The huge sectional in the middle and the big screen TV were just her style.

She toured the rest of the bunker. Connected to the great room, the full kitchen boasted dark cherry wood cabinets and stainless steel appliances. He had even put in a breakfast bar. No wonder Chase had been busy on this project for so long. He'd spared no expense to make this place feel just like home.

B5 was located five floors underground with plenty of living space, five bedrooms, lots of bathrooms, and several other rooms that were sure to come in handy. Chase had outfitted it with a state of the art security room, laundry room, and even a playroom for the children. The only problem was the lack of windows.

"There's a security room to the right with surveillance equipment," Nicholas said. "I'm going to go see if I can get things up and running. Once I do, I should be able to see what's going on in the house."

Although she was relieved they were safe, Alexa couldn't help but be irritated. Sure, it was nice that B5 was available to them in times like this, but it was a basement—an exceptional basement, but still...

The fact that she didn't know what was going on also annoyed her. She glanced at her children. Thank God they were safe. The need to hold them overtook her thirst for answers. She grabbed them and hugged them close.

"Where's Papa?" Ky asked.

Alexa smiled and stroked her daughter's long black hair. "He should be here soon. No te preocupes."

Sara cleared her throat. "How long do we have to be here?"

Alexa paused. She hated that Sara was in this situation, hiding in a basement when she should be enjoying college life with her friends. But Alexa wouldn't lie to her. "I don't know. I wish I had a better answer for you. Hopefully, once Chase gets here, I'll be able to tell you more. I'm sorry you have to be here at all."

"Don't apologize. I love you all. You've been like my family for so long. There's nowhere else I'd rather be. Do you need me to do anything?"

Alexa shook her head and sat down, hoping to keep the tears in her eyes from falling. "We should be good."

"Are we going to be safe?" Alex asked, climbing on her lap.

She ran her hand over his dark curls and down his plump, golden cheek. "We're going to be okay, baby. You know I wouldn't let anything happen to you, right? And neither will your Papa. We'll always protect you."

Briefly, she wondered if she should even make that promise. She'd told the kids not to worry earlier, but there were no guarantees at this point. Forcing her mind from such thoughts, she pulled both kids and Sara into a hug.

CHASE TURNED his headlights off and drove into a remote garage, hidden behind a wall of trees about a mile from the massive estate. Turning the engine off, he jumped out of the car, hurried around to the backseat, and yanked the door open.

"Wake up, CJ," he whispered, nudging him. "We're here."

CJ, his eleven-year-old son, wiped his eyes and peered up at him. "Where are we?"

"We're at a safe place. Come on, we need to hurry."

Once CJ climbed out of the car, Chase rushed to the garage window and scanned the grounds. The rain had picked up again, which reduced visibility to almost nil.

He wondered who had found the safe house and how. Sighing deeply, he crouched and lifted an old rug, uncovering a trap door. He pulled out a key, unlocked the door, and stared down the long, dark stairway. Motioning CJ to enter, he followed the boy down the stairs, locking the heavy trap door behind him.

At the bottom of the stairs were two tunnels. Grabbing CJ's hand, Chase took the tunnel on the right. The passageways were clean, dry, and well lit.

He had made sure of that when he built them. Being underground this deep had its limitations, but his background in construction and architecture proved invaluable when designing B5.

His parents were safe in Canada, and he was glad he didn't have to worry about them. He had called his father to let him know not to come back to the States unless Chase gave him the "all clear".

However, Kendrick was another story. Chase couldn't help but worry about him. His brother was smart, but he didn't have any back up. Not to mention, he had the added distraction of trying to protect his wife and kids. And although Nicholas was with Alexa, Chase worried about her most of all. He hoped she'd made it to B5 safely.

After about a half a mile, he and CJ came to a wall. Chase swiped his hand over the wall, and found the hidden ridge. He pulled out a green key, inserted it in the keyhole under the ridge, turned it, and the wall opened.

The smell of fresh paint invaded his nostrils as he walked through the door with CJ right behind him. B5 had two entrances and this one was connected to the laundry room.

He heard a gasp and spun around. Alexa stood in the doorway. Her eyes were red and puffy, and her hair was in a simple, but messy ponytail. Her clothes were dusty, probably from one of the unfinished hallways leading to B5. But she was alive.

CJ broke away from him and ran into her open arms. "Hi," he squealed.

Alexa hugged him tightly. "I'm so glad you're here safely. I missed you." She gave CJ a big kiss and pointed toward a door. "The kids are through there and past the kitchen. They're watching a movie. Go on in and I'll be right along."

His son ran from the room, calling for Ky and Alex. Chase smiled at Alexa as she rushed into his arms.

"I was so worried," she cried. "I prayed you and CJ wouldn't walk into an ambush. I'm so happy you got here safely."

ALEXA WANTED to hold onto Chase forever, but she realized they needed to talk about what had happened. She pulled back and kissed him on the cheek.

"I'm fine," he said. "You don't look so good, though."

She nodded absently, wiping the tears that had spilled onto her cheeks. "I was scared. I won't lie about that. It's a good thing you finally finished this place." It still amazed her that the construction of B5 had been completed just two short months ago.

"You did well." He ran a finger down the side of her face. "Everyone should be on their way here."

She nodded and pulled him into the great room. When they entered, the kids ran up to him, wanting hugs.

Chase knelt down to their level. "Are you guys okay?"

Ky and Alex nodded.

"It took a long time to get here," Ky said. "But we held hands the whole time."

"Nicholas is in the security room getting things up and running," Alexa informed him.

"I'm glad he was here with you," Chase said. He patted Alex on the head and squeezed Ky's hand.

Alexa couldn't help but smile. "How about you three go get a bath and put on fresh pajamas?" she told the kids. "Sara, can you help them out?"

Alex frowned. "Mama, we don't have any pajamas."

She smiled. "If you go into the room with the big bunk beds and look in one of the drawers, I'm sure you will find some. You'll also find clothes, toys, and games. That's going to be your room for a bit."

Alex cheered and proceeded to pull Sara toward the room with the big bunk beds. Ky and CJ followed.

Once the children disappeared from sight, Alexa pulled Chase into another hug.

Chapter Four

PARKING NEAR THE ESTATE, Kendrick tapped his fingers on the steering wheel. The kids and Kara had settled down on the drive over, but he knew they were all scared. Gunfire and high-speed chases weren't an everyday occurrence, even considering his past. He peered at his wife, sitting in the back seat, biting her nails, with both kids tucked into her sides.

He sighed and wondered what he could say that would make this all better. *Nothing.* He heard a noise and immediately tensed up. Pulling his gun, he checked his rearview mirrors. Lei's black Lincoln MKT pulled up behind him, lights off. Ten minutes later, Dro's black Cadillac Escalade stopped behind Lei.

"Okay, kids," Kendrick said, turning to his children. "We need to be extra quiet. When you get out of the car, go straight to Uncle Dro's truck, you hear me?" When they nodded, he unlocked the doors. He waited for them to get out before he hopped out and followed them to Dro's truck.

Dro jumped out of his truck and headed toward

Kendrick and Lei. "We need to move fast—through the garage," he said. "We don't want to be seen. Kids, remember, no talking."

Kendrick took up the rear and followed Dro down a dark path, through the trees to the remote garage where Chase's car was parked.

INSIDE B5, Alexa struggled to hold it together. Just thinking about what could have happened made her tremble with fear—and anger. "I guess we should talk now," Alexa told Chase.

He pulled her into another hug. "Alexa, it's okay. We're safe."

She gripped his shirt. "I know Chase, but not everyone is safe yet. I won't feel better until they're all here."

"They're on the way. No worries." He swiped a thumb under her eye, catching a stray tear. "Listen, why don't you take a shower and get a change of clothes on? The others should be here shortly."

"That sounds good." He was right. It didn't make any sense to sit there worrying when there was nothing she could do. She turned and headed toward her room.

A blast of cool air hit her as she walked in. She looked around, still in awe over everything Chase had done. No matter how real this situation was, she just couldn't believe they were actually in B5. When the idea first came up all those years ago, she thought it was impossible, but Chase had made it work—like he always did. That was one of the things she loved about him. Still, B5 was like life insurance —it was great to have it if she needed it, but she'd hoped she would never have to use it.

This wasn't the first time she'd had to hide from danger. As a child, her father had shipped her off to different remote locations whenever there was a threat of danger or violence relating to the Martinez Organization. The family business's success didn't come from baking cookies.

Those who dared to compete with the company were met with murder and mayhem. Even those who had branched out into the more legitimate Martinez Security, like her immediate family had, weren't safe from the violence caused by the Martinez Organization's activities.

The question was—were their attackers here because of something the security personnel had done or because of someone in the other part of the family organization?

She walked into the master bathroom, stripping her dirty clothes to the floor as she went. She turned on the shower and waited until steam filled the room. Stepping in, she leaned against the tile and let the water flow over her body.

CHASE CHECKED on the kids then headed to the security room. Nicholas was busy at the computer. He stood up when Chase walked in. "Glad to see you. We were worried."

Chase nodded. "Have you been able to get the cameras up?"

"They're just running through their startup procedures now. It's a good thing there was nothing important on the computers in the house."

"A very good thing," Chase agreed. Once Kendrick arrived, he could deal with the computer situation, since that was his specialty. "The sooner we can get those cameras up, the better. The others should be here shortly. In the meantime, what the hell happened?"

"Well—"

A shrill alarm interrupted Nicholas' explanation. He stepped into the hall with Chase right behind him. Logically, Chase knew it had to be the others, but he was still on edge. He waited cautiously, his hand on his gun.

When Lei walked into the large great room, Chase let out a breath he didn't realize he was holding. As the others streamed in quietly, Ky, Alex, and CJ came out of their rooms. They ran up to their Uncle Lei and gave him big hugs.

Dro appeared last. Chase finally took his hand off his gun and smiled at the sight of his *family*.

DRO GRIPPED the phone against his ear and tried to listen to Alexa's father on the other end. "Pop, I can't really hear you because I'm underground. Chase will be there when your plane lands." He hung up just as Ky and Alex latched on to him, clinging to his legs. CJ followed suit shortly after.

Dro bent down to address his son. "What's up, Alex?"

Alex grabbed his outstretched hand. "I had pajamas in my room, and games."

Dro tousled his hair. "Good. Did you take care of Mama?"

"Uh-huh," Alex replied, his head held high. "And I held Ky's hand the whole time."

Dro reached out to stroke Ky's cheek. "You took care of your brother?"

She nodded, standing taller and looking straight into

his eyes. "Yes. Mama said not to let go of him, and I didn't."

"Good." Dro pulled her into a hug. "Can you, Alana, and CJ make sure the little kids don't get too out of control? It's late and it's going to be time for bed soon. I love you, baby girl," he added in Spanish. "And you, too, son."

"I love you too," Ky said, wrapping her arms around him again.

Alex nodded his agreement and jumped into his father's arms for a quick embrace before running off with Ky to help get the other kids settled.

Dro looked over at Chase. "Where is she?"

"She's in the shower."

Dro walked into the kitchen and pulled a six pack of beer from the fridge. He turned to find Chase standing behind him. Handing over a cold beer, he asked, "Have we gotten the cameras up yet?"

"Not quite. Nicholas is still working on it."

After making sure everyone was occupied, Dro asked Kendrick, Chase, and Lei to join him in the security room. They all took a seat in front of the still picture-less monitors.

Kendrick set his beer on the counter. "What the hell is going on? I had about seven men come at me tonight with serious gun play. One of my kids could've been hit."

Dro pulled his eyes from the uninformative monitors. "Whoever planned this knows too much," he said, pounding his fist on the table. "Nicholas, I want everyone under my employment checked out. This has to be nipped in the bud as soon as possible."

Nicholas nodded and began punching keys on the computer. "You got it, Dro."

Kendrick patted Dro on the back. "Okay, *jefe*, now what?"

Dro cringed at the name *jefe*. It meant "the boss". He had hoped no one would have to use that name again. When they were younger, it was a harmless way for his friends to address him. As they grew into adulthood, he used the moniker to conduct certain Martinez business until he felt it wasn't necessary anymore.

Dro narrowed his eyes at Kendrick. "I want them found and handled. They come into my house; they walk right into the barrel of my shotgun. I'll stop at nothing to ensure my family's safety."

Kendrick nodded. "Then let's get to work. Since, there's no telling how long these assholes are going to be ransacking the safe house, we should wait to make a move at dawn. They'll probably be gone by then."

"I agree," Chase said. "The cameras are up—pictures anyway."

"How long before we get sound?" Dro asked.

"I'm working on it now." Nicholas frowned. "Kendrick, can you give me a hand?"

Kendrick traded seats with Nicholas and tapped at the keys. Without looking away from the computer, he addressed the group. "The attack on my house was a red herring. We all know who the real target is. It's time she dealt with that."

Silence echoed in the room. Dro clenched his fists. It may have been easier to believe otherwise after the grocery store incident two weeks ago, but now they had no choice. Alexa was the target and they needed to figure out who was after her and why.

Chapter Five

ALEXA SAT ON HER BED, her hair wrapped in a towel. A soft knock on the door penetrated her thoughts. She pulled her thick terry cloth robe around her. "Come in."

"Alexa?" Veronica called, poking her head in the door.

"Hi, Ma!"

Veronica rushed to embrace her daughter. "I was very worried about you," she said and held on tighter. "When Lei called, I couldn't stand it. I called your father earlier. He's on the plane now."

"No!" Alexa pulled back to look into her mother's expressive brown eyes. "Daddy shouldn't be coming back right now. It's not safe."

"You know there's nowhere else he would consent to be. He has always protected you before, and he'll continue to do so until his dying breath."

"I guess you're right." Alexa bowed her head, tears escaping from her eyes. "I feel the same way about my children."

"I love you, Alexa," Veronica told her, wiping the tears from her cheeks.

"I love you too, Ma." She couldn't help but admire her mother. The years had been hard on her, but she was still beautiful, her Native American heritage showing in her high cheekbones and exotic features. She had beautiful, caramel-colored skin, and her jet black hair hung long and straight.

Veronica squeezed her hand. "Get some rest. I'm going to check on the others."

As her mother walked away, Alexa plopped down on the edge of the bed. When she heard the door close, she looked down at her feet and smiled as she squished her toes into the plush carpet. Chase had thought of everything. He knew she needed a carpet plush enough that she could run her toes through it.

At the faint creak of the door, she closed her eyes. The warmth of his presence filled her senses. She didn't need to see Dro to know he was there. She looked up into his steely-gray orbs. Her gaze moved on to travel over his six-foot-three-inch frame—a truly gorgeous sight.

Her husband.

Her Love.

DRO GAZED at his precious wife.

"Do the kids know you're here?" she asked.

He nodded and stared into her gorgeous dark eyes. She looked tired, but as beautiful as always. "Come here."

As she slipped into his waiting arms, he pulled her close, afraid to let her go. The smell of fresh citrus filled his nostrils. He unraveled the towel from her hair. When the dark, curly locks tumbled down, he ran his fingers through the thick waves.

"Look at me," he urged.

She complied. His eyes never left hers as he trailed a thumb down her cheek. Then he brushed the fingers of one hand over her full bottom lip and tightened his hold on her hair with the other.

"I missed you," she said, burrowing into his embrace.

He tilted his head back, drinking in the sight of her. When he'd gotten the call from Chase, it felt as if his heart had been ripped from his chest. The thought of her and his children in danger had made his blood run cold. If something had happened to them, he wouldn't have stopped until he'd ripped every last person responsible to shreds.

"Dro?"

He rested his forehead against hers and closed his eyes. "I don't know what I would have done if something had happened to you." Caressing her face with both hands, he whispered, "I love you, *mi corazón*."

"Dro..." His name came out in a breathless whisper.

"Shhh. No words, baby. I just need to feel you," he murmured against her lips. "Let me love you."

Tenderly, he brushed his lips against hers then deepened the kiss, demanding that she open to his probing tongue. When her lips parted, he held her face in his hands and ravaged her mouth.

She tugged at his shirt, shoving it up and caressing his skin. His stomach quivered under her roaming hands and a low groan escaped his throat.

He only broke off for an instant to breathe before he went back for more, crushing his lips to hers before taking her bottom lip into his mouth. She gasped as his teeth nipped her lip, but he quickly soothed the soft bite with his tongue.

They fell back on the bed with him straddling her legs.

She pulled his shirt over his head, breaking the kiss, but he wouldn't be deterred.

He immediately recaptured her lips, using just the right amount of tongue and teeth he knew would drive her into a frenzy. Placing his hands on either side of her head, he made love to her mouth.

Finally, he broke the kiss and blazed a trail along her jaw to ear as he slowly untied her heavy robe. Pressing his mouth against her ear, he nipped at the sensitive spot beneath her ear lobe and whispered, "*Te quiero, te necesito, te amo.*"

He knew she loved it when he spoke to her in Spanish, so he repeated his affection for her over and over, telling her how badly he wanted her, how much he needed her, and loved her.

"Dro, please…" She raked her fingernails over his back, and he hissed in sweet pain.

He stared down at her. "So beautiful." Her mouth was red and swollen from his kisses and a blush was beginning to overtake her golden skin.

Dro couldn't get enough of her, he couldn't stop touching her. He moved his right hand to the edge of the robe and slowly pulled it off her shoulder. Leaning down, he brushed his lips across her collarbone. As she pulled her arms out of the robe, he turned his attention to her breasts, nipping and sucking until she was a writhing bundle of need.

Alexa fiddled with his belt, unbuttoned his pants, and slid them past his hips in one smooth motion. He kicked them off the rest of the way, along with his underwear, and then shifted until he rested between her legs.

He brushed a gentle kiss over her swollen lips, as he inched inside her, enjoying the soft purr that escaped her mouth. He loved her to distraction. Everything about her made him want to do better, be better. For her.

"I'll always love you," he whispered through the emotion that seemed to overtake him when she was wrapped around him, when she let him love her this way. Leaning his forehead against hers, he closed his eyes. "Always, Alexa."

Soon, he set a pace of intense lovemaking—slow and tender, fast and deep. Dro was so caught up in her, in the way they moved together, he couldn't think straight. He couldn't hear anything but her frenzied gasps and hoarse cries. He could see nothing but her.

He relished every minute, every second of their love-making. He didn't know when the next time would come, and a small part of him feared he might never get another opportunity.

He bit her earlobe lightly. "*Te amo.*"

"I love you too, baby," she whispered.

Dro bumped her nose with his before taking her lips in a long, sensual kiss. Alexa ran one finger down the side of his face and then caressed his cheek with her hand.

Bright lights pricked his vision and he felt himself unraveling. She squeezed his hips with her legs. He fell over the cliff, spilling himself inside her. Her walls tightened around him as she shattered with him, calling out his name.

MAKING love to Dro was an adventure all in itself, Alexa thought as she lay next to him. He was an amazing lover. That had not changed in all the years they had been together. From the first time when she was seventeen, to now, he had always set her heart on fire, giving her exactly what she wanted every time.

"*Te amo,*" he repeated against her hair.

"I love you, too." She brushed the stubble on his jaw with her thumb. She couldn't remember a time when she hadn't loved him. Of course, this was the wrong time to be taking time out for this, but she didn't know when they would have another chance.

He pulled her close. "I was so scared, baby."

She traced small circles on his chest with her finger. "I know. But we're okay."

"What happened?"

"I had a bad dream," she said, sitting up, although she loved the feel of Dro's hand stroking her back. "When I woke up, I decided to look outside. I looked for the guard. I didn't see him, but I did see a strange man dressed in all black. The house was dark, so I don't think he saw me. I woke the kids, and we came down here."

"Ky told me she held Alex's hand the whole time."

She smiled. "She did, although Alex was surprisingly calm, just like you."

He laughed softly.

"Everything was so surreal," she continued. "We took the elevator down to the basement to get Nicholas, and he was asleep."

"Asleep?"

"Yes. I was so irritated with him. If I was younger, I probably would've kicked his ass. If he'd been watching the damn security monitors, maybe this could've been avoided."

"I'll have to talk to him about his sleeping on the job. It doesn't sit right with me either. Which staircase did you use from the attic?" he asked, in an abrupt change of subject.

"The hidden set behind the curtain. I know Chase told

me not to use them yet because they weren't finished, but we didn't have any choice."

"Were the kids scared?"

She sighed, thinking of the frightened looks on their faces. "They were. And Sara was terrified, especially when I told her where we were going. Everything worked great, though. All the walls and doors worked. I have to give Chase another hug and thank him for giving me such good instructions."

Dro ran his fingers through her hair and down her back again. She lay back on his chest as he pulled a blanket around them.

"We got here and Chase came shortly after with CJ," she said. "I was so worried, Dro. I hate to think what would have happened if that dream hadn't woken me."

"Me, too." He kissed forehead, then her nose. "My life would have been over."

She swept her hand across his chest. "I can't believe they came here. Someone from inside the Martinez Organization has to be helping them. How else would they have known where we were?"

He arched a brow. "Nicholas is already running a check on all the employees. I want to find out who it is and make them pay. I'm just glad you were able to get out of there before anyone got hurt. If anything ever happened to you, I wouldn't be able to take it." He ran the back of his fingers down her face. "I might as well die too because I can't see myself living without you."

"Dro, you know I feel the same way. But we don't know what's going on, or who they were even after. We've done a lot of dirt throughout our lives. It could conceivably be anybody. And I hate to say it, but—"

He held a finger against her lips. "Then don't say it." Sitting up on the edge of the bed, he bowed his head.

"Baby, we know who they're after. We just don't know why."

She leaned her head against his shoulder. "We have to be prepared for anything. Dro? Look at me."

"So you can tell me to prepare for living without you? There's no way in hell that's going to happen. I'm not going to sit here and listen to you give me dying wishes, Alexa. My life doesn't work without you, so *we* are going to have to take steps to prevent that from happening. And we're going to start by recognizing who this is really about."

She tried to pull away from him, but he wrapped his hand around her wrist. "Dro, I—"

"Don't. Don't pull away from me now."

"I can't do this right now," she whispered.

As he turned to face her, she swore when he looked at her, he could see every part of her soul.

"Yes you can," he said. "You have to do whatever it takes to protect our family."

She tried to escape his gaze. "I promised myself and my children I would never—"

"You promised them you would protect them at all costs."

She shook her head, ready to argue.

"Alexa, you promised me," he insisted in a lethal tone. "You promised me you would be here with me. You promised that we would live and die together. Live and die. Together. That means you can't die unless I'm dying, too."

"Dro, that's not fair. You know things aren't the same as they were then. I'm not the same person."

"Do you deny there is a problem here?"

"No, of course not. But—"

"No buts. This problem has to be solved. I need you here to solve it with me—no matter what it takes."

"Dro—"

He grabbed her face between his massive hands. "Stop. Masked men came into a safe house and threatened to take away everything we've worked so hard for. Now, it's true that things are different, but there's no way the woman I love would sit down and take this. I know you're scared, but this is who you are. This is the life we lead. It doesn't matter how much we want it to be different, we were born into this legacy. And we have to protect the people around us at all costs. And I need you with me fighting for everything we have to lose."

He was right, and she knew it just as surely as she knew her name. But it didn't stop her from worrying. It didn't stop her from wishing this could all simply go away.

He wiped the tears from her face. "We want to go into the house as soon as it's clear." She closed her eyes, but he didn't let up. "Can you pull that box out from under the bed?"

Frowning, she leaned over and felt under the bed until her hands skimmed a hard edge. Slowly, she pulled out a wooden box. She knew what was inside. Her eyes flicked to Dro as she set it on the bed. She ran her hands over the intricate detailing. It had a ladybug engraved on the top. Taking a deep breath, she undid the latch and lifted the top, revealing the contents.

He placed his hand on top of hers. "She's been here waiting for you. I knew if we ever had to come to B5, you would need her."

She picked it up and ran her fingers over it. A quick push of a button and the clip dropped into her lap. She traced the engraving on the side then snapped the clip back into place.

She noticed the gleam in Dro's eyes as she admired her first baby—her gun, Lady.

Chapter Six

AUGUST 23, 1993, Alexa's thirteenth birthday:

ALEXA WAS SO excited she ran across the street to Dro's house. She sprinted into Dro's room smiling. It was her thirteenth birthday and her mother had straightened her hair. It was almost as long as she was tall.

Dro looked up from his school book. "What are you smiling about, Alexa?"

She was glad everyone had stopped calling her lady. Her father started it when he nicknamed her ladybug. As she grew older, she dropped the bug from her nickname and became known as lady. Now that she was thirteen, she wanted to be called by her true name.

She smirked as she sauntered over to him and perched herself on the edge of the desk. "I got my birthday present from Daddy."

He removed his glasses and set them on the desk. "What did he get you?"

She pulled out her brand new Sig Sauer .380 caliber semi-automatic pistol. "This. I'm going to call her Lady."

"How original."

She smacked him on the arm. "Stop teasing me. I figure she can be called Lady. I mean, she's my gun."

"She?"

"Of course, it's a she. I'm a lady and so is she."

"Whatever you say. So, you didn't want a Barbie for your birthday?"

"Why would I want a Barbie when I can have one of these?" She held it up to the light and studied it proudly. "Besides, I'm too old for a Barbie doll and you know it."

He shrugged. "Don't thirteen-year-old girls still play with Barbie dolls?"

"Ha Ha. You're so funny. But Daddy says it's time to train. And you know my goal is to be the best in the business."

"Good luck with that. You may have to beat out your brother for that title."

"Lei? Yeah right. I already have him on my agility and ability to get into tight places. Not to mention my sex appeal."

He laughed. "Sex appeal? You're thirteen. What do you know about sex appeal?"

She smirked. "I know plenty. I've already had my first kiss."

She watched his eyes turn a shade darker.

"Oh really? Who needs their ass kicked?"

"No comment." She grinned and changed the subject. "Anyway, I know plenty about sex appeal. Ari said I have to be sexy in order to lure men into my trap. That way I can get anything I want out of them."

"What does Ari know about it? Alexa, you shouldn't be worried about being sexy for anyone, yet."

"What do you know about it? You're only sixteen."

"I know way more than you do." He finally closed his book and pushed it to the side. He was giving her his undivided attention now, and she couldn't help but feel nervous. "Sex appeal is overrated. If you really want to be the best, you have to make sure you can shoot that thing."

"Daddy is taking me out this afternoon to practice. You want to come?"

He took a sip from a glass of water. "I wouldn't miss it. Maybe I could teach you a few tricks, too."

She didn't know why, but in the pit of her stomach, she started to feel very warm. Clearing her throat, she hopped off the desk. "I can't wait to get started."

"I'll be there." He stood. "Just let me know when you want to go."

She walked toward the door then turned around and found herself staring right into his smoky eyes. She swallowed. "Dro?"

"Yes?"

"Do you think I have what it takes?"

"For what?"

"To be the best?"

He sighed. "Well, I'm probably biased, but yes. You just have to be focused, because the minute you lose focus, everything can fall apart. And we don't want that, right?"

"Right. I definitely don't want everything to fall apart. I think I can handle it." She couldn't help but smile. She had waited for so long to get her first gun so she could go with the boys to the gun range.

"Well, then I believe you can be the best."

She gave him a quick hug. "Thanks. You always believe in me."

He wrapped his arms around her waist and squeezed, lifting her off the floor. She had a massive crush on Dro.

And some days, she swore he knew it. But then there were the days when he was too entranced with his flavor of the month to give her the time of day. Not to mention the other days, when he treated her like an annoying little sister.

She pulled back and gazed into his eyes. She couldn't help but wish he had given her her first kiss. But that was all in due time. "Dro?"

"Yes?"

"Are you sure sex appeal is overrated?"

"Why? Did someone else tell you something different?"

There was that spark in his eyes again. *Was it too much to hope he was jealous?* "No. I was just wondering why sex appeal is overrated when everyone is having sex."

He laughed and ran his hand through her hair, causing her stomach to flip flop. "Don't worry about it. You just focus on your training."

That was *such* a "little sister" move. "For now, but I'll figure it out."

"I'm sure you will. Get out." He pushed her toward the door. "You have plenty of time, Alexa."

Before she could think of a response, he'd shut the door in her face.

NOVEMBER 4, 2011, B5:

ALEXA WRAPPED the sheet around her and walked over to the dresser. Placing *Lady* on the top of it, she bowed her head and took a deep breath. She turned around to face Dro. "You're right. I'll do whatever I have to do to keep my family safe. Don't worry about it."

He hopped out of bed, crossed to her, and braced his hands on the top of the dresser, one on each side of her, caging her in. "I'm not worried. I trust you more than I trust myself sometimes. You'll do what you have to do to protect our life just like I will."

She kissed his chin. "I'm not going to lie. I don't want to take it there. But it's necessary."

"You know what else is necessary?" he asked, placing a gentle kiss on her lips.

"What's that?" She wrapped her arms around his neck, letting the sheet fall.

He kissed her deeply and perched her on the edge of the dresser. "A repeat."

AN HOUR LATER, Dro walked into the computer room. Kendrick was still working. Dro set a hot cup of coffee in front of him and took a seat.

Kendrick remained focused on the monitor, but he picked up the coffee and took a sip. "Thanks. I managed to get sound, but I still can't make out any voices. The men seem inexperienced, but that doesn't really matter. They have guns and numbers. More men have come in and out of the house in the last hour. At this point, there's no real way to determine how many men are on the grounds. Honestly, B5 wasn't ready to be used yet. We're pretty limited down here. We were never able to fully test everything. As a result, there are still some issues with security cameras."

Dro peered at the monitors. "How's Nicholas doing with those background checks?"

"We should have a preliminary report done within the hour. We're kind of limited on some things down here. I'm hoping we can figure out more once we are able to get into the house."

"I explained the situation to Alexa. She's down for whatever."

Kendrick arched an eyebrow at Dro. "Is she? Are you sure about that?"

Dro smirked, knowing Kendrick wanted more details. Kendrick stopped what he was doing and watched him. "What?"

Kendrick snorted. "You're not going to elaborate?"

"What for?"

"You just said she was down for whatever? What exactly did you tell her?"

Dro took a sip of his coffee. "I told her the truth. We don't know much, but we do know these people were looking for her."

"Shit. I know it wasn't that easy. Alexa was firmly in denial the last time I checked."

"And I thought it was time she embraced her inner self. I gave her a little present."

"I'm assuming from your cryptic jargon that you gave her Lady."

Dro nodded. "I did. She needs it."

"I agree she needs a gun. But more than that, we need her."

"And we have her."

Kendrick sipped the hot coffee. "I'm glad you got through to her."

"It didn't take much. She wants a resolution to the problem. And as much as I love her, I need her to stop hiding from the past."

Chapter Seven

OCTOBER 19, 1997, Homecoming:

AFTER LEAVING THE PARTY, Kendrick and Alexa waited in the hotel lobby for Dro and Lei. They had a situation— a threat against Alexa at the party—which left all of them on edge. Alexa was the only one still in high school and the threat had come from a classmate of hers, Steve Hall.

Kendrick had decided to stay local for college, so he was in charge of keeping an eye on Alexa. He made himself available when she needed him. Dro and Chase were away at school for much of the time. Lei was busy with a full load at college and working closely with Pop.

Kendrick had known Steve was trouble the first time he saw him. Steve was a cocky football player who gained some popularity in school and thought he had a right to cause problems. He looked for trouble wherever he went and that was bad news because Alexa never shied away from trouble.

She resented the fact that her father required one of

the boys to be with her when she was hanging out with her high school crew. She complained about it constantly. But Pop didn't play with safety and insisted she have a chaperone whenever she partied. Kendrick understood where she was coming from. Every new friend she made was met with tons of scrutiny.

Now she tapped her foot against the floor and glared at him. "Kendrick, stop breathing all heavy. It's okay."

"It's not, Alexa. I'm not going to get killed because you refuse to take your safety seriously. That asshole shouldn't be threatening you. And what is with that punk you're dating—Erik? You're with him, but he can't even defend you?"

She rolled her eyes. "Look, I don't need Erik to defend me. I can defend myself."

"You shouldn't have to, especially when you have a date."

"You're worse than Lei and Dro. These are high school students, Kendrick, not hardened criminals out for revenge. You're overreacting."

He shook his head incredulously. "You're serious? What part of 'threat' don't you understand? You know there's history between Steve's father and Pop. That's nothing to take lightly."

"I'm not taking it lightly. I can beat Steve in my sleep. He's weak, all talk and no action."

Kendrick pinched the bridge of his nose. "You realize the others are not going to see it that way, right?"

"Yeah." She shrugged. "So what?"

He ran his hand down his face and took a deep breath. She was really starting to get on his nerves. "You're playing with serious fire, Lex. Why would you risk it?"

She studied him with amusement on her face then placed a hand on his shoulder and squeezed. "Steve is

Erik's best friend. I have to see him every day at school. It would be more dangerous for me to act like he's a leper. You always told me to keep my enemies close, so that's what I'm doing."

She was right, Kendrick thought, but Dro was still going to kill her—*after he kills me for not keeping a better eye on her.* The Martinez family didn't like to take chances, especially when Alexa was out in a social setting. They had many enemies, most of which stemmed from Dro's father, Enrique, and his illegitimate businesses.

Kendrick wondered briefly why he'd volunteered to come with her to the high school homecoming dance in the first place. Lei had been all set to come, but Kendrick had volunteered at Alexa's request.

Security was supposed to be a cinch because the dance was in a Martinez hotel, but he should've known better. "Cinch" and "Alexa" never went hand in hand. Normally, a threat from another student would be of no concern, but considering the source, it gave Kendrick cause for alarm. He was uncomfortable and didn't like it.

When he'd called Dro to break the news, he had expected Dro to blow his ear drum out on the phone. Surprisingly, Dro remained composed during the whole conversation. He was so calm Kendrick was forced to question his own reaction. However, once Kendrick had relayed all the details to him, Dro had finally blown his lid.

Steve had threatened to teach Alexa a lesson in "more ways than one." Kendrick had had the overwhelming urge to hang up when Dro refused to stop yelling and cursing in his ear. Dro, who was pretty even-tempered most of the time, became a deranged lunatic when Alexa was involved. Kendrick remembered wanting to throw his phone into the pool as Dro ranted on the other end.

It got even worse once Dro found out Alexa had

shrugged it off as nothing because she was too busy with her boy toy, Erik, to give a damn. She hadn't even told Kendrick about the threat. He'd just happened to overhear a couple of students talking about it in the hotel lobby. *Damn, was the girl daft?*

Dro and Alexa had been sleeping together for a while, but they were keeping it light. According to Dro, that meant they could each see other people. It gave Dro the freedom to see whomever he wanted while he was away at school. But he apparently hadn't realized it also meant Alexa could see whomever she wanted. And she wanted Erik.

Dro had a severe jealous streak when it came to her, so Kendrick had known "keeping it light" wouldn't last long. He could personally vouch for that since he'd been on the receiving end of this jealousy once Dro found out he was the one who had given Alexa her infamous first kiss.

Alexa's curse jolted Kendrick out of his thoughts. Looking up, he saw Dro burst into the hotel lobby, with Lei and Chase on his heels.

Dro marched up to Alexa, who didn't even flinch. "Get your ass upstairs, Alexa. We need to talk." Dro's father reserved a suite especially for them when they were partying at the hotel. It was convenient, especially when they'd been drinking.

Alexa rolled her eyes. "Can you please not order me around like I'm your child?"

"Do you even realize what happened?"

"Yes. I heard about what he said."

"And you don't give a damn?" Dro yelled.

"That's not what I said. Don't put words in my mouth."

He stepped closer to her, and they all knew how much

45

she hated being crowded. "Well then what would possess you not to take this threat seriously?"

She placed her hands against his chest and pushed him back. "Because I can handle Steve. I don't need you to protect me."

"So, someone threatens to rape you, and you say you can handle yourself? I hate to break this to you, but that shit isn't going to fly. And—"

She turned her back on him, interrupting him mid-tirade. Kendrick snorted and Dro glared at him.

"Did you just turn your back on me?" he roared incredulously.

Instead of answering him, she walked away, back into the crowded party.

Dro growled and followed her into the ballroom. Kendrick and the others had no choice but to follow, too.

Kendrick glanced at Lei as they entered the ballroom. "Dro is going to blow. You get him and I'll get her." He knew it was best if he stayed away from Dro. The man would choke him if given half a chance. He still hadn't gotten over the news of that first kiss.

Lei snorted. "That would be best."

As they hurried after Dro and Alexa, Kendrick knew this was only the beginning. Alexa was one of the two people that could get under Dro's skin. The only other person able to do that was Enrique, Dro's father.

ALEXA TOOK a seat at the bar and waited. When Dro caught up to her, she ignored him. She was tired of everyone treating her like she couldn't take care of herself.

"Why did you walk away from me?" His voice was a low growl in her ear. "You know I hate that."

She glared at him and spotted the others waiting quietly behind him.

"Really, Dro? You brought backup. What are you going to do, drag me out of the party against my will?"

"Why would I do that? You're going to get up and walk out with me."

"In whose world? Yours?"

"Exactly."

She had expected his anger, but not the gentle kiss he placed on her neck. She shivered. He was playing hardball. Bracing her hands on his shoulders, she shoved him away. "Stop that. I have a date."

"And I should care because..."

She held him at bay with her hand on his chest. "We said we weren't going public, Dro. That's what you said, right? You made up the rules."

He swept a strand of her hair out of her face, ran a finger along her jaw. "Rules were made to be broken."

"You can't have it both ways. I can see who I want, and you can't act like I'm with you in public. I have a date with Erik. That's who I'm going to be with tonight."

"Really?" He swept her hand out of his way, moved in, and brushed his lips against hers. "You're with *him* tonight?"

She swallowed and tried to push him away again. He didn't budge. "Dro, st—" The word "Stop" wedged in her throat when his tongue darted out to trace her lips.

"Answer the question," he whispered. "Are you with him tonight?"

She swooned as his warm breath breezed over her mouth. But she wasn't about to let him off that easily. Using all her strength, she propelled him back a step. "Stop crowding me. I'll see you later tonight—*after* the party."

"I don't think so. Steve is volatile. He's already threatened you once tonight. If you think I'm going to leave you here at this party by yourself without protection, you're wrong."

"Kendrick can stay with me." She knew he wouldn't go for it since Kendrick was with her tonight when the incident happened, but she refused to give up.

He scowled at Kendrick then turned back to her. "Kendrick is not staying with you because you're not staying here."

"You're ruining my date, Dro. What if Erik sees you all over me like this. He'll never come near me again."

"I don't give a damn."

"Of course you don't. You get to go back to college, and I'm going to be stuck here dateless because no one with any brains will go up against you." She smacked him on the shoulder. "Jerk."

He barked out a laugh, which infuriated her even more. "Listen, if you're the player I think you are you can make anyone want to risk going up against me just to get a taste of you."

The wheels started turning in her head. She scanned the crowd, looking for Erik.

"And trust me," he continued in a low tone. "If you can get someone to want you even after seeing you with me, nothing will stand in your way." Slyly, his right hand slipped into her hair and he pressed a tentative kiss to her mouth, prompting a sharp intake of breath.

Alexa tried to fight her attraction to him, but she knew it was a no-win situation. Making the decision to roll with it, she cradled his head in her hands and pulled him into a quick, but intense kiss.

"Okay," she purred against his lips. "I'll accept your challenge. But I'll still see you later."

DRO ADMIRED Alexa for her ability to turn things around in her favor, and he was looking forward to watching her get out of this situation. It was very likely her classmates had witnessed their little interaction. He was pretty sure Erik had already received the news that his date was flirting with someone else.

Dro dipped his head, ready to capture her lips with his.

"Alexa?" a voice called out.

He knew it was her simpering date, Erik, but he refused to move. Alexa peeked around him.

"Alexa, what are you doing?" Erik demanded. "Who the hell is this?"

Dro straightened to his full height and turned around then smirked at Erik's mortified expression.

"Dro—I—I didn't know it was you."

Dro cracked his knuckles. "What the hell is your problem? And who the hell do you think you're talking to?"

"Uh—I thought Alexa was—" Erik stammered. "I didn't know it was you, but anyway, she's with me."

"And that makes it okay for you to speak to her like that?" Dro crossed his arms over his chest. "She's with you so you have the right to disrespect her? Sounds to me like you're feeling yourself a little too much."

A small crowd had gathered around them.

Erik sighed. "She's my date. I thought—"

"I don't give a damn what you thought," Dro snarled. "And I don't care what you think you are to Alexa. You will never disrespect her like that again. Never talk to her like you're crazy."

"Dro," Alexa interjected.

He ignored her, keeping his eyes on Erik. "Do you understand?"

Erik bowed his head and nodded slightly.

Dro enjoyed making the punk squirm. "Good, because I don't repeat myself, and I don't make idle threats. If I ever hear that you disrespected her again in any way, I won't warn or threaten you—I'll just kill you."

Erik dropped his head.

"If you insist on staying here," Dro said, turning back to Alexa. "I'm staying too. Don't worry, I won't crowd you." He glanced back at Erik, who was standing with his hands shoved in his pockets. "Something tells me your date is over anyway unless you can work some of your magic," he whispered and walked away.

HOW THE HELL had he ended up in this mess? Kendrick wondered as he watched Dro storm off. Alexa was probably mad as hell, and a pissed off Alexa didn't bode well for him. For the life of him, he couldn't understand why Dro had acted the way he did. And since Alexa was never one to shy away from a challenge, this was only going to get worse.

Kendrick sighed and approached Alexa at the bar. "I'm sorry about that, Erik," he heard her tell the dummy.

"What the hell was that about?" Erik demanded. "Are you with Dro?"

"No, we were just talking."

Kendrick snorted. Anyone with eyes could see they'd been doing more than just talking, but Erik was a fool. Alexa had once confided to Kendrick that Erik was different than her other suitors, so he knew she cared for the boy. *What would Dro think about that?*

She frowned at Kendrick. "Can you give me a minute?"

He nodded and stepped back far enough not to crowd them while remaining close enough to hear what they said.

"If you believe that, Erik, you're dumb," Steve said, approaching them.

"Get the hell out of here, Steve," Alexa growled. "This is none of your business."

Erik backed away from her. "No, he's right. Why would Dro be all up in your face like that? Someone told me he even kissed you."

"And you believed them?" she asked innocently. "I'm telling you that's not what happened. My relationship with Dro is complicated, but nothing was going on." She placed her hands on his shoulders. "Erik, believe me, it's not what you think. Dro and I are friends, more like family."

"I want to believe you," he admitted. "But I don't want to get hurt—physically or emotionally."

She cupped his jaw with her hand. "Erik, trust me. I'm with you—nobody else."

Kendrick wanted to slap Erik. *What an idiot!* He watched her pull the clueless man into a hug and couldn't help but roll his eyes. *She is good.* Erik buried his face in her neck. *She's really good.*

Scanning the room, Kendrick noticed Dro tip his drink toward Alexa. Alexa and Dro communicated with their eyes. He couldn't understand why Dro didn't just tell Alexa he wanted only her. They all knew it. Just like they all knew she wanted only him.

"What the..." Steve scoffed. "Erik, I don't know why you bother with her. She's full of shit."

Kendrick balled his hands into a fist, ready to pummel the bastard to a pulp.

"I told you to stay out of it, Steve," Alexa snarled, holding a hand against Kendrick's chest. "You don't want to start something you can't finish."

As much as she infuriated him, Kendrick wouldn't think twice about killing anyone who dared to disrespect her.

Erik backed away as Dro and the others converged on the scene.

"So, if it isn't Dro Martinez?" Steve sneered, folding his arms across his chest. He and Erik obviously had the dummy thing in common. "What are you doing at a high school party anyway?"

"Are you talking to me?" Dro challenged.

Steve moved closer, sandwiching Alexa between them. "I don't stutter like my friend Erik."

Dro snatched Alexa out of the middle and exchanged glances with Lei and Chase. "Apparently not. I heard you have plenty to say about Alexa. You mind repeating it to me?"

Cracking his knuckles, Kendrick willed Steve to say something stupid. They hadn't had a good fight in almost two years. He looked around at his "brothers". They all had reputations around town that resulted in widespread fear among their peers.

Chase was small in stature, but the last person who'd crossed him ended up in traction. Around town, Lei was known as cold and calculating. And Dro wasn't called *jefe* for nothing. No one challenged—or crossed—him.

Steve puffed his chest out. "I didn't say anything about Alexa. And even if I did, it's a free country. I can say what I want."

Kendrick had to hand it to Steve. The punk didn't back down. That should make this all the more interesting.

Lei grinned. "You're a smart ass, huh? You think that's funny?"

Steve shrugged. "Like I said, I didn't stutter."

"I would tell you like I told your friend, Erik, I hate it

when people disrespect Alexa. It pisses me off," Dro grumbled. Barely-controlled fury radiated from him, making his last statement superfluous. "Something tells me that I can tell you that, but it won't matter. You'll still continue to do what you want. And that's your mistake."

Before Steve could respond, Dro's fist connected with his face. Kendrick cringed as Steve fell to the ground holding his shattered jaw. The crowd buzzed; their shocked gasps punctuated with a couple of screams.

Dro stood over Steve. "That's your first warning. Don't test me." Dro grabbed Alexa by the arm and pulled her out of the room.

Kendrick yanked out his phone and dialed the front desk. "It's Kendrick. There's been an accident. Call an ambulance." Dropping his phone back into his pocket, he stepped around the wailing Steve. *Oh well, maybe next time.*

Chapter Eight

NOVEMBER 4, 2011, B5:

DRO GLANCED up when the security room door clicked and Chase and Lei walked in.

Lei dropped his gloves on a table. "We did a quick check of the grounds and found the guard lying dead against the side of the house. We noticed there were four dark colored trucks. There were two men standing at the back door and two men at the front, an unknown number inside."

"Did they see you?" Kendrick asked.

Chase pulled off his coat and dropped it on an empty chair. "No, but we didn't stay long enough to get seen. Have you heard anything from the house?"

"No," Kendrick said. "I don't recognize anyone. But they're still inside. Probably trying to figure out where Alexa is."

"Speaking of Alexa," Lei said. "Is she up to date on what we discussed?"

Kendrick chuckled. "According to *jefe*, she's down for 'whatever'."

"Good." Lei pushed a button on the wall next to the light switch, opening up a small panel. "We're going to need her help. I'm glad *jefe* got through to her."

"I am in the room," Dro snapped, still peering at the monitors. "And someone needs to light a fire under Nicholas's ass. I need that report in my hands ASAP."

Lei pulled a lockbox out of the panel and set his gun in it. "I'll talk to him. You just make sure Alexa's ready when we need her."

Dro closed a notebook he had been jotting in and picked up his now-empty coffee mug. "I got this. No worries."

A FEW HOURS LATER, Alexa and Dro were awakened by a knock on their door. She stretched and perched herself up on her elbows. "What time is it?"

"Time to go up to the house." Dro hopped out of bed, slipped on his pants, and picked up the .45 caliber pistol on the nightstand. "You need to get up."

She rubbed her eyes. "I'm thinking I should probably stay back with Nicholas and keep an eye on the cameras."

"You still need to get up. It shouldn't take too long to go through the house." He slipped on a shirt and exited the room without another word.

Later, when she stepped into the security room, Nicholas was watching the monitors and sipping a cup of coffee. He nearly dropped his mug when she walked in. "What are you doing up?"

"Watching the action," she said, taking a seat.

"You don't have to. I have everything under control."

"I do have to," Alexa insisted. "I want to make sure everything's all right."

"Okay."

Even if he had questions, Alexa knew he wouldn't ask. Dro made sure all their employees knew to never question either one of them. Although, Martinez Security veered away from the old business ways, the people who worked for them had learned to never underestimate her or Dro.

UPSTAIRS IN THE SAFE HOUSE, Dro split them up into twos. He and Lei started in the attic and worked their way down, while Chase and Kendrick began on the ground floor and worked their way up.

The house had been ransacked. Every piece of furniture was either in shreds or completely smashed. It was obvious their faceless enemy intended to leave a clear message.

Dro peeked into the kitchen and assessed the damage. All the dishes were on the floor. He shook his head and continued into the room.

Behind him, Lei kicked a piece of broken glass and sent it skittering across the floor. "This is overkill, don't you think?"

"Pretty much. But we already figured they were inexperienced."

They continued to roam the house, checking every closet. Eventually, they ended up in the home office. Dro stepped over a pile of wood—that used to be a desk—to examine a smashed file cabinet. "Good thing we don't keep anything important here."

Lei tossed aside a couch cushion. "If they came here for Alexa, why destroy the house? Idiots."

"Dro?" Nicholas's voice crackled in Dro's earpiece. "I see movement in Ky's bedroom."

"We're on our way over there," Dro said and motioned for Lei to follow him into the hallway.

"What kind of movement, Nicholas?" Dro asked as he approached Ky's room.

"Behind the curtain."

Stepping into the room with his gun drawn, Lei walked over to the swaying curtains and yanked them open. The window was open, the shutter banging against the house. "It's nothing," he told Dro.

Dro stilled when he heard footsteps in the hall and gripped the handle of his pistol.

Kendrick barged into the room then stopped in his tracks and raised his hands. "Easy, it's just us."

Dro cursed and stuffed his own gun back in its holster. "Did you find anything?"

"Just a big mess," Chase said as he entered the room. He picked up one of Ky's stuffed animals and ran a finger over the torn fabric. "The computer was untouched, which is further confirmation that they weren't here for information."

"Well, we still have to check the play room," Lei said. He headed into the hall.

When the others eventually followed, they were greeted by a masked man with a gun against Lei's temple.

"Who the hell are you?" Dro demanded, stepping closer to Lei and the stranger.

The man laughed. "What makes you think I have to answer you? I'm the one with the upper hand, here. You'll answer my questions, or your friend gets shot."

Dro glanced at Kendrick then Chase. "Listen, whoever you are, let him go and maybe you'll get out of here alive."

"I may not get out alive, but I'll take at least one of you with me."

"Who are you?" Kendrick snapped.

The man snorted. "Wouldn't you like to know?"

Dro rolled his eyes. "I don't have time for this. If you're going to do something, do it. But I can guarantee you won't make it out of here alive if you do. Make it easy on yourself and tell me what you want."

"You know what I want."

"How would I know that?" Dro felt his patience unraveling. "Stop playing games and tell me what you want." The masked man seemed familiar to him, but he couldn't place him.

"I want that bitch, Alexa."

Dro's jaw clenched. "What do you want with her?"

"I want her up here now." The man scanned the corridor. "Where did she go? I have waited years to face her."

Kendrick snorted. "What, are you stupid? Do you really think we're just going to tell you where she is?"

"If you want him alive, you will. I want to see her. Now!"

"What do you want with my wife?" Dro tried to keep his temper under control, but it was becoming harder by the minute.

He noticed a trickle of blood coming from Lei's temple and the dazed look in his eyes. The stranger had obviously clocked him in the head with the butt of his gun. When the man didn't answer, Dro repeated his question. "What. Do. You. Want. With. My. Wife?"

"She killed my brother. I want to return the favor."

So the bastard knows Lei is Alexa's brother. "Then what?" Dro wondered aloud. "You just let us kill you? Or better yet, we let her kill you for killing her brother."

"I want her to suffer the way I've suffered." The man's

voice was shaky and he'd started to fidget. He pointed the gun at Dro. "Knowing there was nothing she could do for her brother."

"What the hell is that supposed to prove?" Dro asked, keeping his eye on the man's gun.

"I don't need to prove anything. When she gets here, all will be explained. Who knows? Maybe she'll be happy to see me."

"I doubt that," Chase mumbled.

The stranger glared at Chase. "Alejandro, tell Chase and Kendrick to back up."

Kendrick, who was steadily inching closer to the masked man, stopped in his tracks. Chase froze as well.

"You didn't know I knew who you were, did you?" the bastard asked.

Chase smirked. "It doesn't matter. You won't leave here alive."

"Damn it," Lei cursed. "Just kill this asshole and let's go."

"Listen." Dro raised both hands and tried to keep his voice calm. "You should probably just get on with whatever you plan to do because there's no way that Alexa is coming here."

"Where the hell is she?" The man was becoming more and more frantic. "She was supposed to be here. That's the only reason I agreed to come."

Dro stalled, hoping the man would reveal more. "Well, it's obvious someone told you wrong. Is that why you stayed around after everyone left? Trying to get to her? That's not going to happen. Who are you working for?"

"Shut up! You don't call the shots. I do. You did this to my brother, too. Alexa told him you were extremely controlling. She said you wouldn't let her go without a fight. But my brother couldn't see past what he wanted, and he wanted her. He wanted to save her from you, but you made her choose between her life and his. So, of course, she chose to save herself."

Dro clenched his teeth together. It took every ounce of restraint he had not to shoot the stupid man where he stood. But he had to know more. "You don't know what you're talking about. I have never had to make Alexa choose me. It was innate for her—like seeing, hearing, or smelling. There was no choice to make."

"Obviously you don't know your wife. My brother did. They made plans together. They were going to leave and take my family with them."

Dro snorted. "If you believe that, then you need serious help." He assessed Lei, who grunted occasionally, and figured his brother-in-law was as tired of this charade as he was. But if Dro could keep the frazzled man talking, he might get everything he needed from him.

The gunman tapped Lei's temple with his pistol. "I don't need any help—you do. My brother told me all about you. He said Alexa was suffering in silence and needed to get out. She was pre—"

The light dawned and Dro knew the rest, even though the idiot abruptly shut up. "She was pregnant and your brother, Paul, thought she was unhappy and wanted to leave me."

Paul's brother yanked the mask off his face. "You figured it out, huh?"

Dro sighed. Paul had been hired as an accountant with Martinez Security and worked for the company for three years until he was caught embezzling money.

Dro had been hesitant to let Alexa get involved in the case, but she wouldn't be deterred. Pregnant with Ky at the time, she had used tears and fake fear to gather evidence against Paul. He had believed all of her lies—most men did—and didn't realize her true intentions until it was too late.

That's why Alexa was one of the best operatives in the business. She was an excellent actress, extremely efficient, and completed most jobs without breaking a sweat. When they were children, Dro had told her she overestimated sex appeal. But *he* had underestimated her.

"So, Paul told you she was in a prison of sorts?" Dro asked, rolling his neck. "And you believed him, of course, because he was your older brother and hero. But what he didn't tell you was that Alexa didn't give a damn about him. You know why he didn't tell you that? He didn't know that until he was staring down the barrel of her gun. Paul was so entranced with her legs and her butt that he didn't see her weapon until it was too late." He glanced over the idiot's shoulder. "I see you're about to make the same mistake."

Chapter Nine

THE CLICK of a gun echoed in the corridor. Dro recognized the moment Paul's brother realized someone was behind him. He froze, but didn't turn around. Instead, he wrapped his free hand around Lei's throat.

"Drop your gun, Tommy, or I'll blow you to hell," Alexa commanded softly.

Dro couldn't help but smirk at the sight of his wife. She was beautiful—top to bottom. Dressed in black pants that hugged her body like a second skin, a short, black leather jacket, and knee-high leather boots, she had her hair pulled back into a long ponytail.

"Did you hear what I said?" she repeated. "Drop it. I won't tell you again."

"I knew you would come," the man breathed.

"Really? You knew that? Did you also know that when I came, I would kill you?"

Kendrick snorted.

"Shut up." Tommy glared at Kendrick a moment before adding, "I have been waiting for you, Alexa."

"Good. I've been waiting to kill you. Now. Let. Him. Go."

"Paul said you were tough, but that you had a heart. You won't shoot me. You're just a trapped, scared woman."

She tilted her head to the side. "Really?" Gunfire erupted, reverberating in the small space. Two quick bursts. Tommy released Lei and slid to the floor.

Lei touched a finger to his temple then glared at Alexa. "I guess it's a good thing you still go to the range occasionally."

She shrugged. "Sorry."

Tommy screamed in pain as blood gushed from his kneecaps. Cursing, he rolled over on his back.

Alexa stood over him, her feet on either side of his body. She bent down, practically straddling him.

You know," she said sweetly. "I hate men who think that just because I'm a woman, I'm scared. You made many mistakes in your attempt to avenge your brother's death. First, you underestimated me because I'm female." A right hook to his face snapped his neck to the right. "Then you held my brother at gun point." The ball of her fist snapped the cartilage in his nose.

He screamed again, blood dripping from his nose and into his mouth.

She tipped his chin up with her gun. "Look at me."

He slowly opened his eyes, whimpering in pain.

She ran a gloved finger down the arch of his nose and pushed down hard, causing him to scream again. "Then you walked into my house and ruined all my furniture—" She clocked him hard with the butt of her gun. "—smashed all the dishes."

She stood and stomped on his groin, twisting her heel. His shrill screams bounced off the walls. "You believed that punk-ass brother of yours." She lifted his head and slammed it on the wood floor. "And you frightened my children."

Whipping out a knife from somewhere on her body, she pressed it against his neck. "But you know what's funny? After doing all those things, you still cry like a little bitch. Poor baby. You're upset because Paul died? Well, your brother was a grown-ass man who made some very bad decisions and became a thief. My children *aren't* grown and you scared them when you and your asshole friends charged in here and terrorized us. I don't like it when my children are scared."

Tommy visibly flinched when the knife dug into the skin below his ear.

"Looks like you made one too many mistakes," she said. "Do you have something to say for yourself? Huh? Are you ready to apologize for all the trouble you caused my family?"

Tommy coughed and blood seeped out of his mouth, but the fool remained silent.

Alexa backhanded him. "You don't have anything to say?" She pressed her forearm against his throat causing him to gasp for air. "So, you're okay with me slicing your throat from ear to ear?"

"B—bitch," he hissed between grunts.

"Bitch, huh?" she snorted. "Is that all you got? Well, judging by the amount of blood you've lost, you don't have long to live, anyway. And just to show you I'm not totally heartless, I'm going to give you the chance to die with some dignity. Tell me what you know and I'll end your life quickly and efficiently. But if you choose to remain mute, I'll put a few more holes in you then leave you here to die a slow painful death—after I let these fellas have a shot at breaking you. So which would you prefer?"

Tommy's eyes drifted closed.

ALEXA STOOD and pointed her gun at Tommy. As much as what she was doing turned her stomach, she knew her family's safety depended on getting all information he had before it was too late. She placed her foot on his chest and stabbed him with the four-inch heel of her boot. "Look at this bloody mess. You even bleed sloppy. You know, Tommy, on second thought, I'll let them handle it anyway because I don't want to mess up my outfit."

His eyes widened. "Wait—"

"Do you finally have something worthwhile to say?"

"She offered..." He coughed, his voice raspy. "They offered me a hundred thousand dollars to do this. But I would've done it for free after what you did to my brother."

"Can you make up your mind? One minute you're demanding revenge and the next minute you're trying to appeal to the scared woman hiding inside me. But I'm not surprised you're confused. You thought Paul walked on water. But he was flawed and didn't think things through. He acted on emotions. And you took after him. So. Who. Hired. You?"

"Wouldn't you like to know?" he snickered.

"I imagine your sister, Margaret, and your mother, Pamela, will tell me what I want to know."

The little bit of color left drained from Tommy's face. "You wouldn't."

"Tommy, Tommy, Tommy—didn't we have this discussion about you underestimating me? Ask yourself that question again and see what answer you come up with."

"Leave my family alone," he choked out.

"Too bad you won't be here to protect them." Alexa shuddered inside as she said it. She hated torture, but sometimes it was a necessary evil—the only thing some people understood.

"Don't hurt them," he sputtered, blood spurting out of his mouth. "Please. I'll tell you what you want to know." She backed away as the others crowded around Tommy. "I don't know her name, but she's working with someone else," he admitted. "She contacted me about six months ago, told me that she had a job with a little revenge for me as a side bonus."

"Was that someone else a man?" Dro asked impatiently.

Tommy nodded. "I heard her on the phone with him one day. I could hear his voice over the receiver."

"You've seen this woman?" Alexa asked.

Tommy coughed again. "Yes, she hired me in person, but she would never give me her name."

Kendrick rolled his eyes. "And you were so blood thirsty for revenge you didn't bother to check her out?"

Tommy scowled at him. "I didn't care. I just wanted to see Alexa suffer. The woman's got money, but she doesn't have much power. The man is calling all the shots."

Dro appeared ready to end the man's misery himself. "Where are they located? Where did you meet her?"

"She met me in a coffee shop on the edge of town," Tommy mumbled. "Misti's coffee."

"I know where that is," Chase said. "Describe this woman."

"I heard about all of you from Paul." Tommy coughed again and cleared his throat. "He told me the Martinez clan was known for its viciousness and said you wouldn't think twice about killing as a means to an end."

Lei stepped on his chest. "You're losing focus, Tommy. Describe her."

Tommy gulped and coughed up more blood. "You won't hurt my family?"

"No," Alexa answered. "Sister and Mom will be okay if you just tell us what we want to know."

Tommy sighed. "Light skinned, short hair, hour glass figure. She did tell all of us that when we caught you, we should tell you something."

"What?" Alexa kicked him again.

"She told me to tell you that 'your day is coming, little girl'."

"Melissa," Dro snapped. He eyed Alexa as he asked, "And she never said who she was working with?"

Tommy shook his head. "No, but I get the feeling they're intimate with each other, maybe her husband or something."

JANUARY 15, 1998:

DRO SAT with Alexa on his lap at the local bar one evening, his arms wrapped possessively around her. "I'm glad you're here, baby," he said. "I needed to see you."

They'd been seeing each other semi-privately for longer than he wanted to admit. It was common knowledge she was his girl, but they hadn't made a complete commitment yet.

"I'm glad you can admit that to me," she whispered, nipping his bottom lip.

"Hey, I'm nothing if not honest, especially with you." He watched her mull over his words and figured they were quickly heading off a cliff—a point of no return. Surprisingly, he was okay with that. He always knew they were destined to be together, but he hadn't realized he would be anticipating that destiny with anything other than resignation.

After the debacle during her high school homecoming party, he had suggested that they continue to see other people with one stipulation—when he was in town, she was with him. Period. She'd had a stipulation of her own —the same thing held when she was visiting him on campus.

Over the past couple of months, he'd come to rely on her for more than just sex. Although they'd been close before, he'd never expected her to become his best friend. But they'd now reached the point where he confided in her and trusted her explicitly. She was quickly becoming the most important person in his life.

"Where did you go?" she asked, running her fingers through his hair. "We should head back to your apartment."

He sighed. *No use in prolonging the inevitable.* "Yeah, let's get out of here."

As she slid off his lap, he dropped a fifty-dollar bill on the bar. She reached out, grasped his hand, and began pulling him out of the bar. When he heard a loud gasp and realized who had come up behind them, he groaned in frustration. *This isn't going to be good.*

"Hi Dro," Melissa said then pointed at Alexa. "Who is this?"

"I'm Alexa." She held out her hand to shake Melissa's. "Who are you?"

Melissa eyed her with an air of superiority, which Dro knew would infuriate Alexa. "I'm Melissa. And I believe I was talking to Dro."

Alexa folded her arms over her breasts. "You asked who I am, and I told you."

Melissa sneered at her. "Listen, little girl, I don't know who you think you are, but this is my turf. My family runs this town. And I'm talking to Dro, not you."

Alexa glanced at Dro again out of the corner of her eye. "Dro? Can you get your little friend to leave before I do something I won't regret?"

He jammed his hands into his pockets. "Melissa, what do you want?"

She smiled at him and placed her hand on his arm. "Who is she, Dro?"

"She just told you who she was."

Melissa snickered and turned to Alexa. "I'm sorry, little girl, but Dro is my man."

"Really?" Alexa turned to him. "Is that true?"

He prided himself on his ability to remain calm in any circumstance, but right now he couldn't think of anything to say. Alexa was going to hurt the fool if he didn't get her out of there. He motioned for Kendrick who was watching with amusement on his face. Ari and Lei joined them as well.

"Well, Dro?" Alexa repeated. "Are you her man?"

He frowned. "What do you think?"

She turned back to Melissa. "I don't know who you are, but I'm thinking it's time you know who I am."

Melissa smirked. "I could care less who you are. It really doesn't matter. I run this place and I've had enough of you. Go back to the playground and play with someone your own age. Dro has his hands full with a grown woman."

Alexa laughed. "You're a regular comedian. I'm not going to argue with you about Dro. The clear fact is he's leaving with me. It really doesn't matter who you *think* you are to him." She elbowed him in the gut. "I suggest you tell this person to get the hell out of my face."

Dro wrapped his arm around Alexa's shoulders. "Melissa, I'm trying hard not to embarrass you in public, but you're acting like an idiot right now. I'm not your man. I've never been your man. I don't know why you insist on making our relationship more than it was."

"What?" she screeched. "How can you say that after everything we've done?"

Pinching the bridge of his nose, he took a deep breath. "This conversation is getting old. I haven't seen you since Thanksgiving. What makes you think you were more than a one-night stand?"

"Ouch," Alexa murmured.

Dro cursed, his annoyance tripling instantly when he noticed the small crowd gathering around them.

Alexa squeezed his arm. "You really don't want a scene, do you, Melissa? If I were you, I'd just walk away."

Melissa shook her finger in Alexa's face. "Bitch, you don't know shit about me. You better watch your back."

Alexa sighed and dug her nails into Dro's arm as Melissa ranted about her family and her town, shoving that damn finger in Alexa's face.

Finally, Alexa removed her nails from his skin, grabbed Melissa's finger, and snapped it back.

Damn. Dro winced as Melissa screamed in pain and dropped to her knees while Alexa held on to her finger.

"I'm tired of you calling me names," she said calmly. "My name is not little girl or bitch. My name is Alexa. And if you can't remember that shit, I'll tattoo it on your ass."

NOVEMBER 4, 2011, the safe house:

. . .

DRO KNEW Tommy was barely clinging to consciousness at this point.

"Tommy," Alexa said, her voice almost a whisper. "Do you know what your brother did to me?"

He didn't answer.

"He tried to rape me when I wouldn't give him what he wanted. And when I fought him back, he cut me in my stomach, even though I was pregnant with my daughter. He threatened to kill me and my unborn child and shoot himself if I didn't choose him over Dro. There was never any choice. But I pretended to agree. He already thought I was unhappy, so I told him that I would leave Dro. When he let go of me slightly, I pulled my gun out and I shot him right between the eyes."

Dro looked at Tommy when she finished her story. His eyes were closed, his breathing shallow. When Dro glanced at Alexa, her eyes looked dead.

"Since then," she continued. "I told myself I would never put them in harm's way again. I would never place my children at risk. I was never scared of anything until your brother threatened my child's life."

"Why are you telling me this?" Tommy asked.

She picked up her gun again and aimed at his head. "Because you threatened my children's lives by coming here—all in the name of your brother. I just thought you should know who your brother really was. He stole from us for over three years and he worked with a competitor who was trying to put us out of business. He was a coward in every way. And you want to be just like him. The way I see it, I'm giving you what you want—to be like Paul."

Although Alexa had rage on her face and her gun aimed at Tommy's heart, Dro knew she couldn't kill him in cold blood.

She was a fierce defender of those she loved, yet the

days of sweeping her own emotions under the rug for a job were long gone. But before he could tell her he understood and he'd handle it from here, Nicholas stormed in and put two bullets in Tommy's head.

"What the hell was that?" Alexa growled. She whirled around and trained her gun on Nicholas, pressing the tip to his temple.

Nicholas' eyes widened. "I just wanted to help. I thought—"

"Why are you here?" she asked. "I told you to monitor the cameras. What makes you think *we* need *your* help? We had this situation under control and you jeopardized our safety by leaving your post and coming here."

Dro glared at Nicholas. "I'd really like to know the answer to that myself. But now is not the time. Take your ass back down to B5. Now."

Nicholas turned and left without a word. Dro stepped over to Alexa and gently squeezed her arm. When her arm grew lax, he gripped her hand and took her gun. He secured the safety and tossed it over to Chase.

"Clean this up," Dro ordered.

Chapter Ten

ALEXA FLED TOWARD THE STAIRS, leaving them to clean up the mess.

"Baby?" Dro's voice stopped her in her tracks. She clinched her fists together and forced herself to breath slowly. "Baby, don't run from me," he said. "Remember, I'm the only one who knows you cry after every mission."

With tears in her eyes, she whirled around to face him. His thumb caught the first teardrop that escaped as he gathered her close. She sobbed openly into his shirt while he whispered nonsensical words in her ear.

It seemed like they had stood there forever when she eventually broke away and gazed into his smoky eyes.

He stroked her moist cheeks. "It's okay, baby."

"It's not, Dro." She cleared her throat when her voice cracked. "I told myself I would never raise a gun to kill again. That I would never put my family in harm's way again, never put myself in the position to have to do something like that!"

"You didn't put yourself in that position. He came here to kill you. That's on him, not you."

"Dro, you can't seriously believe that. He came here to avenge his brother's death. You know as well as I do that was a direct result of my actions."

"That's not true. Paul tried to rape you. He knocked you down. He ripped your underwear off. He cut your stomach. Killing him was self-defense."

"Maybe," she admitted. "But there were many others that weren't self-defense. Besides, Paul flipped out because I made him think I wanted him. I played him just like all the others. Others who didn't deserve what I did to them. I told you, we have done so much dirt. It was bound to come back on us. And I can't—" She swallowed, trying to ease the lump in her throat. "—I can't help but feel like we deserve everything that comes to us."

"Alexa, you heard what Tommy said. The person who hired him was Melissa. This has nothing to do with our business."

"That we know of. We don't know who the other person is, the man she's working with."

"But we'll find out and stop them." He rested his hands on her folded arms. "Don't do this to yourself. We made decisions based on the life we led then and the choices our parents made for us. We're trying to make it better, and sometimes it just doesn't work. But we can't give up on that dream. And we can't stop fighting."

She shook her head and stepped back from him. But when she tried to turn away from him, he grabbed her head with his hands so she couldn't avoid eye contact. She sighed. "Dro, please, you know I'm right. That's why I can't do this anymore." She pushed him back, pulled her knife out, and dropped it on the floor. "I promised myself I wouldn't harm another human being. I made that promise for my children. We made these changes so our kids could have a better life."

"You're right," he agreed. "We're parents, and no, we can't act like we used to. We've done things in our lives that...I don't even need to say it. I understand where you're coming from. I don't like that the kids are involved. And I know you don't want Ky and Alex to see this side of you or to grow up striving to be like you. But we do want them to grow up, baby. That means we have to protect them." He searched her face. "It's fine to want something better for our children. I do too, baby. But you can't keep hiding, running from the past. You shouldn't deny who you are, Alexa."

She choked back another sob. "I'm a killer, Dro. Do you want me to wear an assassin's badge? If there was ever a past someone should hide from, it's mine. What if Ky sees me like this and decides she wants to follow in my footsteps?"

"So what? She would do good to follow in your footsteps. She doesn't have to kill to be like you. Somewhere along the line you forgot who you are because you were so busy pretending. The fact that you've killed does not define you. Our kids could do so much worse than to be like you." Dro cradled her face again, smoothing his hands over her hair. "You're intelligent, fearless, and strong. You're everything I've ever wanted. And you're never more beautiful to me than when you are being yourself. I love everything about you, even the worse parts. I've known since I was ten years old that you would be my wife. I've loved you for so long, I can barely remember what it was like to not love you. And our children love you, too. They need us to fight for them."

"Dro, I'm scared."

He smiled down at her and placed a sweet kiss on her lips. "No, you're not. Remember, you are never scared."

She appreciated his attempt to lighten the situation. "I

am, baby. We have so much to lose. If something were to happen to our kids because of me, I don't think I could survive it."

He pulled her back into his arms. "I know. But it's going to be alright. We just have to believe that."

AUGUST 22, 1997:

DRO STIFLED a groan when Alexa walked into his room and hopped up on his desk. At seventeen, she was even more beautiful. He had to remember to breathe every time she smiled. Her hair was styled in a long, layered cut. But he preferred it in a mound of messy curls, like it was today.

She closed the book he was reading. "It's my birthday tomorrow, Dro. What are you getting me?"

"Do I ever tell you what I'm going to get you?"

"No, but do I ever stop trying?"

"I guess not." He leaned back in his chair. "What's up?"

She picked at the torn edges of his textbook. "I have a question to ask you."

"What is it?"

She fidgeted, a rare occurrence. "As you know I'm turning seventeen tomorrow, and there are some things I want to accomplish."

He took a sip from his glass of water. "Like what?"

"I want to lose my virginity."

Choking on the water in his mouth, he pounded on his chest. "W—What?"

"I'm ready to lose my virginity."

Trying to compose himself, he rubbed the back of his

neck "I heard you, but I'm wondering what the hell your problem is?"

She shrugged then giggled when he rubbed his hand down his face. "I don't have a problem, Dro. I'm the only one I know that hasn't had sex. It's time."

He frowned, wondering where the hell this was leading. "So, what does this have to do with me?"

"Well...I want you to be my first."

Immediately, his gaze traveled down her body. "Okay, let's just pencil that in between cake and ice cream." Clearing his throat, he sat up straight. "You're really trippin'."

"No, I'm not." She slid off the desk and onto his lap, straddling him. "I'm ready. And I trust you, so I want you to be the first."

His hands fell to her thighs. "I don't think that's a good idea."

"Why not? You're not attracted to me?"

He gazed into her expressive brown eyes, tilting his head. "That's not what I'm saying. It's just...I don't know if we should..."

She placed her finger against his lips and he had to fight the urge to suck the digit into his mouth. "I have a reason for this request. I already had Kendrick give me my first kiss." He was so distracted by her finger lingering over his lips that he almost missed her comment about who gave her that kiss. Almost.

Dro arched an eyebrow at her. "So Kendrick was the first kiss?"

She trailed her tiny fingers up his arms, distracting him from planning Kendrick's beat-down. "And then Chase took me to second base," she continued, obviously not realizing that she'd just sealed Chase's fate as well.

Alexa adjusted her position on his lap, not realizing she

was dangerously close to feeling just how attracted he was to her. He gripped her thighs tighter.

She placed her hands on his shoulders. "So I figured I might as well skip third base, cause...Ewww. I don't want to do that with just anybody. And since we're already supposed to get married, I figured you should be my first."

Dro mulled over her words. When they were children, their parents agreed they should marry. Pop thought of it as a way to ensure Alexa's protection. And Dro's father agreed. Dro found out about this on his tenth birthday. But his father always told him he would never force him to marry her if Dro felt strongly against it.

In Dro's mind, however, he never thought he would marry anyone other than Alexa no matter what his father said. He knew Pop would still insist she marry someone in the Organization, and Dro wasn't going to let it be Chase or Kendrick—or anyone else for that matter. He knew she trusted him and he wouldn't let her marry someone she didn't trust.

Dro realized Alexa was staring at him quietly. "What?"

"Are you thinking about it?" She traced small circles on his shoulder. "Because I know you have women—a lot of women. But the thing is I trust you—you know that. And more importantly, I trust you with my body."

Instinctively, his gaze slid over that lovely body again. "Sex isn't something we can turn back from. Once we do it, it's going to change things."

She smiled, and Dro...melted a little? He frowned at that realization, but tried to remain focused.

"Well," she whispered, leaning in. "I figured it would change a few things. I'm ready, though. I want my first time to be soon. With you."

His focus shifted to her plump lips. For a second, he wondered if she was wearing that fruit flavored lip gloss she was always gushing about. It wouldn't be much trouble for him to lean in just a little bit more and taste her. "I'm not sure you're ready to be with me."

She rubbed his chin with her thumb and he prayed she would just stop touching him. His mind was already in the gutter. One more push and her virginity would be a long lost memory.

She arched a brow at him. "I know I am. But maybe it's the other way around. Maybe you're not ready to be with me?"

"Lex..." he sighed. "I'm not sure. I have to think about it."

She shrugged and jumped off his lap. "Okay, but don't think too long though. I may decide to ask someone else. Something tells me whomever else I ask may not be so noble."

He watched her walk out of his room then dropped his forehead on the desk and took a few cleansing breaths, willing himself not to focus on the temptation that was Alexa.

NOVEMBER 4, 2011, B5:

B5 WAS STILL quiet when Alexa and Dro arrived. Chase, Kendrick, and Lei were still up in the house. Nicholas met them in the foyer. They stood in silence for a few minutes. She surveyed Nicholas, still suspicious of his motives for charging in and killing Tommy—especially when it wasn't necessary. The situation was obviously under control. Even if she wouldn't pull trigger herself, one of them would have done it. She wanted to give Nicholas the benefit of the doubt, though. He'd been there for her more times than she could count, proving himself loyal to the family.

"The background checks came back," he said softly. "I went through the report quickly and highlighted some things I thought you should look at." He handed a file to Dro.

Dro scanned the documents briefly, and gave the folder back. "Do me a favor and give it to Lei first. I'll look at it later."

"Will do. I have to get back in the security room and make sure everything is okay."

"Aside from that, your actions tonight were inappropriate and I don't appreciate it. If you can't do the job I hired you for, you're no good to me. You're certainly not gaining any trust by disregarding my orders, despite your intent. Do what you're told. Period."

"Nicholas?" Alexa said, clearing her throat. "You've never given me reason not to trust you. I'm choosing to accept your reason for coming up to the house. But don't let it happen again. It's been a long day. When they get back, why don't you get some sleep? You haven't had much rest."

Nicholas nodded and walked into the security room without a word. Alexa hurried to her bedroom, leaving Dro to finish the conversation.

Chapter Eleven

LEI QUIETLY OPENED the door to B5. His head was pounding courtesy of Tommy. He was irritated, so he left Kendrick and Chase to clean up. He skimmed his temple with his fingers and frowned when he felt the blood. Stalking into a small bathroom, he surveyed the damage on his head.

"What happened to you?" a soft voice asked.

Lei peered at Ari's reflection in the mirror. "Nothing. Don't worry about it. What are you doing up?"

Ari watched him in the mirror. "Don't tell me not to worry about you? What happened?"

"I got caught sleeping, Ari." He turned to face her. "Someone clocked me in the head."

Ari gasped and pulled Lei down the hall into her bedroom. Pushing him down on the toilet, she grabbed her medical bag and immediately went to work on his head. As her fingers skirted over his wound, he gripped the edge of the commode. She stilled, but eventually continued to clean it.

He held his breath as she dabbed antiseptic over the

cut. Closing his eyes, he waited for more pain, but it never came. Instead, he felt her cool breath against the cut. He opened his eyes, and she smiled at him. He could tell she wanted to say something, but he knew she wouldn't make the first move.

She rummaged around in her bag and pulled out some gauze and tape. After rubbing salve on his cut, she gently placed the gauze on top and taped it. She held his gaze for a minute before tossing the waste in the trash can.

Lei continued to watch her as she moved around, throwing away more soiled cloths, and cleaning her instruments. He knew she was aware of his scrutiny, but she still remained quiet. She only stopped when he placed his hand on her arm.

He moved his fingers down her arm to her hand and squeezed gently. "Ari...Stop."

"You need to go," she whispered.

He pulled her down on his lap. "I'm okay."

She looked at him then, tears standing in her beautiful brown eyes. Although Ari and Dro were siblings, Dro was the only one who inherited his mother's startling bluish-gray ones. But Lei didn't care because he loved Ari's expressive brown eyes. They were eyes he saw in his dreams, too many times to count.

"Lei, what if...never mind." She tried to get off of his lap, but he wrapped his arms around her waist and held her there.

"I'm all right," he repeated softly. He placed a gentle kiss below her ear. "It's okay."

She wiped an errant tear from her cheek. "Lei, I can't do this."

Lei whispered to her, "Yes you can. I need you." He kissed her again, this time on her neck.

ARI CLOSED her eyes and sighed deeply. There was one thing she was sure of in her life and that was Lei. He'd always been there for her, since they were children and she loved him with all her heart. But theirs was not a love story for the books. Most of their romantic relationship existed behind closed doors.

He was a married man. And she hated herself for needing him the way she did. Makayla was one of her closest friends in the world, but Ari would sooner die than ever give Lei up. She opened her eyes to find him watching her intently. Lifting her hand, she stroked his brow. "Makayla is in the other room. You should go to her. She's probably worried."

"You're worried, and I'm concerned about you, Ariana."

She knew he was telling the truth. Even though they couldn't be together like they wanted, he always made sure she remembered what she meant to him. They had both made decisions long ago that prevented them from exploring a full relationship. Ari married, at the young age of nineteen, to Makayla's brother, Jackson. She was pregnant with Alana and she thought it was Jackson's baby. Once Alana was born, however, her striking resemblance to Lei was unmistakable. But it was too late. Her father forced her to marry Jackson before the baby was born, even though she begged him not to.

For a while, Lei and Ari continued to see each other, with her sneaking out to see him on occasion so they could be together.

When Jackson died, she finally thought she and Lei would be together. But he had already committed himself to Makayla, offering to stand by her side because she had no family left.

When he married Makayla, Ari tried to get over him, but she couldn't. Although she dated other men, she knew she would die still loving Lei.

She forced her mind away from her thoughts and traced his jaw with her fingers. "I couldn't sleep. I knew you and the others went up to search the house, so I thought I would wait for you to come back."

He stayed silent while she shifted her position on his lap and ran the back of her hand down his cheek.

"I heard Alexa and Dro come back," she continued softly. "I panicked initially. I just had to see if you were alright."

"I'm fine. Alexa had to come and rescue me, though." He laughed faintly. "She came at just the right time."

She giggled as she relaxed into him. "So, Alexa, saved you? That's...different."

"I think Dro had something to do with that."

Ari smiled, thinking of her brother and Alexa. "Well, I'm glad he did. She's pretty stubborn."

"You're not lying," he said, running his fingers through her hair. "I'm glad she decided hiding was no longer an option because I was glad to see her."

She intertwined her fingers with his and squeezed. "I'm glad you're okay. Are you any closer to figuring out who did this?"

He shook his head. "The only thing we do know is that Melissa is involved."

"Melissa?" She sat upright. "Who's that?"

"Don't you remember her, Dro's one night stand from hell? Alexa broke her finger at the bar?"

"Oh yeah, I remember that." She leaned back against his hard chest. "How do you know she's involved?"

"She left a message for Alexa."

"Well, she better hope Alexa's not the one who finds her. She would have better luck with Kendrick."

They both laughed at that because Kendrick was considered the violent one of the group. And they both knew he would be a piece of cake compared to Alexa. She wasn't as violent as Kendrick, but Melissa had threatened her children, and that wasn't something someone could do and get away unscathed.

Ari rose and stepped away from him. "You need to go."

As much as she wanted him to stay, she knew Makayla was probably waiting for him. He grasped her hand again and stood up. "I don't know how long we have to be down here." He cradled her face in his hands. "But I want you to know how much I—"

"Shhh. Don't say it. I know."

He leaned down and brushed his lips against hers, then pulled her closer, and deepened the kiss. She stood on the tips of her toes and wrapped her arms around his neck, taking what she could in the moment. But eventually, reluctantly, she broke the kiss and pulled away.

Turning away from him, she held back the tears until she heard the soft click of the door.

WHEN LEI WALKED into his room, he was glad Makayla was asleep. He just wanted to put this day behind him. He slowly slipped his shirt off, then his pants, and crawled into bed next to her.

Lei loved Makayla, but not like he should. She was his wife, but his mind was constantly on Ari. He didn't believe in regrets, but the longer he stayed married to Makayla, the more he resented the choices they all made so long ago. For once, he just wanted to be happy with the woman he loved more than his own life. He wanted that undying kind of love Dro and Alexa had. But he made a promise to stay by Makayla's side for better or worse. And he would keep that promise to her because he did love her and wanted her to be safe and happy.

Makayla turned to face him. She hadn't been asleep after all.

"I thought you were sleeping," he whispered.

She reached up and touched the bandage on his temple. "Are you okay?"

"I'm okay. It's nothing big."

There were tears shining in her eyes. "But you're hurt, Lei."

"It's just a cut."

"Did Ari clean you up?"

"Yeah, she saw me when I was coming in and insisted on tending me."

Although Makayla never said anything about it, he knew she was well aware of his past—and present—with Ari. After all, Makayla and Lei had been friends since Kindergarten. They had grown up together. And Makayla had made a few comments on how much Alana resembled him.

"Good. I'm glad you're okay. I was worried," she said and kissed him.

He pulled her into his arms. "I know, baby."

MAKAYLA SIGHED and willed the tears not to fall. She waited until she heard Lei's soft snores then pulled away from him. She'd known he was with Ari. She could smell her on him. It was no secret that Lei and Ari had a connection. She knew he secretly wished he could be with the other woman.

If she was selfless, she would have let him go a long time ago so he could be happy with Ari. But she wasn't. She couldn't help it, she loved him, even though she had long ago accepted the fact he would never love her like he did Ari. She didn't think that he realized she knew about them. But she did—all too well. She also knew Alana was Lei's daughter and every chance Lei got, he was with Ari.

Makayla was okay with that. Really. She figured she was damaged goods anyway. She couldn't give Lei a child, but he had still agreed to marry and protect her. He had never wavered on his oath, and she knew he would die keeping that promise.

She fell in love with him when she was twenty years-old and had never stopped. At first she had hoped he would love her the same way. Ultimately, she chose to give up that dream and just enjoy the piece of him he was willing to give her. She rolled over and smiled at her husband. Reaching out, she skimmed the bandage on his head with her fingers. "I love you, Lei."

"I love you, too."

Startled that he'd heard her, she burrowed into his open arms and smiled when he placed a chaste kiss to her forehead.

Chapter Twelve

_____

ALEXA NIBBLED on a ham sandwich and waited for Dro to arrive. She had just come from the hotel with Lei. Over the past couple of weeks, she had been trying to break up with Erik. But he wasn't taking the hint. It wasn't her choice to hurt him like that, but Steve had shown his true colors a couple of weeks before. They heard Steve had threatened Erik as a means of getting to her. And she wasn't about to let Erik get caught up in this mess.

She felt that by limiting contact with him, Steve would back off. But Erik was holding on. She had told him on numerous occasions she didn't want him anymore, even going so far as to pretend she and Kendrick were together, which Dro wasn't too happy about. But that was another story.

Things were getting hot between her family and Steve's. Dro had broken Steve's jaw at the homecoming dance, and Steve's father was hell bent on revenge. Pop had been trying to handle the situation, but he was also dealing with important Martinez business, so he couldn't devote the time he needed to the situation. Dro was managing security as best he could, but there was only so much he could do from college. Lei picked up the slack for Dro, and no one had made a move against them yet—which was good.

At the hotel earlier, Alexa had noticed Erik hanging around with Steve and his father. Lei accused her of being too nice to Erik and suggested she ask Dro to handle him. She had her doubts about that. For all his talk of keeping things light, Dro seemed to enjoy scaring all her potential dates away and keeping her for himself.

She heard a knock at the door and bellowed, "Come in."

Dro stepped into her room. "You need to stop being so nice to Erik." He must have talked to Lei.

She glared at him as he approached her. "Hi, to you too, Dro."

"Lei told me what happened this afternoon. You need to stop being so nice and just break up with that idiot."

"I know you probably don't want to hear this, but I care about Erik. I don't want to hurt him."

"Do you want him *hurt*?"

She sighed and stood then paced back and forth across the room. "No I don't. But I also don't want to break his heart."

"At this point, it doesn't matter. You said you wanted him safe, and we all agreed you would dump him so he doesn't get entangled in this bullshit."

"Dro, I did dump him. I've told him I don't want him. He doesn't believe me."

"Well, he'll believe me. I'll talk to him." He plopped down on the bed, picked up her half-eaten sandwich, and took a bite. "But I can see why he doesn't believe you. Besides the fact that you're being too nice, you're one hell of a liar." When she rolled her eyes, he grinned. "You've been lying to him from day one, and he's believed every single one of your lies."

Alexa felt bad for leading Erik on, and that was a first for her. Erik was different from other boys. Besides, they had been friends since middle school. She snatched the sandwich from his hands. "Fine. Do your worst. I guess I'll just have to deal with him hating me forever."

"Is that the problem? You don't want him to hate you? What the hell is wrong with this picture?"

"Don't start, Dro. I just told you to do your worst. But no, I don't want him to hate me. I've known Erik for a long time and he's been a good friend to me." She pushed her hair out of her face. "I don't want him involved either. Steve is up to something and I want Erik to be far away from me when this goes down."

Dro stood and slowly walked up behind her. "Lei told me you guys saw Steve and his father today." He rested his chin on her shoulder. "I want you to stay away from them. Steve is mad. He lost serious cool points when I snapped his jaw. And he's not very smart. But with his dad backing him, we could have some serious trouble. Pop wants us to keep everything tight until he can take care of Steve's father."

She tilted her head to the side, resting it on his. "Okay, Dro. You don't have to understand about Erik, but I do care for him."

"I don't understand. I'll never understand. If you haven't figured it out by now, I don't want to understand anything about you and someone else. But I'll tell you this. When I do talk to him, you have to roll with me, whatever I say."

"What are you going to say?"

"I don't know yet, but I'm going to make it convincing. As long as it gets the job done, right?"

"Like I said, do your worst."

MARCH 19, 1998, Martinez Hotel:

LATER ON THAT SAME EVENING, Dro was in the hotel bar with Alexa. When Erik arrived with another classmate of theirs, Janine, Dro felt Alexa nudge him with her elbow.

"He's walking in now," she said.

"I see that." He jerked her into an intense kiss, tangling his hand in her dark hair. When he broke it off, he couldn't help but smirk at the blush creeping up her neck to her face. He ran a finger along her jaw and she closed her eyes in response.

He glanced in the mirror behind the bar. Erik was gaping at them. *Perfect.* Dro turned back to Alexa, who was staring at the ceiling.

She stood up abruptly. "Make it quick. I'm ready to go home," she said and dashed out of the bar.

He noticed Janine chase after Alexa as Erik approached the bar.

Erik ordered a shot, drank it down, and slammed the tiny glass on the bar. "Keep 'em coming," he told the bartender.

Dro moved over and slid onto the barstool next to him. "Cut him off, Drew," Dro told the bartender.

Erik glared at Dro. "What the hell are you doing?"

"He's underage. Stop serving him. He's done."

Erik slammed his fist on the bar. "Says who? I showed him my ID and who the hell do you think you are?"

Dro smirked. "You don't know? *Soy el jefe*."

Erik fiddled with his empty shot glass. "I know what your 'crew' calls you, but what does that have to do with me? I don't have to answer to you."

Dro motioned the bartender away. The man set a cold beer in front of Dro and headed to the other end of the bar.

"You really are an idiot," Dro told Erik. "I guess you didn't take Spanish. *El jefe* means 'the boss'. This is a Martinez hotel and the last thing we need is to get busted for serving a minor."

"I saw you with your tongue all down Alexa's throat like you own her."

Dro shrugged and took a sip from his bottle. "How do you know I don't? You don't know anything about my relationship with Alexa. And if you saw me with my tongue down her throat, then you also saw that she wasn't objecting in any way."

"Whatever."

"I don't like you," Dro said. "I've never liked you."

"Well, it's good that it's not up to you to like me. She likes me and that's all that matters."

Dro tapped a finger against the counter. "There you go, feeling yourself too much."

"She's with me when you are away at school."

"Not anymore. From now on, she's only with me. This is not a competition, Erik. If it was, you wouldn't stand a chance."

"What do you want?" Erik asked.

"Just wanted to give you a little friendly advice. This infatuation you have with Alexa has to stop. Stay away from her. Don't see her again, don't even look her way."

"What if she doesn't want me to leave her alone?" Erik asked. "See, from where I'm sitting, you don't know a hell of a lot about my relationship with Alexa."

"I know all I need to know."

Erik seemed to ponder that. "Well, I know Alexa. Something's up. She confides in me."

"Oh, you mean her little sob story? 'Dro and I are supposed to be married...my father has determined I have to be with him...I like you, but there are things you'll never understand about my family...obligations that have to be kept.' Am I close?"

Erik's eyes widened. "Too close," he mumbled.

Dro rolled his eyes. This really was too easy. "You don't get it, do you? Alexa is a player and you got played."

Erik shook his head. "She may surprise you."

"Nothing about her surprises me. But you're obviously surprised I know what your average conversation with her was about. Like I said, just let her go. It'll be better for you in the end. And don't think she'll care when you're gone. That's what a player does. You're nothing special to her. She finds some unsuspecting idiot so enamored with her they fail to see the game she plays on them, until she walks away with their dignity."

Erik scowled at him. "Are you telling me this to help me or to keep her to yourself?"

Dro smirked. "I already told you that I don't need to try to keep Alexa to myself. She's already with me. This is just my way of helping you not to get on my bad side. She told you she was done with you. She means it. And now that I have to get involved, I'm irritated. It's a waste of my time to be having this conversation with you right now. I don't like talking to you. Stay away from her. Period. If you don't, then I'm going to have to use other means to get the message across. We both know I don't make idle threats."

He finished the rest of his beer, stood up, and walked out of the bar.

When he entered the lobby, Alexa was waiting with Lei and Kendrick.

"It's done. Let's get out of here." Dro took Alexa's hand in his as they headed out of the hotel with Lei ahead of them and Kendrick bringing up the rear.

As they walked to the garage, he noticed a black car heading toward them. It was too late to warn the others as the back window lowered and bullets sprayed in their direction.

From that point, everything happened in slow motion. Lei cursed and fell to the ground. Kendrick yelled for Alexa to get down, but she had reached under her dress for her own gun and dived behind a car. Dro grabbed his gun and fired at the car, while he headed for Lei who was already moaning on the ground.

Dodging bullets, Kendrick and Alexa returned fire, each from behind a parked sedan. Moments later, the enemy's vehicle crashed into a nearby telephone pole. Assuming one of his crew shot a tire out, Dro signaled to Kendrick who rushed over to check the occupants of the car.

By the time Dro reached Lei, Alexa was shouting to someone on her cell phone and the blood oozing from Lei's wound had pooled on the cement. He grabbed Lei's ankle and dragged him away from the street. But before he could examine the wound, Alexa was at his side.

She dropped to her knees beside Lei. "Is he okay?"

"Did you call Chase?" Dro asked. He couldn't meet her eyes. He was no doctor, but Lei was losing a lot of blood. "We need to get out of here."

"Yes. He's on his way. Luckily, he was right around the corner."

"Good." Dro pressed his jacket over the wound on Lei's chest.

"There were two of them and they're both dead," Kendrick said from behind them. "I don't know who they are or who sent them."

The sound of screeching tires had everyone but Lei spinning around, guns at the ready as Chase braked to a halt in a dark Expedition. Dro and Kendrick lifted Lei up, set him in the back seat then climbed in beside him as Alexa hopped in the front. The faint sounds of police sirens could be heard as they sped off into the night.

NOVEMBER 4, 2011, B5:

ALEXA LAY IN BED, facing Dro.

He reached out and tucked a stand of her hair behind her ear. "I was ten when I saw my father kill someone for the first time."

She gasped.

"From that moment on, I knew I was never going to have a normal life. I mean, how could I if my father was willing to kill someone right in front of me. After he murdered the man, he told me it was just the way of life. Your father was there, but he didn't say anything. Instead, Pop just gave the order to clean up the mess."

"You never told me this story before," she admitted softly.

She knew that when Dro's grandfather arrived in the States from Puerto Rico, he had founded Martinez Organization and opened a neighborhood store. But he quickly realized he could make more money by branching out into some illegal activities. So he began making hooch, or moonshine, and smuggling it to neighboring states. Eventually, he expanded into narcotics, using the store as a front for business.

Dro's father, Enrique Martinez, a shrewd business man, took over business when his father retired. He established many legitimate businesses under the Martinez Organization umbrella, but the biggest money maker continued to be their illegal activities. Enrique delved further into the drug trade, becoming the main supplier for Tri-State area. But that wasn't enough. He also wanted to become a major player in the selling and distribution of weapons and made millions smuggling guns to Puerto Rico and other nearby countries.

Alexa knew all this, but she knew very little of Dro's early brushes with the dark side of the family profession. Surprised and interested, she gestured for him to continue.

"When we were younger," he said. "I kind of embraced the life. We all did. We all knew that our name gave us power. My father built the company by stealing, manipulating, and murdering people who crossed him. Because of that, we were untouchable. It wasn't until I fell in love with you that I realized I had so much to lose."

She wrapped her arms around him and nuzzled into his neck.

He pressed his lips to her hair. "Then my priorities changed and I took steps to distance you and me from that side of the business as much as possible. And now, I'm faced with the real possibility that all of the decisions we made when we were younger—and all the lives my father and yours ruined—are coming back to haunt us and our children. It's hard. So I do understand where you're coming from."

She kissed him gently. "I guess when I think back on

our lives, and all the people our family has hurt, I can't help but worry. There are too many secrets, too many lies. Someone is waiting in the wings to get revenge, and it could be anybody."

"We still have to fight, though. We can't afford to bury our heads in the sand and hope this goes away."

"I know, Dro." She sighed and sat up. "I guess I should make some calls."

"You probably should."

"After this is over, maybe we will finally be able to retire to an island somewhere like we dreamed about."

"And ensure Ky and Alex have the life we didn't." He wrapped an arm around her shoulders. "Make love all night, every night, without me having to run around and make sure security is tight."

She skimmed her fingers across the hair at his nape. "Are you getting soft in your old age?"

"Never that, Lex," he murmured with a soft chuckle, and then he fisted a hand in her hair and jerked her to him for a passionate kiss.

Chapter Thirteen

MARCH 19, 1998, a Martinez Organization safe house:

AFTER THE SHOOTOUT in front of Martinez Hotel that wounded Lei, Dro told Chase to drive to the closest refuge. A remote cottage outside of town, it was used by the family for various activities, but mostly as a place where employees could lay low for any reason.

Several hours after arriving at the farm, Dro sat at the small table nursing a glass filled with cognac when Alexa entered the kitchen. She stared at him and he shrugged. He didn't drink often, but he was wound tight. Lei was more like a brother to him than a friend. At this point, the doctors weren't sure he would survive. Dro heard Alexa's shoes on the linoleum floors as she approached him.

She smoothed her hand through his hair. "You okay?"

Dro studied her, focusing on her blood stained dress. It was a reminder that Lei had damn near bled to death. It looked like she'd tried to wash her neck and arms, but he could still see Lei's blood on her skin.

Dro finished the rest of his drink. "When I was younger, your father told me to never let my guard down. He told me the minute I stop paying attention, someone dies."

She knelt in front of him and placed her hands on his knees. "Lei is going to be okay. You have to believe that."

He traced a spot of dried blood on her bare shoulder with his fingers. "What I believe is beside the point. I never wanted to be the type of person my father was. But your father...when he told me he wanted me to marry you, I felt honored. I felt like he trusted me with his most precious asset. That felt good to me. He taught me everything I know. He's been more of a father to me than my own. And I let his son get shot."

"Stop it, Dro."

He stood and paced back and forth. "Lei could die and what was I doing? I was so busy looking after you that I failed to pay attention to my surroundings. What if I hadn't seen that car when I did?"

"It's not your fault."

"You're getting a guard."

"A guard?" She frowned. "What? No."

"I'm not taking any more chances," he told her. "I'm going to get someone to protect you."

"I don't need a guard," she yelled. "And don't treat me like I can't defend myself."

"Will you just shut the hell up and take the damn guard?"

Her eyes widened then narrowed with intent. "Did you just tell me to shut the hell up?"

"Is that what you heard?"

She nodded.

He lifted his hands up to his sides. "So what part don't you understand?"

Fury radiated from her, flushing her fair skin a dark shade of red. "First off, you don't tell me to shut up. Second, you need to trust me and my ability to take care of myself."

"This isn't about you anymore. Your father and my father trusted me and Lei to handle security for all of us. None of us want guards, but we're going to have them now."

She glared at him. "Yeah, right. Kendrick will never agree to a guard."

"He will if I tell him to. This isn't up for discussion. Do you realize what could have happened tonight? We were involved in a drive by shooting in front of our fucking hotel. Any one of us could have been shot and killed. I'm not willing to take any more chances with our lives. This has nothing to do with whether or not I think you can handle yourself. I know you can, but you're still getting a guard."

"Dro, I'm still in high school. What do I look like having a guard shadow me all damn day?"

He shrugged. "I couldn't care less. Our parents are on their way here, and this is the only thing I can think of to appease them. We don't know who came after us tonight. It's not like we lead pristine lives here. My father made his fortune off the misfortune of others. And your father...he's basically a hired assassin."

She turned away from him and he immediately felt guilty. He knew her father was the most important person in her life. But she knew who he was and what he did, even if she didn't feel like hearing it.

Dro grabbed her shoulders and turned her to face him. "Alexa, don't turn your back on me. We both know how our parents got to be so powerful. My father is a criminal. And yours..." He couldn't finish his sentence. "They've done many things in their lives to cause someone to want to gun Lei down. I mean, we tell ourselves your father is different because he works as a CIA operative. But he's done plenty of jobs that didn't have anything to do with the government."

Dro sighed. As much as he loved Leiland Sr., or Pop, the man was a cold-blooded killer. At a young age, he'd enlisted with the marines and quickly gained the respect of more than a few high ranking officials. These same officials thought it was a good idea to send him out to complete some "hard tasks". He excelled and eventually began doing jobs for other government agencies.

When Pop was discharged from the marines, he immediately went to work for Martinez Organization and formed Martinez Security with Enrique's blessing. While the security branch specialized in training bodyguards for celebrities and politicians and developing security systems for high profile companies, it was mainly a cover for Pop's work with the CIA. And he'd made a lot of enemies over the years.

"It's not forever," Dro assured her. "But I do need you to stand by me, Alexa. Don't give me a hard time with this."

Kendrick stepped into the kitchen "Dro?"

"Did you get the truck out of the garage?" Dro asked him, keeping a firm grip on Alexa.

"What was left of it," Kendrick said. "Someone did a nice job vandalizing it."

"Probably trying to make sure we had no transportation out of there," Dro mused. "We need to figure out who did this."

"I'm trying to gain access to the hotel's security cameras to see if someone in the hotel looks suspicious,"

Kendrick told him. "Whoever it was knew we were there and coming out at that time."

"My father will be here any minute—and so will Pop."

Kendrick nodded and left the kitchen.

When Dro turned back to Alexa, she had her arms crossed and was scowling at him. "What?" he asked, though he already knew. With a shrug, he picked up the open fifth of cognac on the table, poured himself another glass, and downed the contents in one gulp. "Kendrick is getting a guard, too."

"So why didn't you tell him that?" she growled.

"I don't need to. Kendrick, unlike you, realizes I have to make hard choices to appease my father—and yours. He won't care."

"Don't." She snatched his glass from him and slammed it on the table. "Don't act like I'm this pain in your side."

He refilled it again. "You're *acting* like a pain in my side. I get that you feel like you have something to prove. But you don't have to prove anything to me. I've never underestimated your ability to take care of yourself. And this isn't some sinister plan to make you feel less than Kendrick or anyone else."

She softened her stance a little, dropping her hands to her side.

He took another sip of his drink and eyed her. "Robert will be your guard."

She gasped. "Robert? No! I want Julio."

"Hell no. You're getting Robert. He's older with plenty of experience, and he won't fall for your charms like Julio will."

"Fuck you, Dro," she growled, stomping her foot and bolting for the door.

Dro caught her with an arm around her waist, pulling her against him.

"Let me go," she demanded, trying to break away from his hold.

He'd given up trying to convince her he was right. He needed her in a different way at that point. His fingertips tingled with the need to touch her and take her, to make sure she knew just how much he loved her. The thought of losing her scared him more than anything had in his life. His lips skimmed the skin under her ear as he dipped his head and inhaled her scent. "I don't want to fight with you," he whispered against her ear. "I don't see any other way. Just trust me. Trust me to know what I'm doing."

"I do trust you, Dro. I just...you're right. I do feel like I have something to prove. I'm not sure why, but I do. I'm a woman, and I feel like people will always discount me."

"That's not true. I never discount you. So trust me."

"Okay," she agreed. "I'll accept the guard, if it's what you want."

He nipped at her ear. "It's what I want."

She turned in his arms to face him. "Robert still thinks of me as a child. Daddy might as well be guarding me. Does it have to be him, Dro?"

He smirked and rested his hands on her ass. "Yes."

"Fine. Whatever you say."

He leaned in to give her a kiss. She placed her well-manicured forefinger over his lips. "Not so fast. I'm sure you think that by making nice all is forgotten. But you did tell me to shut the hell up. And while I may accept the guard, I won't accept that. I'm going to bed."

NOVEMBER 4, 2011, B5:

. . .

POP FOLLOWED Chase into B5 at eight o'clock in the morning.

After one look at the place, he smiled. "Chase, you did one hell of a job here. I'm proud of you."

"Thanks, Pop. I appreciate it more than you know."

Pop rubbed his graying beard. "Which room is my wife in?"

"She's the first door on the right," Chase told him, pointing him in the general direction.

"Ladybug and Dro?"

Chase pointed in the opposite direction. "Third door on the left. Lei and Makayla are the second door on the left."

Pop nodded. "I won't wake them up now. Thanks for coming to pick me up."

"How was your trip?"

"It was tough. I didn't know what I would find when I got back. I want to be briefed on the situation as soon as everyone's up. We need to develop a plan of action."

"Well, I'm ready. They should be up in a few."

Dro burst into the kitchen, wearing only sweatpants. "You're here," he said, embracing Pop. "Good to see you."

"Good to see you, too. Where's my ladybug?"

"In the bed. Rough night."

"I bet. I was just telling Chase I want to know everything that's happened."

"That's fine," Dro agreed. "Let me finish getting dressed. I actually came out here because Chase only brought soap for Alexa." He glared at Chase. "And there's no way I'm using cinnamon fruit drop or anything like that."

Pop laughed as Dro hurried off in search of soap.

Chapter Fourteen

ALEXA ROLLED OVER, expecting to burrow into Dro's warm body, but all she found was cold sheets. Opening her eyes, she spotted him on the far side of the room, slipping on his pants.

She sat up straight. "Is everything okay? Where are you going?"

"Pop is here. He wants to talk."

Alexa couldn't help but feel excited at the news of her father's arrival. She had missed him. Hopping out of bed, she headed for the closet. "Well, then let's not keep him waiting."

"Wow, when I came in last night, you wouldn't even look at me. Your father comes, and you jump right out of bed."

She brushed passed him and bumped him away from the dresser so she could retrieve a bra. "That's not true. I remember very well what I did when I saw you." She looked over her shoulder at him and winked. She rushed to the bathroom, bumping into him again. "Dro, can you please not start this discussion without me?"

He followed her into the bathroom. "You know I won't. We're in this together, baby," he said and started to shave as she stepped into the shower.

"I've been thinking," she said. "Daddy is probably going to want to come up with a game plan and wait before we make a move. But I think we need to make a move first and then see what happens."

"I think we need to wait until we have more information. We definitely need to set up surveillance on Melissa's family and do some digging around to see if we can figure out who her partner is."

"Yeah, but Melissa is a ding-a-ling. If we get to her first, we may be able to break her."

Dro cleared his throat. "I know you want to see her suffer, but we have to think about her family. Her parents are very wealthy and have a lot of influence. We don't want to make a move too quickly."

"Dro, she hired men to come into our house and kill us. Didn't you tell me it was time to fight? I want to fight that bitch."

He laughed. "Oh, you'll get your chance, but not until we know more. You told me you were going to make some calls. Did you get that done?"

Pretending she didn't hear him, she sighed and turned off the water. "What about the kids?"

"We'll play it by ear. We're pretty secure here, but we should still consider other options." He tossed her a towel as she stepped out of the shower. "Are you going to answer my question?"

She dried her body then wrapped her hair up in another towel. "I put in a call to my contact. He's checking into it. And that's what makes this so hard. We know Melissa isn't smart enough to do this by herself. It could be anybody."

"It's important to narrow this down though. Are these thugs after you for your work with Martinez Security or is this connected to some outside job you did for the CIA?"

A chill ran up her spine. Could this have something to do with the Company? It wasn't common knowledge that she'd been recruited by one of her father's friends to do freelance work for them. In fact, the only people who knew were Dro and Kendrick. Even her father had no idea she'd done freelance work for the government.

Pop had made it clear to his contacts that all jobs contracted with Martinez Security went through him. He funneled them to the group because he didn't want them involved in the politics. When Alexa was contacted directly, she'd thought long and hard about betraying her father to work with the CIA.

Ultimately, she chose the money and the adrenaline rush they provided. But there wasn't a single day that she didn't wish she could share that side of herself with her father.

"You're right," she said, running a brush through her hair. "We need more information before we go any further." She stopped when she noticed Dro watching her. "Baby, what's up?"

"Nothing." He wrapped his arms around her and placed a quick kiss on her lips. "Just looking at you. I can't look at you?"

She smiled. "You can look at me anytime you want. But are you sure you're okay?"

"I'm good now that I know you're good. Once we figure out what's going on, we can end this and live our lives the way we planned."

"Then let's get to work."

———

AUGUST 23, 1998, Alexa's eighteenth birthday:

"DADDY," Alexa cried as she ran into Pop's arms. "You're here. I didn't think you were coming in until tomorrow."

Pop smiled as he embraced her. "I wouldn't miss your birthday for the world, sweetheart."

She beamed with pride as he kissed her forehead and handed her a gift box. "Why don't you wait until later to give this to me? At the dinner?"

"No, ladybug. I need to give this to you now."

She glanced up at him. "You're going to be at dinner aren't you?"

"Of course, but this is not a gift for the dinner table."

She tore the gift wrap off the small package and gasped when she noticed the small antique locket. "Oh Daddy, it's so beautiful."

He sat down on the bed and pulled her next him. "I bought this locket when you were first born," he said, as he took her hand in his and squeezed. "I always knew I would give it to you on your eighteenth birthday."

Tears sprang up in her eyes when she opened it. Inside was a tiny braid of hair, a picture of her as a baby, and a baby picture of him as well. "Is this my hair?"

"Mine and yours, braided together. I gave your brother one too—well not a locket—but I did give him a braid to symbolize our bond together. I always dreamed of having a little girl. But you've turned out to be so much more than I ever hoped for. You've grown into a competent and wonderful young lady. I'm so proud of you." He reached into the briefcase sitting next to him and pulled out another box. "This is for you too."

She ripped the gold wrapping paper and tossed it on the floor. "Daddy, you got it?"

"I got it."

The semi-automatic .45 caliber pistol finished in titanium gleamed at her. She lifted it out of the box and gripped the handle. "It's beautiful."

"I bought your first gun when you were a little girl. Now you're a woman, and you need a woman's gun."

She hugged him again. "I love you, Daddy."

"I love you too, ladybug. I'll take you out tomorrow so you can practice with it. I want you to do your first job next week."

She grinned, excited about her first job. She had dreamed of being a part of this growing up and the anticipation was killing her. Would she have to do a kidnapping or a robbery—a murder? "Did you get the knife I wanted too?"

She knew the men did plenty of different jobs for her father. Pop was hired to assassinate, to infiltrate, to kidnap, to secure—whatever his country needed. The men learned a great deal from each experience.

Now it was her turn.

"Of course I did," he said, handing her another box. "Keep this in a special place. Make sure that when you whip it out, no one knows where you pulled it from. Always leave them guessing, ladybug."

She grinned and snatched it from his hands. "You're the best, Daddy."

NOVEMBER 4, 2011, B5:

. . .

POP WAS STANDING at the breakfast bar when Alexa entered the kitchen, followed by Dro. She ran straight to her father's waiting arms, just like she had when she was a little girl.

Pop wrapped his arms around her and held on tight. "I'm glad you're okay."

"I'm glad you're here. I've missed you." She pulled away and scanned the room. "The kids aren't up yet? Where's everybody?"

Pop shrugged. "My guess is everyone is still sleeping. I heard you had a rough night."

"Coffee?" Kendrick was leaning against the counter in the kitchen. "I filled Pop in on some of the details of last night, but we should probably talk in another room in case the kids decide to make an appearance."

Alexa held out a coffee mug for Chase to fill then handed the piping hot liquid to Dro before fetching another mug for herself. When everyone was served, they all headed to the security room.

Once everyone was seated, Pop addressed the group. "Kendrick told me about this woman, Melissa. Is her family into some kind of shady business?"

"Her family is very wealthy," Dro answered. "But as far as I know, they're legit. She used to always walk around acting like her family owned the town, but it wasn't because they were criminals or anything."

Pop rubbed his beard. "Well, the first thing we need to do is check out her family. I already asked Kendrick to get going on that with Nicholas."

"I went over the employee list," Lei added. "There were a few names that popped out to me—one in particular. I don't know how we missed it, but it seems there's a connection between one employee and the Neal Family."

Alexa gasped. "The Neals?" *Erik's family?*

"Naomi Gardner, who works in the records division of Martinez Security," Lei continued. "She could have had access to our security routines."

"How is she related to the Neals?" Alexa wondered. "That name should have never gotten through our checks."

"She married..." Lei scanned through the folder. "Adam. This was months after she was hired, though. And she kept her maiden name."

"Damn." Alexa winced when Pop frowned at her. "Sorry, Daddy."

Dro glanced at Alexa. "We're going to have to bring Naomi in," he said to Lei. "If she's connected to Adam, chances are this could be some sort of revenge."

Alexa set her mug on the table. "I want to talk to her."

Dro shook his head. "Kendrick and Chase will talk to her. You don't need to be there."

"Why the hell not? If she's involved, I want to talk to her."

"There's no reason to change how we do things," Dro said calmly. "Kendrick and Chase can handle it. It's too personal for you, and if you piss her off, she might withhold her cooperation."

"Under normal circumstances, I'd agree with you. But this *is* personal," she insisted. "It's personal for all of us, even Kendrick and Chase."

Kendrick cleared his throat. "I don't see why she can't come with us. If the bitch is in on the attacks, she's not likely to cooperate anyway. Alexa may be able to persuade her."

Alexa loved Kendrick for always having her back, but

she wished he hadn't stuck his nose in. Dro glared at him like he wanted to fling him across the room. But then they always had a love-hate sort of friendship.

"I just don't think it's a good idea," Dro growled through clenched teeth. "They're after Alexa and right now it's best that no one knows what happened to her. If we bring her into this too soon, they'll be prepared for her."

"He's right," Chase agreed. "Alexa, you might have to sit this one out. You can watch the whole thing on the monitors, but you're better off not being involved in the interrogation."

"I agree, ladybug stays behind," Pop concurred. "But we have something more pressing to discuss. I don't think it's wise to keep the kids here. They need fresh air. They need to be able to play. There's no telling how long this will last. And I would feel better if we got them out of the country."

"I was thinking the same thing," Dro said. "We can send the kids, Ma, Makayla, and Ari away. One of us has to go with them, though."

"That's going to leave us vulnerable up here," Lei said. "You don't think we can send Nicholas or someone else down there?"

"No," Dro said. "I'm not sending my family out of the country without adequate protection. And I don't trust anyone else. We're going to send others, but I need one of us there too."

"Kendrick should go," Pop suggested.

"No," Alexa stated.

Dro sighed, but remained silent.

"Kendrick would be best," Pop argued. "His kids and his wife are going too. He may want to be in control of the situation."

"No!" Alexa was adamant. "Kendrick should stay here. We need him here."

"Ladybug." Pop rubbed his neck. "I don't think you understand—"

"I understand perfectly, Daddy. Kendrick should stay here." She kept eye contact with him. "I actually think you should go with the kids." When everyone stared at her, she shrugged. In the past, she would never have said something like that to her father. But with her kids at stake, she couldn't afford to back down. "It's not like I don't want you here. I just think as far as resources go, you're the best bet to go with them. You're more than capable of handling problems, even more so than Kendrick. If we send Nicholas, we're going to need Kendrick here in case we have computer issues. Chase can go with you."

Alexa hated to throw Chase under the bus, but she needed Kendrick by her side. They were partners in crime. Obviously irritated, Dro turned his back on her and whispered something in Lei's ear. He never really understood her relationship with Kendrick, and she couldn't explain it to him.

"You may have a point, ladybug," Pop said after a minute. "I just don't want to leave you here to fight this enemy alone. I feel like I should be here."

She smiled. "I know, Daddy. I also know you won't let anything happen to the kids—neither will Chase."

"Lay it on thick," Dro said to her.

"I don't know what you mean," she replied innocently. "It's the truth. I trust both of them with the kids."

Dro arched a brow at her. "Whatever."

She narrowed her eyes as she assessed him then decided to table their personal disagreements for later. "Daddy? What do you think?"

"I'll go," he stated. "Chase and I will take care of the

family. But I want to be kept in the loop. You hear me? I want to know every move you make."

Lei nodded. "Sure. No problem. Kendrick can set up a secure line so we can keep in touch."

Chase stalked out of the room, slamming the door behind him. Kendrick moved to follow him. After giving Alexa another hug, Pop left the room, motioning for Lei to join him.

"You know you're wrong," Dro said, once they were alone.

"Why?"

He set his mug down on the table. "You just can't be away from Kendrick."

"You know it's not like that."

"Do I?" he asked, his tone reeking with sarcasm.

"Yes."

His steely gray eyes narrowed on her. "What I know is that you just shipped the most experienced one of us out of the country? What if something goes wrong with B5 and Chase isn't here to fix it, all because you don't want to be without Kendrick?"

"You know we need Kendrick here," she persisted. "There's no other way around it."

"Whatever." Dro started toward the door. "You got what you wanted. All is well, huh?"

"Dro—"

He held up his hand. "No, Alexa. Don't even bother explaining. I already know." Then he walked away from her without another word.

Chapter Fifteen

APRIL 12, 1998, Victoria's Secret:

ALEXA HAD WALKED around the lingerie store forever, or so it seemed. It was Dro's birthday the next day and she wanted to get something he would like. She knew her guard, Robert, was a few feet behind her.

"Robert?" she called, holding up a particularly risqué piece of lingerie. "I need your opinion please. You think Dro would like this?"

Robert coughed, cleared his throat, and pulled at his dress shirt. "Ms. Richardson, I don't want to give you any opinions on anything in this store. Your father is liable to kill me."

She hummed softly as she looked through the racks. "I thought we had an understanding. You're my guard. You accompany me everywhere I go. Can't you just humor me? I need a second opinion. If you had a woman, and it was your birthday, would you like your woman to wear something like this?"

Alexa smirked, enjoying the uncomfortable look on the older man's face. She knew Robert hated this detail as much as she did. And even though he was a pain in her ass, she couldn't help but love him. The fifty-year-old guard was one of the only people her father trusted with her safety.

Every birthday, Robert would buy her a charm for her bracelet. He never had any kids, so he treated her like she was one of his own. Reluctantly, she had to admit that Dro's assigning him to guard her was the right move. Robert would die before he let anything happen to her.

"Well?" She tapped her foot, trying to hide her smile.

He nodded slightly. "It's fine."

She shifted and held the piece up to her body again before sliding it back into place on the rack. "Maybe I'll get the other set I saw in the front of the store."

He glanced toward the front and his eyes narrowed. "Wait here. I'll be right back."

As he walked off in the direction of the bathroom—presumably to check out something suspicious—she scanned her surroundings, but saw nothing wrong. Robert was probably just being overly cautious.

She liked shopping in the evening after the high school crowd left the mall, liked having the store to herself. Only three other people were in the store, two saleswomen and an older woman, browsing through the bra section.

Deciding on the black lace at the front of the store, she strolled over to register. Once she settled the bill, she stood by the door waiting for Robert.

Glancing around her, she noticed the store had emptied out and checked her watch. It had been twenty minutes since Robert left her. The saleswomen were preparing to close. Hurrying to the bathroom door, she knocked. "Robert!"

No answer.

She slowly turned the knob and stepped into the bathroom.

"Robert?"

Searching the bathroom, she saw a pool of blood on the floor near the handicapped stall.

She dropped her shopping bag on the floor, pushed the stall door open, and gasped. Robert lay on the floor, blood oozing from his neck.

She knelt down next to him. "Robert?" When he didn't respond, she grabbed up his wrist and felt for a pulse. It was faint, but at least he was alive.

Immediately, she sprang up and locked the bathroom door. Then she hurried to the sink and yanked the paper dispenser open, grabbing a bunch of towels.

Kneeling next to Robert again, she held the paper towel over the gaping neck wound.

She placed a hand on his arm and shook him. "Robert?"

He moaned quietly. "Alexa?"

She sighed, grateful he was semi-conscious. "I'm going to call someone and get you some help."

"No," he groaned, pushing her away from him. "You need to get out of here-"

"Stop. You need to be still, Robert. Who did this to you?"

"They got me from behind. Didn't see them." He tried to push her away again, but she wouldn't budge. "Go now. You need to leave-"

"You're losing too much blood." She pushed the paper towels harder against his neck. "And no, I'm not leaving you here."

"It's too late for me," he murmured. "Go before they come back."

She dug her cell phone out. *Damn! No signal.* Tossing the phone back into her purse, she wondered what to do next.

Someone jiggled the doorknob. Alexa scrambled to her feet, slid her leather jacket off, and laid it over Robert. "I'll call someone. Hang in there." Opening his suit jacket, she took the car keys out of the inside pocket.

The jiggling on the knob was replaced by loud knocks. There was no way of knowing who was on the other side of the door without opening it. It was either one of the saleswomen doing a bathroom check or the person who hurt Robert. She scanned the bathroom for another way out and noted a high window in the corner. *Shit!* Kicking off her shoes, she hopped on top of a sink and used the heel of her shoe as a hammer to break the glass.

She glanced back at the door then pulled herself up to the window sill. The cool April breeze hit her skin, sending a chill through her body. She peered down at the ground, said a prayer, and jumped.

"Shit!" she hissed as she hit the ground and landed on something sharp. She took a minute to look at her foot and pulled a piece of glass from it, moaning as pain shot through her ankle. Cringing, she slid both of her four-inch pumps back on. *Why didn't I wear comfortable shoes?*

She tore through her purse for her phone and yanked it out. There was a faint signal. She dialed.

"What's up?" Kendrick answered.

"Kendrick," she whispered. "I need you."

"What's going on, Alexa?"

"Robert was stabbed. I'm not sure who did it. He's barely hanging on, though. I need you to send someone to the Victoria's Secret on Bush."

Kendrick cursed. "Where exactly are you?"

"I'm in the alley behind the store." She limped toward

the car, careful not to put too much pressure on her injured foot. "I'm heading to the car."

"Come straight home. Hurry. I'll send someone for Robert."

As she neared the street, a shadowy figure turned into the alley. Alexa froze. The sun had already gone down, so she wasn't sure if he'd noticed her. Cautiously, she slipped behind a trash can and leaned against the wall of the store.

"Did you see her?" a male voice asked.

"No, I didn't," responded a different man. "I checked the whole store. She's nowhere in sight."

"How did she slip past us?"

"I don't know."

She closed her eyes and wondered how she was going to get out of this. Grabbing an empty pop bottle, she pitched it behind her. Footsteps raced toward the sound. Once they were past her, she bolted for the street as fast as she could go. It seemed too easy, but she went with it— until she ran right into a third man, who grabbed and hauled her off her feet.

She struggled, kicking and punching him. Finally, he lost his grip and dropped her. She immediately socked him in the balls. It stunned him, but not enough to disable him. He grabbed her hair as she slammed him in the knee with her good foot. His leg buckled, but his grip remained steady. She grabbed another stray bottle and bashed him in the face. Releasing her, he collapsed to the ground with a thud.

Another man advanced toward her and she kicked him in the chest. Yanking her knife from its hiding place, she thrust it into his neck. As a third man charged her, she pulled the knife out and plunged it into that man's leg. Before he could retaliate, she jerked her gun from its holster and shot him.

A groan pulled her attention back to the first man, who was struggling to his feet. She slapped him across the cheek with the butt of her gun. He slumped back to the ground.

She leaned down and peered at his face. "Who the hell sent you?"

Placing her gun beneath his chin, she waited.

"Who are you?" he croaked.

She pressed the gun harder into his skin. "*You* came after *me*. Shouldn't you *know* who I am?"

"His name's Steve," the man confessed. "He and his father paid us to grab you and bring you back to him. Please," he begged. "I have children. I only took this job to support them. Let me go. I'll tell you anything you want to know. He also said he may have other jobs for us that have to do with you."

"What types of jobs?"

The man took a deep breath. "He didn't want a hair harmed on your head because he was going to use you as leverage against someone. He had plans for someone else too, but I didn't catch a name. He told us he had been watching you for a long time."

"Thanks," she said and patted him on the shoulder.

As she started to rise, he slid a gun from his pocket, cocking it as his hand came up. Instinctively, her finger tightened on the trigger of her own gun, the bullet went straight through his heart.

Sirens roared in the distance as she hurried to the car. She said a quick prayer for Robert, slid into the driver's seat, and sped off into the night.

Kendrick had said to come straight home, but Alexa decided to make a quick stop on the way. Kendrick wouldn't like it, but that couldn't be helped.

When she reached her destination, she immediately turned off her headlights and got out of the car. Taking a deep breath, she ran up to the house and knocked on the door.

A tall lanky man answered the door. Alexa smiled. "Hi. I'm looking for Steve."

"Steve isn't here. I'm the housekeeper. Is there something I can help you with?"

She beamed at him. "Thank God, you're here. I had a study date with Steve today, and I accidentally let him walk away with my book and all my notes. Can I just go to his room and get it? I promise it won't take long."

She couldn't tell if he believed her story or not, but he didn't let her in. "How about I have Steve just call you when he gets in."

"Please," she pleaded. "I really need to study. I'm trying to get into MIT next year. This test can make or break my grade this semester."

The man sighed. "I'll go to his room and see if I can find it for you. Wait here."

She nodded, and waited until he turned around. Spying a vase on a small table next to the door, she pushed it off the stand. When the housekeeper rushed over to the broken vase, she smashed him in the head with the butt of her gun. He slumped to the floor, unconscious.

Alexa dashed up the massive staircase and down a long hallway. Since she had been to Steve's house one time, with Erik, she knew where his room was. She reached his door and cautiously pushed it open. Lying on Steve's bed was his brother, Aaron. *Even better.* Aaron was too busy listening to his stereo to notice her enter the room until it was too late.

She placed the muzzle of her gun against his forehead. Aaron's eyes popped open, widening with fear.

"Sit up," she commanded. "I need to give your brother a little message."

NOVEMBER 4, 2011, B5:

ALEXA FOUND Chase in the kitchen. "Hi," she said, sliding into the seat next to him.

"I know you're mad," she said. "I'm sorry."

"I'm not mad. And you're not sorry." He finished a bottle of water. "Kendrick is your best friend. You always choose him."

"Actually, I chose you."

He shot her a sidelong glance. "Don't try to play me, Alexa."

"I'm not." She grabbed one of his hands and squeezed. "I'm choosing you to take care of my kids. I trust you with them. I know you'll protect them. That's important to me."

Alexa closed her eyes and sighed. If she had her way, she'd want all of them there battling this enemy together. But it wasn't possible.

"I wanted to be here," Chase said. "But it's not feasible, and I understand that. I told you I'm not mad."

She patted his hand gently. "I hope you're not, because I love you, Chase."

"Isn't that sweet?" Kendrick said, strutting into the kitchen.

"Kendrick, this is a private conversation," she said.

He opened the refrigerator and pulled out a beer. "Then go somewhere private."

She rolled her eyes and looked at Chase, who was watching her closely. "Chase, you've been there for me every single time it mattered. I can't thank you enough for just being who you are."

Chase raised a brow. "But you want Kendrick to stay here, to be by your side." He smirked. "Just go ahead and admit it."

"I want all of you to stay here with me," she groaned, throwing up her hands in frustration. "Okay. The only thing I'll admit is that Kendrick is my partner, and we always work better together. Other than that, I meant everything I said to you. This isn't some sort of competition between you and Kendrick."

"Because we all know who would win that contest," Dro murmured as he entered the kitchen.

Alexa sighed. "Can I please talk to Chase alone?"

Dro took the beer Kendrick held out for him. "Why are you in the kitchen if you want privacy?"

Kendrick laughed and she glared at him. "You really get on my nerves. Maybe you *should* go."

Chase chuckled. Standing, he said, "I'm just playing with you. Alexa, we're good. Love you, too." He turned to Dro. "I looked into Naomi's background a little further. She was hired right out of college. Before that, there was nothing—no high school records, birth certificate, or anything. Also, I'm almost finished with that project you asked me to do. Want to check it out?"

Alexa watched Chase leave the kitchen. Dro shook his head then followed after him. Kendrick pulled another beer out of the refrigerator. He held it out for her. She grabbed it and took a swig.

Setting it on the counter, she rubbed the side of her face. "I don't know what his problem is."

"Yes, you do. It's the same one he's had since you were kids."

Kendrick had always maintained that Chase was in love with her, but she refused to entertain that idea. She smacked his shoulder. "I'm talking about Dro, dummy."

"You know what his problem is, too."

"You?" she offered.

"More like *you* needing me."

Taking another swig of her beer, she raked her free hand through her hair, trying to ignore the pain in her heart. "Go spend some time with your wife and kids before they leave."

Chapter Sixteen

APRIL 12, 1998, *Pop's house*:

KENDRICK PACED the foyer at Pop's house, waiting on Alexa to arrive. He glanced at his watch for the fiftieth time in the last half hour. She had called hours ago. She was supposed to be on her way home, but she hadn't made it yet. Someone had attacked her guard, and she was out on the town. What the hell was she thinking?

He heard keys in the door and whirled around as Alexa slipped in. Not wanting to alert the whole house to her presence before he had sufficient time to scold her, he grabbed her arm, dragged her into the sitting room, and softly closed the door.

"Where the hell have you been?" he hissed.

"I—"

"What the hell is your problem? When I talked to you, I assumed you were on your way here. Now here it is an hour later, and you're just strolling through the door? But hey, I guess that's what I get for assuming because you keep making an ass out of me!"

"Kendrick, I'm sorry. I had to make a stop."

"A stop?" He pinched the bridge of his nose, certain his head would burst from the pressure building behind his eyes. "In whose reality could you possibly think that was okay? Shit, Lex, what the hell were you thinking? Everyone has been worried sick about you. Dro is livid—practically insane—and you made a stop?"

"Calm down so I can explain myself, damn it."

He took a deep breath, shoving his hands into his pockets to keep from strangling her. But his attempt to calm his nerves didn't work. "Where were you?"

She twisted her fingers together and he groaned out loud. *This can't be good.* When she looked up at him with puppy dog eyes, he braced himself.

"I went to Steve's house," she whispered.

And just like that, this whole situation got worse. If he was a lesser man, he would've fallen on the ground in frustration and had a full blown temper tantrum like a toddler.

"You *what*?"

"I went to Steve's house."

"You—" He took a deep breath, willing himself to take it down a notch. The house was crawling with people and he didn't want to draw attention to them. "You went to Steve's house? What on earth would possess you to do that?"

"I wanted to leave him a message—let him know I could get to him just as easily as he thinks he can get to me."

"A message?"

"Yes. I went to his house, tied his brother up—after I made him strip—and left him there. I didn't hurt him."

Kendrick couldn't help it. Unable to control his temper,

he hurled his brand new cell phone into the wall. It shattered. "Shit!"

He hated losing his temper, but when dealing with Alexa it seemed unavoidable. The girl might be his best friend, but at times, she drove him mad. And now he'd ruined his brand new cell phone. That sucked. He'd really liked that phone.

He paced the room, feeling like a caged animal, as the same word rolled through his mind over and over. Shit!

"Kendrick, can you please stop pacing back and forth. You're making me nervous."

He whirled, glaring at her. *She has the gall to say that to me*? "Do you really think I give a damn? You're unbelievable. You went to Steve's house—after Robert was killed and you left three dead men in the alley behind Victoria's Secret—and you think I give a damn how you feel?"

She closed her eyes and her lips trembled. "Robert's dead?"

She'd better not cry. Damn it, now he felt like an ass. He was never strong when faced with her tears, and he couldn't help but soften. "He was dead by the time we got there."

"He was alive when I left him. I wanted to stay with him, but he told me to get out of there. I tried to walk away, Kendrick. When I jumped out the window, I headed straight for the car, but I was cornered."

"You do realize you didn't need to go over there and leave any kind of message?" he asked, barely able to conceal his rage. "The message was clear when you killed three of their men by yourself."

"Alexa?" Dro called from the doorway. He stormed into the room, slamming the door behind him. "Where the hell have you been?"

"Dro," she breathed.

"Where were you?" Dro's voice was calm, but Kendrick knew it wouldn't last long once he found out where she'd been.

"I—" She cleared her throat. "I made a stop."

Dro stood silent, his arms folded across his chest. Kendrick assumed Alexa would continue, but she stood mute as well. He hoped she wasn't going to leave it at that. Then *he* would be forced to explain the situation.

"Um," she began again. "I know you're probably upset I didn't come straight here. I know you were worried—"

"Stop," he said, slicing a hand through the air. "I don't need you to try to explain yourself. Just tell me where you were."

"I went to Steve's house," she muttered, under her breath.

The room was silent—so silent it was deafening. Kendrick could tell Dro's infamous control dangled by a very fine thread.

"Three men cornered me in the alley," she continued, sitting on the edge of one of the couches. "One of them told me Steve and his father set the whole thing up. So, I decided to go to Steve's and leave a message-"

"What the hell is your problem?" Dro stopped and took a few deep breaths.

Kendrick wanted to tell him that shit didn't work, but he figured silence was his best option.

"You have no idea how much I want to choke you right now. Why would you go off halfcocked to Steve's house—on his territory—by yourself—to leave an unnecessary message? What the hell kind of message did you leave?"

Alexa peered at Kendrick, swallowing visibly then turned back to Dro. "I figured Steve and his father wouldn't be there because they would be waiting for the men to bring me to them. My plan was to just go there and leave them something, letting them know I was there. His brother was there. I didn't hurt him. I just scared him. I made him strip and tied him to the bed. What?"

Dro rolled his eyes. "Don't say anything else, just listen. What you did will serve no purpose other than to rile them up and force them to step up their game. Did you even think about what would've happened if Steve and his father had hired the men to bring you to their house? You could have been ambushed when you set foot on the property. There could have been hidden guards anywhere. So, again, what were you thinking?" He threw his hands in the air then fisted them on his hips. "Not only that, you knew you were supposed to bring your ass back here as soon as possible. You didn't give a damn about that, though. All you were worried about is proving yourself yet again. And how many times do I have to tell you there's nothing to prove?"

She opened her mouth to speak, but he held up his hand.

"I just don't know what goes on in your head when you make decisions like this," he roared. "You can't even follow simple instructions. You just want to do your own thing. Maybe I should suggest that Pop send you away."

She gasped. "You wouldn't!"

"I would. Don't ever underestimate me."

She walked closer to Dro. "Listen to me-"

"Don't," he said, stepping away from her. "You pissed me the fuck off. I don't even want to look at you right now. Do you realize how worried we were about you? Do you even care? Kendrick told you to bring your ass straight home! And you couldn't even do that. Robert is dead, Alexa. There were three dead men in the alley. We didn't know what the hell happened to you. And you went to Steve's?"

She placed a hand on his arm. "Dro-"

Kendrick tensed, suddenly feeling very protective, when Dro batted her hands away. Of course, he knew Dro would never hit her, but he'd also never seen him this angry before.

"Stop touching me," he growled. "Just leave me the hell alone. There's no explanation good enough. Don't you get it? I don't want to hear how sorry you are 'cause I don't give a damn."

"Alexa, just let him calm down," Kendrick said softly. "Let him go. I don't want to have to beat Dro's ass for talking to you like he's crazy."

"You couldn't beat my ass in your best dream." Dro stalked out of the room and Alexa ran after him.

"Dro," she called as she chased him through the foyer to the spiral staircase.

Kendrick had never seen her behave like this—so desperate. It shocked the hell out of him.

"Please," she begged as Dro headed up the stairs. "I'm sorry."

Pop and Lei entered the foyer.

"Ladybug, where the hell were you?" Pop bellowed. He turned to Dro. "Hold on, Son."

Alexa's shoulder slumped and peered at Kendrick with red eyes. He was willing to go up against Dro, but Pop was a different story.

"Ladybug?" Pop repeated loudly. "Do you realize how worried we were for you?"

"Yes Daddy," she whispered, bowing her head. "I'm sorry."

Pop sighed. "I'm glad you're safe, ladybug. Lei call Chase and tell him she's home. We'll talk about this soon as you get cleaned up." Pop eyed Dro. "Since Enrique is out of town, I want you and Ari to stay here. It would make me feel better."

Dro nodded. "I'm going to bed." His eyes flashed to Alexa before he continued his trek up the stairs.

NOVEMBER 4, 2011, B5:

AFTER ANOTHER DISCUSSION in the security room it was decided that Canada was the best place for Pop and Chase to take the family. It was close enough for them to get back if necessary, or for one of the others to come there.

Kendrick stayed with Alexa while Dro and Lei handled important Martinez business.

"You made Dro mad," he told her, wiping a bit of sweat off her brow.

She smacked his hand. "I didn't mean to."

He wrapped an arm around her and tugged her closer. "You never mean to, but it always seems to happen."

"Please, let's just not talk." She punched his shoulder. "Harder."

He shook his head. "Not until you talk to me."

As he loomed over her, she averted her eyes from his gaze and punched him again. "Kendrick, I need you to go harder."

"I said no. Not until you talk to me."

"Let's just get down to it."

He encircled a hand around her neck. "Alexa," he whispered. "Sometimes you can't have it your way."

She rolled her eyes. "Listen, I told you." She pushed at him at again. "Go harder. I need to do this."

Grabbing her leg, he hooked an arm under her knee. "You need to look at me and answer me."

"You didn't ask a question. And what do you want me to say?" she grumbled. "I know I pissed him off. But I need you here. And you know you want to be here, so why do we even have to talk about this?"

"And what about Chase?"

She frowned. "What about him?"

"You know how he feels about you. He's in love with you."

"Actually, that's not a proven fact, and I wish you'd stop saying that. As far as him going, I can't be sorry about it. The only thing that matters is that I know my kids will be taken care of with Chase and Daddy."

"Back to Dro," Kendrick said. "How are you going to fix it?"

"Give him time. He's...irritated," she admitted.

"Can you blame him?"

"No." She thumped his forehead. "Damn it, Kendrick, stop talking."

He chuckled and pinned her arms to the floor. "I'm glad I'm here with you. I don't think I could have left you here. You and Dro always talk that 'Live and Die' shit. But you're my ride or die."

"You're stupid, Kendrick," she muttered and slapped his arm. "Harder."

He sat up on his knees and pushed against her thighs with his elbows. She was lying flat on her back, one thigh in the air. "You know I'm telling the truth," he said. "The real Bonnie and Clyde we are, without all that silly love stuff."

When they were younger, many people referred to Alexa and Dro as "Bonnie and Clyde". Kendrick always thought it was bullshit. For one, Bonnie and Clyde died in the end. And he worked better with Alexa than Dro ever did. So if anyone was Clyde to her Bonnie it would be him.

She lifted up her other thigh, and he pushed down on both.

"Can you two stop all the yapping and get going?" Lei suggested, entering the small gym. "She's barely broken a sweat."

"Kendrick," Dro added, tossing a bottle of water at him. "Stop trying to sweet talk my wife. This is supposed to be a workout—enough stretching."

She shoved Kendrick, causing him to lose his balance and tumble to the ground. She charged at him once he was on his feet again, but he averted her. A quick roundhouse kick toward his face was blocked right before he knocked her flat on her back.

"You're slipping," he said. He lifted his hands up in the fight stance. "Come on."

She massaged her lower back. "Damn you, Kendrick."

Arms in front of her face, fists closed, she barreled toward him again. When he reached out to strike her, she ducked and spun around with a low kick to his knee. It buckled, but he remained upright. He charged at her, but she flipped away from him. Landing into a split, she punched him below his groin. Then she swept her leg under him and tripped him.

Before he could get up, she was standing over him, with her foot pressed against his neck. He grabbed her other leg and flipped her onto her back. She scrambled to her feet just in time to block his next punch.

He grasped her legs and slammed her on the mat, face down. Rolling over, she kicked at him, wrapped her leg around his neck, and then jabbed him in the stomach.

"Okay," Lei shouted. He tossed a towel at Alexa. "That's good. We need to talk."

She dabbed the sweat from her brow. "What about?"

"Since Chase is gone," Dro said. "Lei is going to take Kendrick and go talk to Naomi. We'll observe the interrogation, Alexa. Pop checked in and they're almost to the border. With Nicolas there, Chase may be available to come back if we need him."

"When are we heading into town to talk to Naomi?" Kendrick asked.

"In the morning," Lei replied. "For now, I need Alexa to take a break and come back in an hour so we can work out. You're a little slow. I need you back in form."

She groaned and slapped him with her towel. "I can still kick your ass, Lei."

"Whatever," he joked. "I'm not taking any chances."

"I don't need another workout," she said, pouting. "I'm good."

"Good?" Dro asked. "Lei is right, baby. You're a little slow. You need to work out with him."

She pushed Dro in the chest. "How about I work out with you?"

"What kind of workout are you trying to do?" he asked, tugging on her towel.

Kendrick rolled his eyes. "Can you two please stop with the sexual innuendos? My wife is gone. I can't get any relief until this is over."

Dro glared at him. "You could've gone with her, but your friend here wouldn't stand for it."

Alexa dropped her towel on the floor. "Do we have to go through this again?" She grabbed Dro's hand. "And I'm talking a real workout, Mr. Martinez."

She swung on Dro, but he caught her wrist. "Ah Ah Ah."

Then she swung her other fist, this time connecting with his jaw.

"Good one." He rubbed his jaw. "But I'm not going to work out with you. That's Lei and Kendrick's department."

She winked at him. "You scared?"

"Only of losing you," he replied. "So, you need to fight with someone who doesn't want to fuck you. We all know that us working out together is not very productive."

She headed toward the door. "Fine, you win. I'm going to take a break. I'll be back in an hour." Before she exited the gym, she glanced back at Dro over her shoulder. "You coming?"

He shrugged when Kendrick and Lei both arched a brow at him. "She'll be back in an hour," he said, following her out.

Chapter Seventeen

APRIL 13, 1998, Pop's house:

ALEXA WAS GOING CRAZY. Dro was still not talking to her after the Victoria Secret debacle. The whole family had gathered to celebrate his birthday, but he wouldn't even look at her. Kendrick told her to give him some time. *But how much time does he need?* It was no secret he was stubborn. If you were on his list, you pretty much stayed there until he took you off.

At dinner, he managed to speak to everyone except her, which drew curious looks from her parents. Dro and Alexa had, pretty much, been inseparable at the house. The fact they weren't speaking was bound to raise a red flag.

After her little adventure at Steve's house, she endured more lectures from her father and Lei. Even her mother and Chase joined the "trash Alexa" brigade. But all she really wanted was to talk to Dro. This had gone on too long. She was forced to take drastic measures.

Alexa slipped into Dro's room later that evening. He

was lying on his stomach asleep—one sheet draped low on his hips, his chest bare. She tiptoed toward his bed.

"What are you doing here?" he asked softly.

She paused and took a deep breath. "I wanted to talk to you."

"You need to leave," he said, peering at her through one eye.

She scooted next to him on the bed. "How did you know it was me?"

"I just did."

He rolled onto his back and sat up. When he started to get out of the bed, she held on to his arm.

"Please, Dro. Let me talk to you. You don't have to say anything, but can you just hear me out?"

He leaned against the headboard and crossed his arms over his chest.

"Happy Birthday." She sighed in frustration when he remained silent. "I know how you feel."

He snickered.

She rubbed her sweaty palms on her legs. *He's making this hard.* "I can tell when you walk in a room, too. I don't know why, but I always know when you're near me. It's like a sixth sense."

He remained silent.

She touched his knee. "Come on, Dro. Are you going to ignore me for the rest of our lives? I'm sorry. I was wrong. I made a stupid decision. Don't punish me forever."

He moved her hand away.

Needing to find something to do with her hands, she smoothed them over a stray pillow. "Dro, I miss you. I don't think you've ever gone this long without talking to me. You've never been this upset with me. Talk to me, Dro. This is ridiculous. You can't just ignore me forever." Alexa realized that she had never felt this desperate before. It made her angrier—at herself.

His gaze was fixed on the wall.

"I had such plans for your birthday," she said with a nervous giggle. "I bought this lingerie at Victoria's Secret last night before..." *No reason to bring up last night.* Besides, she'd left her purchase in the bathroom when she found Robert. "I want to get past this, but we can't if you don't talk to me."

They sat there in uncomfortable silence for a few more minutes. Giving up, she started to get off the bed, but he placed his hands on hers.

DRO GLANCED at Alexa out of the corner of his eye and noticed a tear slide down her cheek. *Tears?* Alexa and tears were not synonymous with each other. She wasn't the type to just let them fall, unlike other women he had known. He'd only seen her cry a few times, under specific circumstances—but never because of him. And that was his downfall. "I miss you, too, but I'm still pissed. I want to let this go, but I can't—not when you did something so careless that you could have been hurt."

She turned her palm to his and squeezed. "I know, and I promise I won't do it again. I won't take unnecessary risks anymore. Just talk to me. Let me spend some time with you on your birthday."

"It's not my birthday anymore," he murmured.

She peered at the clock on the nightstand. "It's eleven-thirty. I still have time."

"Alexa, you can't just apologize and expect everything to be okay. What you did wasn't cool with me."

"I know, but I can't change it. The only thing I can do is promise never to do it again."

He wanted to forgive her, but her little stunt had scared the hell out of him. He pinched the bridge of his nose and groaned. "But can I trust that? Can I trust you not to take those types of risks with your life?" He hopped out of the bed and headed to the other side of the room, needing to put some distance between them. He knew he wouldn't be able to sit next to her without touching her. "I need to believe you won't do that again."

"I won't." She stood up. "I promise. Have I ever lied to you?"

"You can't promise me that!"

Staring at the ceiling, he sighed deeply. *She's too close.*

She placed her hands over his crossed arms. "Despite what you think, I didn't do it to prove anything. I just reacted when that man told me Steve hired them. I went there without thinking and I know how wrong it was. I know how costly that decision could have been."

"But I know you. I know how you think. And you take chances you don't need to take. You've been like this all your life."

"But Dro, that's our life. We all risk something to do the job. You know what we do—what I do. How can I do that if you are going to be mad at me every time I take a risk?"

"Risk is one thing, but unnecessary risk is another. I'm not stupid, so don't play me. I know there's some type of risk in everything. But going to Steve's house was just stupid. You always want to play the odds and I can't stand it. I hated waiting for you to come home last night. I didn't know what happened to you. I wondered if they got you, where you were, what they were doing to you."

Images he'd conjured up in his head last night popped

L R WRIGHT

into his mind again and he turned away from her.

Her shoulders slumped. "I'll admit it was a stupid thing to do. But nothing happened. I'm here. My boneheaded plan didn't get me killed—"

"This time." He walked around her over to the opposite wall. "You can come in here and promise me you won't do it again, but I know you will. It's in your nature."

She ran her fingers through her hair. "You're right. I can't promise I'll never do something like that again. I *can* promise that I'll call someone first."

His eyes narrowed. "Not Kendrick. Stop calling Kendrick first. He lets you get away with too much."

She smirked. "Are you jealous?"

"I'm not jealous of Kendrick. I just would appreciate it if you called me."

"I will. I haven't broken a promise to you before."

"Don't let this be the first." He sat on the edge of the bed.

She approached him. "You don't have to worry about that. Are we good?"

"We're good. You know, I couldn't stop thinking about what I would do if something happened to you. I feel like if I'm still here, you have to be here, too." He massaged the back of his neck. "I watched my Mom die right in front of my eyes. I don't want to lose another person that I love."

"Love?" she asked.

He understood why she seemed surprised. He'd always spurned love after his mother committed suicide. He said he was never going to let love destroy him like it did his mother. As far as he was concerned, his mother's main flaw was her love for his father. She loved him so much she lost herself. She kept waiting for him to love her back. It cost him and Ari in the end when she took her own life because she finally realized Enrique would never love her.

He also knew what he felt for Alexa was damn close to love. In fact, he was pretty sure it was headed there quickly. He was still cynical, though. When she didn't come home, he was hit with this uncontrollable and blinding fear in the pit of his stomach. Nothing had prepared him for the feeling caused by his fear for her life, or the relief he felt when he saw her talking to Kendrick. All he wanted to do was hold her in his arms and make sure she was really standing there, before he let his anger at her consume him. He knew it was only a reaction to the fear, but he'd let the anger rule.

He studied her. "Why are you acting surprised? You know how I feel about you." He knew what she was asking.

"Oh yeah, I know you love me—like you love Ari." She smirked and he knew she was playing with him. He also knew she was a woman. A part of her was probably curious, though.

"That would be pretty incestuous. Don't you think?"

"Very incestuous," she giggled.

"No, I don't love you like I love Ari."

"I was just wondering."

"I know what you're wondering," he admitted, lowering his head and looking at the ground.

She stepped between his legs and braced her hands on his shoulders. He smoothed his hand up the back of her leg to her upper thighs.

"I love you," she whispered.

Dro's eyes flashed to hers, searching her face and losing himself in her brown eyes. He knew she loved him, but her words weren't a simple "I love you".

She trailed one of her fingers across his forehead, down the slope of his nose. He closed his eyes as her cool fingertips moved sensually over his face.

Dro wasn't ready to admit he was in love with her, but

in that moment, he knew he couldn't live without her. Normally, a woman admitting that she loved him was enough to send him running far away, but not Alexa. Not today. Not ever.

"I'm in love with you," she breathed, with a nervous giggle. "Sometimes I think I've loved you my whole life. I can't be sure of most things, but I'm sure of that. Last night had to be one of the worst nights of my life. I promised myself I would tell you how I felt even if you never talked to me again. But I'm not afraid. I'm never scared."

He laughed softly and pulled her into him. "That's right. You're not scared. Come here."

She touched her lips to his lightly.

"Alexa, you know I—"

A finger over his mouth prevented him from finishing his thought. "Shhh! You don't need to say anything because I said it or because you think I want to hear it. I don't need words, Dro. Like you said, I know how you feel about me."

He skimmed her jaw with the back of one hand while drawing circles behind her knee with the other. She was right. He could feel her when she was near. Every bone and muscle reacted to her presence, clenched in anticipation of her touch. He knew if he wasn't careful, she would consume him. In many ways, she already did.

"I gave you those words because I wanted to," she whispered. "Not to get something in return. I love you because of who you are. And I know exactly who you are. I love everything about you—your past, your present, and your future."

He closed his eyes as he let her words wrap around him like a tight embrace. Her voice had soothed his soul so many times before. Wrapping a hand around her wrist, he brought her palm to his mouth and kissed it. She sucked in a breath as he placed soft kisses up her arms.

"I know when you're scared," she breathed. "When you're sleepy, when you're irritated, when you're angry, when you want me."

He wanted her all right—more than he ever wanted her before. He snaked a hand around the back of her neck and tugged her closer to him. He felt her soft breath against his lips. She placed a chaste kiss against his mouth. It wasn't enough. He wanted more. When he attempted to deepen the kiss, she pulled away.

"Alexa," he whispered, hoping to say something that was fitting for this moment.

"Dro," she sighed, gazing into his eyes. "You don't need to say the words. I don't need them."

"I need you so much." He rested his head against her stomach. The soft tips of her fingers tickled his scalp. It was true, he did need her.

When he finally peered up at her, he was ready to speak. She silenced him with a quick kiss and this time she let him deepen it.

"Happy Birthday, Dro," she said.

As he pulled her into another intense kiss, they fell back on the bed. "Thank you, baby."

NOVEMBER 4, 2011, B5:

DRO AND ALEXA were wrapped in each other's arms, limbs intertwined, after a taxing *private* workout. He ran his fingers through her curly hair. He couldn't help but love her "bed head" as she called it. She preferred to have her hair straightened, but he loved when it was wild and curly. He wanted to drag her back on top of him and make love to her again, but he knew she needed to meet Lei.

He patted her thigh lightly. "You should probably get ready for your workout."

"I don't want to." She kissed him softly on his chin.

He smoothed his hand down her back. "Lei isn't going to take no for an answer."

"He's going to kick my ass," she groaned, nestling into his side.

He laughed. "You're right. But you need it. It's been awhile."

She traced his six-pack. "I miss the kids."

"Me too, but they're safe. That's all that matters. I'm sure they are having fun just like we used to when we were shipped off somewhere."

He remembered the secret childhood trips they took when Enrique insisted they leave town for their own safety. His father always shipped them off to his resort in Puerto Rico. Dro's family was powerful on both sides and they were well protected.

"I remember," she purred. "We had a lot of fun, especially once we got old enough to really enjoy everything."

He kissed her forehead. "We really did enjoy it—and each other." They spent many nights on his private terrace engulfed in each other. Puerto Rico held so many memories for them. It was where he first proposed to her, at the age of ten. And thirteen years later, he made it official.

She lifted her head up and met his gaze. "I wonder if Adam has anything to do with this."

He squeezed the back of her neck. The last thing he needed was Erik coming back from the grave after all these years. Adam Neal was Erik's younger brother. They hadn't seen Adam since Erik died all those years ago. The boy had been distraught over the untimely death of his brother. Now he was married to one of Martinez' employees—one connected to security with access to information on the family. It couldn't have been a coincidence. "If he is, I'll kill him. And I won't think twice about it."

"I just...I can't figure out why he would be involved."

"Revenge," he offered. "If he's involved, it probably has something to do with revenge."

"For what though?" she asked. "We didn't do anything to him."

"Well he probably figures we had something to do with Erik's death."

"And Melissa? "What the hell is her problem?"

He chuckled, playing with her soft curls. "Well, you kicked her ass so many times, she definitely wants some revenge."

"She provoked me each and every time. You would think you confessed your undying love to the girl, the way she was hanging on. I never cared what she thought of me. It was different with Erik, though. We came to an understanding."

"Perception is in the eye of the beholder. The only way we're going to get answers is if we speak to Adam."

"You're right." She stroked his chest and rolled out of bed. "I guess I better go get my ass kicked."

As she stomped into the bathroom, he thought of the past. He knew she harbored a lot of guilt about Erik. She cried for days after Erik died, which was a shock. Alexa wasn't the type to regret the choices she made. She had admitted to Dro on many occasions that she regretted getting involved with him. Erik ended up another casualty in their war with Steve and his father.

Chapter Eighteen

APRIL 23, 1998:

ALEXA WAITED with Dro in her room. Erik had requested a meeting with them about Steve. She was surprised to hear from him considering Dro's threat at the hotel bar. Erik had taken that threat to heart in the weeks that followed. She hadn't seen or talked to him since then. But she wasn't exactly available to talk to either. Lei had been shot, and then she was attacked outside of Victoria's Secret soon afterward.

The word on the street was that Steve and his father were hell bent on getting to her—a fact that left them all on edge. Pop insisted she be under constant guard. One of the guys had to be with her at all times.

"Thanks for not giving me a hard time about this," she said to Dro.

"I still don't like it, Alexa."

"I think we should hear what he has to say. He

wouldn't contact me if this wasn't important. He doesn't want to antagonize you."

"How do you know that?" Dro asked. "He could be working with Steve."

Alexa was sure Erik would never work with Steve, but Dro wouldn't believe her. He suspected everyone. "Dro, just give him a chance."

"The minute he says something out of line, I'm kicking his ass out of here. And stop worrying. I've never known you to be worried before." He took her bottom lip between his and kissed her.

"I'm not worried, just concerned. Steve won't give up—"

"Until we kill him. And that may happen sooner than later."

"It can't be soon enough." She kissed him again, and they fell into a fervent embrace.

He gently nudged her onto her back and climbed over her. Opening each button of her shirt slowly, he bared her body to his eyes and his kisses. He brushed his lips against her forehead, then her nose, and finally her lips. She sucked in a breath when he nibbled on her chin.

She heard a soft creak. On the far side of the room, a panel opened and Lei stepped into the room. Dro re-buttoned her blouse and rolled off of her.

"I guess it's a good thing I walked in when I did," Lei said. "If you're going to have company you should be decent."

"Whatever," Dro growled.

"What's up?" Alexa asked her brother.

"Erik is here," Lei informed them. "He's with Janine, though."

She frowned. "Why is he with her?"

"Why do you care?" Dro asked, arching a brow at her.

She shrugged. "I don't. I was just wondering why he brought her. We did tell him to come alone."

"I just wanted to let you know," Lei said. "I'll be listening." He disappeared behind the wall again.

Alexa's father had invested a large sum of money building little secret passageways within the house. It helped when they needed a quick escape or, mostly, to do a little dirt. Because of the passageways, Pop had made sure Dro's room wasn't connected to hers since he spent a lot of time at their home. She guessed Pop wasn't thinking too clearly because her room was connected to Lei's room and Dro just used that passageway to get to her.

There was a soft knock on the door. "Come in," she called.

Erik stepped into the room with Janine right behind him. "Thanks for agreeing to meet," he said.

He plopped down on the window seat. Alexa noted the bags under his eyes. He looked tired and must have been under enormous stress. "I really could use your help," he started, motioning Janine to the seat next to him.

"What's up?" Alexa asked.

"Steve is crazy," Erik claimed. "And for some reason, I think you know more about him then you're letting on."

"What makes you think I know anything about Steve?" Alexa said, crossing her arms across her chest.

"I think you and your family are into some shady business. Steve has slipped up on many occasions and admitted your family has a beef with his. I already know Steve's father has some shady dealings. I have known that for as long as I've known Steve."

She sighed. "What makes you think Steve is crazy? And what does this have to do with Janine." She eyed the girl, sitting on the other side of the room.

Janine used to be a friend of hers. Over the past

month, though, Janine had made it a point to be seen with Erik as if they were a couple. Janine was also running around the school spreading rumors about her.

"Alexa," Janine said, twirling her thumb around the strap of her purse. "I know we haven't been cool. And I know you've heard some things, but there is a reason for everything. I really need your help."

Alexa was curious now. "Why? Aren't you and Erik together? Why do you need my help?"

Erik touched Janine's leg. "We're not together," he insisted. "The only reason we're being seen together is to protect Janine. Steve's brother, Aaron, has been harassing her. He's threatened her plenty of times. He only backed off once she told him we were together. I'm not sure how long that will last. They're both on some kind of power trip. They've been hinting that their Dad is on to something big that will give them power in the streets. Steve has also made it very clear that he doesn't care who he has to step on to get it."

Alexa glanced at Dro, who was silently watching Erik. "I have to ask you why you think we can help?" she asked, meeting Erik's gaze again.

Erik swept his hand through the air as he scanned the room. "Look around you. Your family has power. It's the same power that Steve and his family want. I just figured your family could help us. I can't have imagined that you care about me, Alexa. All the years we've known each other and confided in each other, you couldn't have been pretending the whole time."

She averted her eyes from his, letting her guilt soak her to the bone.

"What do you want Erik?" Dro asked finally. "So far, you're just talking in circles. Tell me what you want. What is it?"

"I'm willing to do whatever it takes to protect myself and Janine." Erik cleared his throat. "If that means bringing you information on Steve and his family so you can make them disappear, I'll do it. I'm just tired of living like this."

Alexa shook her head. "You're not getting involved in this."

"Is that why you broke up with me?" Erik asked. "You don't want me involved?"

She rubbed the back of her neck. "What you're asking is just too dangerous. You don't know anything about Steve and his family, or the lengths they will go to get what they want. You need to stay far away from this."

"I always knew you cared about me," Erik uttered. "Now, I know for certain Dro's threat had more to do with you than him. You staged the whole scene at the bar. He did it because you told him to. I had a feeling."

"Is that why you clown on her every time you see her in public?" Dro asked.

Erik's eyes narrowed. "I did that because I was hurt, and I wanted to make it convincing. Deep down, I knew she cared about me."

Alexa elbowed Dro in the side, hoping it would stop him from saying something.

"I'm tired of this shit," Dro said, standing to his feet. "What do you need from us, Erik, because I don't have time for this? Your feelings for Alexa don't matter. You came to us because you said you needed help. What do you want us to do?"

Alexa covered her mouth with her hand to hide her smile. *Jealous much?* Dro couldn't stand Erik, which was rather funny to her. "He's right, Erik. There's no sense in rehashing the past."

"But if that's the reason why you broke up with me—" Erik began.

"Erik." She sliced her hand in the air. "It doesn't matter. I do care about you. I broke it off with you because I didn't want you to get hurt. And not just from Steve. I was hurting you in other ways. I guess what it all boils down to is I just couldn't give you what you wanted or needed."

Erik lifted his chin. "Well, I want to help. I told you, I'll do whatever it takes."

"Whatever." Dro rolled his eyes. "What you want is Alexa. I told you that day in the bar to let it go."

"I know that she's with you," Erik responded. "You have made it perfectly clear. I still want to help with the Steve situation."

"What is it that you think you can do to help us?" Dro challenged.

Alexa thought it was time for her to step in. "What he means is—"

"I meant what I said. What do you think you can do to help?" Dro leaned against the dresser and folded his arms over his chest. "Who are you? Do you have some secret that you think would be interesting to us? Are you privy to some business dealings that we can use to our advantage? Are you willing to walk into Steve's house and kill him? What do you think you can do to help?"

"I don't have any of those things," Erik confessed. "And I'm not a killer."

"What can you do to help us, then?" Dro repeated. "This is bullshit. I'm tired of repeating myself to you. For some reason, you just don't get it. We don't need you to help us do shit. You bring something to the table, other than stupidity, and we can talk. If you don't have anything to contribute, what are you doing here? You asked to meet with us because you said you needed our help. Now you want to help us? Can you pick one and stick with it?"

Erik twisted his hat in his hands. He jumped up abruptly and stalked toward Dro. Alexa hopped off the bed and stepped between them.

Janine touched Erik's arm. "Erik, calm down."

"Janine is right," Alexa said. She placed a hand against Erik's chest. "You need to calm down." She could feel his heart pumping fast beneath her palm. *Dro will eat him alive.*

Dro massaged Alexa's shoulders. He was egging Erik on, in an already tense situation. The vein in Erik's temple throbbed.

"Baby," Dro whispered loud enough for everyone in the room to hear. "You don't need to stand between us. Erik is not stupid."

Erik blew out a deep breath and finally took his seat again. Dro remained standing.

Alexa turned to Dro. "Can you please stop? This isn't helping."

"I told you this was a waste of time," he said to Alexa.

She kissed him on the chin. "Just sit down, baby." Only he didn't sit down like she suggested. He leaned against the dresser again.

Alexa rolled her eyes. Turning to Erik, she said, "Tomorrow, you need to stage a public breakup with Janine. Then, Janine, you're going to pretend to be kicking it with Kendrick. That way, you'll be protected. Erik, it's time for us to step out on the town together."

"Like hell," Dro growled. "There's no way you're going anywhere with him."

She spun around to face Dro. "Listen—"

"No, I'm not going to listen," Dro argued. "I don't have a problem with Kendrick hanging with Janine for protection, but Erik doesn't need protection from you. I'll put someone else on him. For now, Erik, you need to keep a low profile. Stay away from Steve. If he's as crazy as you say, he won't think twice about using you to get what he wants. And that means you better stay the hell away from Alexa. Tell me what you know about Steve and his family and I'll let you know what's going to happen from here."

Alexa smirked as Dro barked more orders. Paying close attention to Dro over the years had finally paid off. She'd known he would react that way. At least she'd accomplished her goal and gotten Erik some protection.

NOVEMBER 5, 2011, Martinez offices:

ALEXA WATCHED through the two-way glass and waited for Naomi to arrive. Kendrick and Lei planned on questioning her and were seated inside the meeting room. Dro stood beside her, stoic and unreadable. When they had arrived at the office earlier, Lei and Kendrick cleared the top floor. It was important that no one knew what they were doing in the office.

A memo had been sent out by "Chase", asking Naomi to meet with him regarding a top secret security matter. All meeting rooms were equipped with cameras. Some had observation glass such as the one Alexa was looking through.

Alexa gasped when Naomi entered the room. She was familiar—too familiar. She was none other than Janine, her high school friend.

Dro let out of gruff curse under his breath.

Kendrick rose from his seat abruptly, tipping his chair

153

on its back. "What the hell are you doing? And why the hell did you change your name?"

Lei had walked up behind Janine while Kendrick was talking. "Sit," he ordered, motioning to a chair. "You have some explaining to do."

Janine complied with his request.

"Answer the question, Janine." Kendrick's tone was even. "What the hell is wrong with this picture?"

Janine crossed her legs and smoothed her skirt. "I changed my name four years ago, right after college. Naomi is my middle name."

"Do you know why you're here?" Kendrick asked.

She lowered her head. "I'm not sure. Chase sent me a memo asking to meet about an important security matter."

"Why hide who you are?" Lei asked from his position behind her. He held up a folder. "I looked at your employment application. You conveniently forgot to disclose any former names."

Janine peered at Lei. "I just wanted to put that side of me to rest. I'm not the same person I was back then."

Kendrick arched a brow. "You look the same to me. The fact that you hid your identity from us when you were hired raises all sorts of flags."

Janine spread her hands flat on the conference room table and tapped the wood with her thumbs.

"We did a check on you," Lei said, taking the seat directly across from her. "You're married to Adam, Erik's brother."

Janine nodded.

"You didn't think that was important to tell us either?" Lei asked.

"We just got married last year," she confessed. "It was after I started working here. He reminded me so much of Erik. He pursued me."

Alexa, from her vantage point, clenched her teeth. Janine was hired under a new name and had been working for Martinez for at least a year. Something wasn't right about this. Janine seemed innocent and scared enough in a room with Kendrick and Lei breathing down her neck, but Alexa knew it was a front.

Out of the corner of her eye, she observed Dro talking heatedly over the phone. He slammed the phone down and sent it flying against the wall. It shattered on impact.

He stomped to the door and jerked it open. "Let's go," he growled.

"Why?" Alexa asked. "I want to hear this."

"We're going in there. Let's go." He moved to her side and grabbed her hand, yanking her out of the room with him.

He barreled into the conference room. Alexa stumbled in behind him. He advanced on Janine, not stopping until he had lifted her out of her seat and slammed her back against the nearest wall. He snaked a hand around her neck. "Stop playing games. What the hell are you doing working for me? And who are you really working for?"

"What's going on Dro?" Lei asked, frowning.

Alexa watched Dro and grew concerned about the choke hold he had on Janine. No matter what was going on in his life, he made an effort to never manhandle any woman. Enrique often hit Dro's mother when he had fits of rage, and Dro vowed never to be anything like Enrique.

Dro didn't take his eyes or his choke hold off of Janine. "Lei, get Pop on the phone."

Alexa's heart pumped fast. "Dro, what's going on?" She placed a hand against her chest. "Why does Lei have to call Pop?"

Dro glanced at Alexa then back at Janine. "I know who hired you. I know who let you get past my security checks.

The problem is I don't know who you're working for. And I want to know now."

All the color drained from Janine's face. Alexa guessed the choke hold was getting to be too much for her.

Janine gasped, trying to catch her breath. "I—I don't know what you're talking about, Dro," she sputtered.

"Janine, don't play with me," Dro sneered.

"Well," Kendrick said. "I suggest you let go of her a minute before she's dead and can't tell us anything."

Dro immediately let her go, and Janine sank to the floor. She heaved loudly, gripped her neck, and coughed violently. Dro stalked over to Lei. "Did you reach Pop?"

Lei's phone was against his ear. He shook his head. "I'm calling Chase now."

Dro took a breath and stared at Alexa. She watched him as he marched back over to Janine, slumped over on the floor.

She scrambled away from him. "Don't hurt me," she begged. "Or you'll never find your children."

Lei slammed his phone on the table. "I can't reach anyone."

"What the hell does that mean?" Alexa panicked. "Keep trying."

"Nicholas," Dro announced. "He hired Janine. He signed off on all of her security passes. He didn't even do the necessary checks."

Alexa gasped. "What?"

"Nicholas?" Kendrick asked.

Dro nodded. "Yes."

Alexa whirled around to face Janine, who was watching them silently. The look of fear she had on her face a few minutes earlier was now replaced with a smug smirk. "How do you know Nicholas?" Alexa asked, gripping the handle of her gun. It took all the strength she had to not beat the shit out of her.

Janine stood up and dusted her suit off. "We were friends in college. He's dating one of my sorority sisters. She convinced him to get me into Martinez. Oh, I'm sure he doesn't realize what he's done, but he's been a big help. By now, your father and your kids are right where we want them."

Alexa drew her gun and smacked Janine in the head, sending her flying back to the ground. "You, Bitch! What have you done with my kids?"

Janine spit her blood back at Alexa. "Doesn't it just kill you to lose something so precious to you?"

"What the hell is that supposed to mean?" Kendrick asked, holding on to Alexa's wrist. "What have you lost?"

Janine stared icily at Kendrick. "I hated that you were involved. Wait, no I didn't. You did a half ass job of protecting me when Steve and Aaron were after me. You were so busy worrying about Alexa and what Alexa was doing that you let Aaron get to me. You let him brutalize me in the worse way. And now you're going to suffer."

Kendrick clutched Janine's fake ponytail and slammed her head against the wall. "Fuck you. You don't know what you're talking about. But know this—if my wife and kids are harmed, you'll wish it was punk ass Aaron brutalizing you."

"Who are you working for?" Dro growled.

Janine winced when Kendrick smashed her head against the wall again. "Wouldn't you like to know?"

"Janine, this is not a joke," Alexa said. "We already know Melissa is in this. Who else? Is it Adam?"

Kendrick released his hold on Janine's hair and she balled up into a fetal position.

"We need to get out of here," Lei said, packing his folders into a briefcase. "Grab her. She's coming with us."

Janine peered at Lei, fear etched in her features. "What?"

Lei stepped over to her, grabbed her by hair, and picked her up off the ground. "You walk out with us right now, or you die where you're standing. Your choice."

"Yeah right," she said, tugging on her suit jacket. "You walk me out, and I'll scream from the rooftop that you beat me."

Alexa couldn't help it. She smacked the twit again, this time with her fist. Janine fell into the conference table. "You don't walk out quietly, I'll throw you from this goddamn building and make it look like you tripped."

Janine's eyes widened with fear. "I thought it was them. I thought it was just them that were crazy. You're crazy too. But you had Erik. You always had him, even when you didn't. He still wanted you. And it cost him his life."

Alexa slapped her again. "You're delusional. Erik died because he befriended that sick, twisted, asshole Steve. Erik died because Steve and his father had a vendetta with my family."

Erik had been in the wrong place when Chase set off a bomb, blowing up the car Steve's father was in. Steve went into a blind rage, and stabbed Erik three times before Dro could stop him. Dro killed Steve, but it was too late for Erik.

Alexa hated to leave Erik, but they had to remove all evidence of themselves at the scene. She left Erik to die by himself. Erik had told her he loved her and always would. Dro handed him the gun he used to kill Steve and they left.

Alexa didn't cry often, but she wept for days over her friend's death. She cared for Erik and hated that he got caught between her and Steve. It was a terrible situation.

In the end, the police assumed Steve stabbed Erik and Erik shot him. He was already dead when they arrived at the scene.

Alexa forced herself to focus on Janine. "If anything happens to my children, you'll wish you died with Erik. Kendrick will be the least of your problems."

Lei dragged Janine off the table and wrapped his coat around her. "We're going out through the private elevator to the garage anyway. It doesn't matter if you scream or not. No one will hear you. No one will even know you're gone. But I would listen to Alexa and be quiet anyway. I can't stand a lot of noise."

THEY DROVE to Alexa and Dro's house instead of back to B5, since it was closer to the Martinez Offices. Inside, they locked Janine, bound and gagged, in the hallway closet.

Alexa paced back and forth in the sitting room, while Dro, Lei and Kendrick talked.

Kendrick took a seat on the couch. "I'm not sure why we brought her back here. This is not going to work. This place isn't secure. Why don't we just kill her now so we won't have to worry about her anymore?"

"Kendrick, just chill," Dro ordered. "We can't kill her until we know more."

Lei shook his head. "That's a waste of time. I agree with Kendrick. She's not talking. And bringing her here is dangerous."

"I needed to come here and pick up some things." Dro took his jacket off and dropped it in a chair. "It's not like we can't take care of more than one thing at a time. It doesn't make sense to kill her before we get more information."

Kendrick shook his head. "I still feel like this is a waste of time. The longer we keep her alive, the easier it'll be for someone to place her with us. We need to kill her now."

Alexa stopped pacing. "Bullshit. That ho knows more than she's saying. And I'm not killing her until I find my kids."

A cell phone rang from inside the closet.

JANINE CRINGED when the door was yanked open. She screamed as Kendrick dragged her out by her feet. Alexa fumbled for her cell phone in her suit jacket.

Alexa pulled the ringing object out of her inside pocket and checked the caller ID. "Well, well, well," she taunted. "It looks like Adam is looking for his wife. Should I answer it or leave it?"

The phone stopped ringing and Janine heaved a sigh of relief. When it started ringing again a couple of seconds later, Alexa pushed it at Janine. "Answer it and don't try anything stupid."

Janine looked at the phone and then at four guns and a knife pointing directly at her. The knife, held by Alexa, was pressed up against her neck. "Hello," she said into the receiver.

Alexa tapped the "Speaker On" button.

"Hey, baby," Adam said. "Where have you been? I've been calling you. We need to meet. Some things have changed."

Janine peered at her captors and swallowed. "What's wrong?"

"We're meeting at Misti's in thirty minutes. Can you get out of work?"

Tears streamed down Janine's face. "I don't think I can."

"Why?" Adam asked with concern in his voice. "Have they asked you to work late or something? Remember we're supposed to pick up Marnie for the birthday party later."

WHEN JANINE'S eyes flashed to Alexa, she didn't miss the smirk that played across her face. She couldn't speak. She watched Kendrick leave the room and wondered where he was going. Lei and Dro kept their guns trained on her.

"Janine," Adam repeated. "What's going on?"

Janine couldn't swallow past the lump in her throat, but she knew she needed to speak. "Adam, why are we meeting?"

"Melissa wants to meet to discuss our next move," Adam sounded irritated.

Alexa yanked the phone from Janine's grasp and hung up. "That's enough. We know enough to take it from here. Too bad, Janine. I guess we can pick Marnie up for you."

"No," Janine cried. "I'll tell you everything you need to know. Just don't hurt her. She's my—"

"Answer this for me," Lei cut in. "Why should I care who Marnie is? You obviously didn't care about my family."

Janine couldn't stop the tears from falling if she tried. She would beg if she had to.

"Can you please stop with the dramatics, Janine?" Alexa snapped. "You said you would tell us everything, so talk. I'm not in the business of hurting kids like you and your buddies. But if I have to, I'll make sure you never see Marnie again."

Janine felt a desperation she had never felt before. Her stomach was flip flopping and her throat seemed like it was closing up. "I met Melissa when I graduated from college," she croaked. She cleared her throat. "I went to work for her family's company. When she found out where I was from, she asked if I knew you. We bonded over our mutual dislike. Eventually, she came to me with a proposition. She would make sure you all paid for everything that happened to me and Erik. By this time, Adam and I were dating and he wanted in. Melissa thought I could use my connection to Nicholas to get into Martinez Security. Nicholas has no idea who I really am. He's totally loyal to you. In fact, I'm pretty sure he would kill me if he found out."

"I don't care about Nicholas," Dro said. "Is Melissa working with anyone else?"

"She is," Janine admitted. "But she hasn't named him."

Alexa rolled her eyes. "You're an idiot. What does she have planned for my family? Where are they?"

Janine shrugged. "I don't know. I just know they were supposed to pick them up. I found out the location of all the safe houses when I hacked into Nicholas' computer. I found out where you were and then we figured out where you sent the kids when I traced Nicholas' phone."

Lei arched a brow. "And you were okay with Melissa just taking innocent children and putting them in harm's way just to get to us?"

"Yes," Janine replied. "I just wanted to bring you down. Melissa assured me the children wouldn't be hurt."

Alexa smacked her. "And you believed her? How did you become such an idiot?"

"It looks like we're going to be getting a little package," Kendrick announced, walking back into the room.

"No," Janine shouted. "Please, don't hurt my little girl. She's just a baby."

Chapter Nineteen

LEI JAMMED a syringe filled with a clear substance into a frantic Janine's neck. She immediately fell on her back, her eyes wide open. He dropped the needle into an orange biochemical bag. "She'll be gone in a few. It's pentobarbital. I didn't feel like cleaning up any blood." He wrapped up the syringe then put it in his bag. "We need to figure out our next move."

Janine's breathing slowed, and Alexa felt a quick tinge of guilt. "I don't need to figure out my next move. I need to get to my kids."

"I agree," Dro added. "We don't do anything until we find out where my family is. For now, we dispose of this." He pointed to Janine's body. "Then we go back to B5."

Kendrick knelt down and picked up Janine's wrist. He pulled a white tarp out of his bag and tossed it over Janine's now dead body. "Lei." He sighed. "I really wish you hadn't killed her yet. We may have needed her."

Lei glared at Kendrick. "We don't need shit from her. Besides, I couldn't stand to look at her any longer. My whole family could be dead because of some high school vendetta she had against Alexa. Who in their right mind would befriend someone as crazy as Melissa and come up with some stupid scheme for revenge? Erik died because Steve killed him—not because of whatever twisted reason they came up with in their minds. And you didn't owe her your protection, Kendrick. You agreed to do it because Alexa talked you into it. It wasn't your fault Aaron raped her. Aaron raped her because he was a sick fuck, not because you didn't protect her. Janine was an idiot for using that to put this stupid revenge thing in motion. But that's what happens when people are crazy. They make things up in their minds. You weren't even with Alexa on the night in question. But Janine has always been jealous of Alexa, and couldn't see past that."

Alexa watched Lei move through the room, gathering up his coat and his briefcase. He was obviously very irritated with this whole situation. And he definitely wasn't the type to sugar coat things. He was one of the best attorneys she ever had the pleasure of knowing. He only looked at the facts. Lei stalked out of the room, mumbling under his breath the whole time.

"I can't stand Lei sometimes," Kendrick said to Alexa.

She smiled slightly. "I'm sure he feels the same way, Kendrick. He was right, though. Janine was an idiot. And as soon as we get the rest of the idiots she's working with and get my children to safety, I'm getting the hell out of dodge."

Dro's eyes flashed to hers. "Alexa—"

"Dro, I'm tired." She grabbed her coat. "I understand all the reasons why we're in this predicament, but I'm tired of living like this."

"Let's get out of here," Lei called from the foyer.

Alexa glanced at Dro briefly, and joined Lei in the foyer. Kendrick rolled an old trash can over to Janine, picked her up, and dropped her in it. Dro threw another tarp over the steel object.

One of Martinez' trusted guards, Julio, appeared in the doorway. "Kendrick called and asked me to take care of something."

Dro pointed to the trash can. "Get rid of this. And take John with you. Send a crew to clean the house."

AS THEY ENTERED the kitchen in B5, Alexa paused at the sight of Chase pointing a gun at them.

Chase let out a deep sigh and dropped his gun on the counter. "Sorry."

She pushed past Dro. "What are you doing here? Where are the kids?"

"I don't know," Chase replied with a sigh. "I was hoping they came back here."

"What do you mean?" Kendrick asked. "You were supposed to be with them, Chase!"

Alexa took in Chase's appearance. He looked haggard. His clothes were burned and he had visible bruises on his face.

"Chase, what happened?" Dro asked.

"We were ambushed," Chase began. "On the way up to the house, I got this feeling we were being followed."

They followed him into the kitchen.

Chase picked up a beer bottle from the counter and took a sip. "I called Pop and told him to go the contingent route. Nicholas and I continued up to the house to secure it. Once we got out of the car, the bullets started flying."

"Oh my God," Alexa gasped. "Were you hit?"

"No. Nicholas didn't make it, though. I tried to get him out of there, but I couldn't."

Kendrick sighed. "Well, it's a good thing you weren't hit. Nicholas getting killed saves me from having to kill him."

Chase frowned at Kendrick. "What are you talking about? Nicholas was one of us."

Kendrick tossed a set of keys on the counter. "No, he sure as hell wasn't. Nicholas is the reason our security was breached. But that's too long a story for right now. What happened to Pop?"

Chase shrugged. "I got out of there as fast as I could. When I tried to call Pop to let him know not to go to the house, I didn't get an answer. I thought he turned back."

Alexa closed her eyes. *Where are my babies?* If she didn't find them soon, she would go crazy.

"If Pop arrived at the safe house and didn't see your car, Chase, he would've gone to another safe place," Dro said. "It makes sense to come here, but maybe he went somewhere else. Lei? Any ideas?"

"Well," Lei said, scratching the stubble on his chin. "Maybe we should check Pop's house. He might have gone there."

"We were just over there," Alexa said. "We didn't see any sign of activity at Daddy's house. Besides, he wouldn't go there. It's not secure. No one has been there at all since we got Ma out of there. We've pulled most of the security teams to this area."

"What about the hotel?" Lei wondered. "He might go there?"

Kendrick shook his head. "That doesn't make any sense. The hotel is too public, even though there are hidden areas there. He wouldn't risk being seen there.

Besides, he knows that we would be here. He should have come here."

"Kendrick is right." Alexa clenched her teeth together. "Daddy wouldn't have gone there or to his house. It's not secure." She knew her father well, but there were some things he kept hidden from them. He could've gone anywhere. He had friends everywhere. Pop's house wasn't an option.

Alexa and Dro were renovating Enrique's old house. That's the reason she had been at the B5 safe house in the first place. Chase was finishing the bunker and it was easier for him to look out for her and the kids in the safe house above B5. They had upped her security in recent months and Dro felt more comfortable when Chase was with her while he had been in Puerto Rico on business.

"Get some men up to the Canadian safe house and go both routes," Dro told Lei. "Maybe we can get an idea of where he went. If he's not in danger, Pop will get in touch with us at some point. That's all I really have to hold on to. Ari is with him. She can handle a gun and so can Ma. I know they'll protect each other."

"I'm sorry," Chase said, bowing his head.

Kendrick placed a hand on Chase's shoulder. "It's okay, bruh. We're just glad you got out of there. Who was driving?"

"They were in two protected trucks," Chase answered. "Ari and Pop were driving behind us. We thought it would be safer if we went first to case out the spot. When they veered off, Pop was leading."

"It doesn't make sense for Pop to go anywhere else except here," Kendrick mused. "That's what makes me worry. It's just not like him to not stay in touch."

"If he thinks it's best that he doesn't stay in touch, he won't," Dro said. "I think we need to assume that Pop is fine until we know differently. If he's lying low, it's probably best if we focus on neutralizing the enemy. We need to go to Misti's."

"Why do we have to go to Misti's?" Chase looked confused.

Kendrick patted him on the shoulder again. "It's a long story. Why don't you get a shower or something and we can discuss our next move."

AN HOUR LATER, they all gathered in the security room. Kendrick had filled Chase in on everything that had happened.

Alexa paced back and forth in the small space. "We're wasting time here. It makes sense that we just go in for the kill. I'm tired of playing around with these people. They don't own us and they don't control me."

Dro frowned. "Will you just calm down, baby? It doesn't make sense to just stroll into a public diner and open fire. I know you're worried and ready to get this over with, but come on."

She sighed heavily then plopped down into a chair. Deep down, she knew Dro was right. But they had no idea where their children were and terror ripped through her gut. It was hard to get a hold of her emotions.

"What if we just buy the diner?" Kendrick suggested. "That way we can control who's there."

"It makes sense." Chase fiddled with his gun. "I'm sure if we approach the owner with enough cash, he'll let us do what we want."

"What if he doesn't?" Dro asked. "We have to have another plan."

"Buying the diner is the wrong move," Lei said, ending

a phone call. "We don't want to be connected if we do have to 'open fire'. The guards just called. They got rid of Janine. I also have some feelers out to some of Pop's contacts. Hopefully, we'll hear something soon."

"Okay." Dro walked over to the wall and punched in a code on the keypad, opening a hidden panel. "I want to make sure we have all the fire power we need. If we get separated for some reason, we meet here. I sent a small group up to the Canadian safe house to check around too. Until we hear differently, we're going to go ahead and get a handle on this enemy."

All of a sudden, Alexa felt like she couldn't breathe in the stuffy room. She stormed out. Little pins pricked her body. She clenched her fist, stretching her neck from side to side. She was frustrated and it wasn't helping the situation. It wasn't like her to let her emotions control her, but these were her children, her parents, and her best friends. If something happened to them, she was sure she wouldn't survive it. A hand on her shoulder jarred her from her thoughts. She whirled around, fists ready, poised to fight. Kendrick was standing there.

She dropped her arms to her side. "Don't you think you should be in there planning?"

"I'm right where I need to be. Alexa, you have to get a hold of yourself. You know that emotions are only going to make this harder. I know it's been a while since you've had to turn them off, but you have to try. Once this is done, we can make some decisions about where you want to be."

She stared at the ceiling. "I already know where I want to be and it's not here. I told you, Kendrick, I've been feeling this way for a while. I need to get out of here. I need to take my children and leave town."

"We can talk about that when this is over," Kendrick said softly.

"Dro will never let me leave," she mumbled, pacing back and forth.

"You're right," Dro agreed, stepping into the hall. "You're not going to run, Alexa. Why would you even want to? I can't just leave. I have a company to run, obligations here. You want to leave so bad, but are you willing to leave me?"

She turned away from him. "If that's the only way I can keep my kids safe..." She didn't finish the sentence, but Dro wasn't stupid. They had been having this conversation for some time now. She was feeling increasingly uncomfortable in their environment. She needed a change, but Dro was adamant against it. He couldn't just pick up and leave. He did have obligations that needed to be met. But she only had one thing keeping her there—him.

"What, Alexa?" he challenged. "If that's the only way you can keep *our* kids safe, what? You would leave me? Walk out on me, and take my family away?"

She glared at him over her shoulder. "You know I don't want to leave you, Dro. It's not like that. I just...forget it. This is not the time to talk about it anyway. We need to end this so I can see my kids again—if they're still alive."

"Stop," Kendrick and Dro shouted simultaneously.

"Don't ever say that to me," Dro roared. "My kids are still alive. Our family is still alive."

"You don't know that, Dro," she cried. "Where are they? Where's my dad? They're not here. We don't know where they are. I know Daddy is good. He can take care of them, but why hasn't he touched base with us?" Fear gripped her throat as she yelled at Dro, cutting off her breath until she had no choice but to fall to her knees. She collapsed onto her stomach and broke down sobbing.

DRO WAVED KENDRICK AWAY, but he didn't move. Lei and Chase stepped out of the security room. Dro was sure the sight of Alexa breaking down stunned all of them. He dropped to his knees, gathered her into his arms, and stroked her back. "Baby, it's okay. The kids are fine. You have to believe that."

"Oh God, I hope so," she sputtered. "Please, God, let them be okay. My babies—"

Dro locked her in his embrace and swayed back and forth, rocking her.

"My babies," she whimpered. "Where are they? It's my fault. All of this is my fault. What if they got daddy? What if they hurt my babies? Ky—what if they—"

Dro tipped her head up and gazed into her swollen red eyes. He wiped an errant tear from her chin. "Don't say it."

"I can't stop thinking it. She's my baby girl. And Alex? Where are my babies, Dro?"

Dro glanced back at Lei and caught him absently wiping tears from his face. "Baby, I don't know where they are," he whispered against her ear. "But you're going to have to get control over this. We have something to do. Pop is taking care of them." He grasped her face with his hands when she tried to bury her face in his chest. "Come on now. Stop crying. We have to take care of this. Do it for me and do it for our children. Be the strong woman I love."

The sound of Lei's phone ringing penetrated the room.

"This is Lei," he said, his voice raspy.

They all remained silent as he spoke on the phone. Dro noted the subtle changes in Lei during the conversation. It wasn't good news, judging by the tense, all business tone in Lei's voice and the vein throbbing on the side of head.

Lei ended the call and massaged the back of his neck.

"They found the two trucks abandoned on an old dirt road off the interstate. There's no sign of the children or anybody else."

Dro held Alexa closer when she started crying again.

"That just means Pop ditched the cars," Kendrick said. "He'll be in touch as soon as he can."

Dro knew Kendrick was just trying to think positively because anything else was unacceptable.

Dro helped Alexa to her feet. "Right. Pop has this under control. I mean, that's why we sent..." His voice cracked.

"Pop is fine," Lei whispered. "We all agreed Pop was the best person to go with the kids. He's fine." With that, Lei returned to the security room. Eventually, they all shuffled in behind him.

Alexa peered into the panel in the wall—the weapons closet. She opened a drawer and pulled out a wig and some colored contacts.

Dro watched her suck in all of her emotions and wondered if he could do the same. He had tried to tell her to get it together. When Lei got the call about the trucks, though, his heart dropped. He had no other choice but to believe Pop had everything under control.

Kendrick grabbed some ammunition out of a drawer and a black duffle bag. "We need to be extra cautious. No splitting up. We do everything together."

Chase packed a few tools into a flat bag. "If something should happen, we know that we meet back here."

They gathered everything they needed and left B5.

Chapter Twenty

NOVEMBER 5, 2011, Misti's Coney Island:

AT MISTI'S, Adam Neal sat by himself in his usual corner booth. He was worried about Janine. She hadn't sounded right when he talked to her on the phone. In fact, she was totally out of character. He tried to chalk it up to her being at work, but the more he thought about it, the more worried he became.

They were too close to their goal to mess up now. Although, parts of him wanted to forget he ever met Melissa, he missed his brother, Erik, too much to back down. He hated the Martinez group because he thought they had destroyed Erik. Even though they didn't technically pull the trigger, they had set the events of that night in motion. Alexa had lied to Erik for months, making him think she loved only him. She played him and never intended to be with him. She only wanted Dro. And Dro had punked Erik too many times to count. Adam hated them both.

He observed the new waitress, on the other side of the diner, waiting on customers. Janine was fifteen minutes late. He had called her numerous times in the last hour, but she didn't pick up. Melissa would be here any minute.

The new waitress sauntered over to his booth. "Refill?" she asked gruffly.

He slid his mug back and forth on the table. "Sure. Are you new here?"

"Yes I am," she replied, smacking on her gum. "Can I get you started on anything?"

He winced at her homely looks. The black waitress wore thick rimmed glasses and a blonde wig, which were quite unattractive. Her eyes, though, were a deep hunter green. When she smiled, he noticed a gold tooth in her mouth. He trailed his eyes down her lumpy body. She was a far cry from the cute little blond that used to wait on him.

"I would like the chopped salad with extra raspberry vinaigrette," he said with an air of superiority.

The waitress scribbled on her small notepad. "Will you be eating alone this evening?"

"No, I'm expecting two more people."

She slipped the pad of paper in the pocket of her apron. "Okay, holla if you need me." She stuck her pencil into her bleached wig.

He rolled his eyes as she walked away. He surmised that the owner must have been desperate to hire the woman. In Adam's opinion, she was horrendous. He hated to see black women with blonde hair. In his mind, black women were some of the most beautiful women on the planet—but this woman was a far cry from beautiful.

He took another sip of coffee and opened the New York Times app on his smart phone while he waited.

The homely waitress brought his food back ten minutes later with a lopsided smile. "Here you go." She set his plate and the extra side of dressing in front of him. Once he picked his fork up, she poured more coffee into his mug. "Enjoy."

As she turned to walk away, the bell chimed and Melissa entered the restaurant in her black mink coat. Adam rolled his eyes again. Melissa was one of the worst women he'd ever known. She reeked of smelly, but expensive, perfume and flaunted her wealth wherever she went. She was disgusting. But she was a means to an end for him.

Melissa skipped the pleasantries and slid into the booth. "Where's Janine?"

"She was held up at work." Or at least that was what he hoped.

She waved her hand to signal the waitress after she pulled her gloves off. "Well, we have to start without her. I have to leave town tonight."

The waitress waltzed over to the table. "What can I get you ma'am?"

Melissa crinkled her nose at the waitress. "Ma'am? I assure you I'm no one's Ma'am. I need a coffee and extra cream."

The waitress pulled out her pad of paper and snatched the pencil out of her hair. "There's cream on the table, Ma'am. Did you want to place an order? Can I interest you in the fish and chips? They're on special today."

Melissa rolled her eyes and snorted. "I wouldn't eat the food here if you paid me. I need plenty of cream with my coffee, thank you."

The waitress scratched her forehead with her pen. Her brow creased. "I'll be right with you, Ma'am."

Adam snickered when he heard Melissa curse under her breath that the waitress dared to call her Ma'am. She went on like that for several minutes until the woman came back with a piping hot coffee dispenser.

She poured the coffee into an empty mug and tossed a new bowl of creamers in front of Melissa. "Is there anything else you need?"

Melissa waved her off as if she was insignificant. "No, I'll call you if I need anything."

The waitress paused for a minute and then shuffled over to the counter.

He watched as the frustrated woman cracked her neck and then proceeded to wipe down some tables. He turned and scrutinized Melissa as she dumped tons of cream into her coffee mug. "What's going on? Why did you need to meet?"

Melissa leaned closer. "We have a problem."

"What kind of problem?" he asked, keeping his tone even. "Janine delivered you their location. What could have possibly happened?"

She shifted in her seat. "We lost some of our men. Apparently, they sent someone ahead to secure the place and there was gun play. The kids never showed up. One of their men is down, though. Nicholas Cass? Do you know him?"

He swallowed a bite of chicken. "He works very closely with them. Janine knew him from a college friend. He's the one who got her into Martinez. She'll be upset to hear this."

Melissa opened five packets of Splenda and emptied them into her coffee. "I'm leaving town tonight, Adam. It's getting too hot here for me."

"What about us?" Adam couldn't believe what he was hearing. "You can't just leave, Melissa. We've come too far."

She stirred her coffee with a spoon. "I haven't abandoned the plan, but I have to assume that stupid ass Tommy sang before he 'disappeared'. Dro may come looking for me. I have to get out of here. Don't worry, I'll be in touch."

Adam was growing more frustrated by the minute. "Cut the crap, Melissa. You walk out of here, and I'll never see you again. In the meantime, you have my assets frozen in that damn bank of yours."

Her eyes flashed to his. "And they'll stay that way until I get what I want."

He leaned forward, clenching his fists together. He wanted to choke the life out of her. "You're lucky I want the same thing you want. Or I would definitely wipe that smirk off of your face."

She pushed her coffee mug toward him as she stood up, spilling some on the table. "You better be careful who you're talking to like that. I can make it so your future is very dismal. Just keep quiet and you'll get your money back in due time, plus some additional funds when I take over Martinez Security."

He rested his back against the booth and twiddled his thumbs. "You're so sure that you're holding all the cards."

She sneered at him, pointing a crooked finger in his face. "Don't be so sure I'm not. You and Janine just stay in line and everything will work out fine."

He grabbed her wrist and jerked her back into the booth. "Look, I don't like this. You said it would be easy once Janine gave you the location to the safe houses. She gave the whole list. You had ample opportunity to grab Alexa and her children. You couldn't do it. Why should I believe that you'll hold up your end of the deal now?"

She struggled to pull her arm away as he dug his fingers into her skin. Smoothing her wiry hair down with her other hand, she swallowed. "Let go of me Adam before I scream bloody murder."

He loosened the grip on her arm and she snatched it

away. He picked up his knife and fork, while she rubbed her arm.

"Just hang tight," she hissed. "Everything will be okay."

He stabbed a piece of lettuce with his fork. "It better be," he warned before taking another bite of his salad.

Just then, the waitress ambled back over to the table. "Are you alright? It looked like things were pretty heated over here."

He lifted his eyes from his plate and assessed the waitress. "We're fine. She was just leaving."

Melissa scowled at the waitress, then Adam. "He's paying for my coffee," she stated as she rose to her feet. She smoothed her skirt and buttoned her coat.

The waitress arched a brow at him. "Is this correct, sir? Are you really paying for her coffee?"

Adam gave Melissa a dirty look. "Yes, I'll take care of it."

Melissa turned to the waitress. "Can you please get me a cup to go?" She eyed Adam. "I'll be in touch." She looked around the diner, her nose turned up. "This place is dead. Do you realize we're the only people here?"

"Who cares?" Adam replied. "I like it when there aren't many people around."

The waitress headed toward the table, fumbling with the "To Go" coffee container. "I hate these things," she confessed. "I'm sorry, Ma'am. I'm having the darnedest time getting the lid to fit on the cup."

Melissa rolled her eyes. "I'm sure it's not rocket science."

The waitress played around with the cup some more. The paper cup slipped from her hand and spattered on the floor and on Melissa's shoes.

"Oh my God," Melissa screeched. "Do you realize I paid fifteen hundred dollars for these shoes?" She grabbed some napkins from the table and bent to wipe her shoes off.

The waitress backed away from her. "I'm sorry, Ma'am. I didn't mean to ruin your shoes."

Adam surveyed the waitress curiously. She didn't look sorry at all. He tilted his head and studied her. She was familiar to him now that he thought about it. He eyed her while she watched Melissa carry on about those damn shoes. She must have felt him looking at her because she turned to him, meeting his stare with her emerald colored eyes.

Next thing he knew, she stepped up to Melissa's bent form and kicked her in the chin, knocking her flat on her back. She was out cold.

The waitress slid into the vacant spot in the booth, across from Adam. Then Adam heard the click of her gun. "Hi, Adam. Glad to see me?"

His eyes widened as the waitress tugged the blond wig off. The glasses came next and then the contacts. He was looking into the eyes of the beautiful, but deadly Alexa.

***

MAY 15, 1998:

ADAM STARED at his brother's casket and he wondered how he got there. His brother, Erik, was never someone he strove to be like, but they were still brothers. He glanced at his weeping mother. Although she was trying to be strong, she was barely holding it together.

Adam faced the casket again. It was a plain oak casket, one of the cheapest ones in the funeral home. It wasn't fancy like some of the ones the funeral home tried to get them to buy. His mother wanted to buy Erik the best casket she could find, but she didn't have the money. It was pointless anyway. Why bury someone in a casket that cost as much as a car? Especially when she needed a new car? But Elizabeth Neal was hurting for her son, and couldn't bear the thought of her baby being lowered underground in a cheap, uncomfortable box.

He scanned the crowd. The sanctuary was filled with tons of high school students, his classmates. They had come to the funeral to catch a glimpse of his dead brother and offer pointless and meaningless words of comfort. They came out in droves and he guessed it was because of his brother's athletic prowess on the football field. Erik Neal was the school's star quarterback after all.

He sat still, wishing time would move a little faster. When he saw Alexa enter the church, he noticed there were plenty of stares—and some glares. Alexa was the most beautiful girl he'd ever seen. And she was looking right at him. Normally she would smile and he would blush profusely, but not this time. She was the reason he was here. She was the reason his brother was dead.

She walked up to the casket. Her dark sunglasses hid her eyes from view, but somehow he knew she'd been crying. He knew that, in some strange way, she was grieving for his brother, too.

Her hair was pulled back into a tight bun and she wore a dark gray suit. Her hand skimmed the casket softly before she turned and exited the church.

The day had been a blur. Adam had watched his stepfather practically pull his mother away as the casket was lowered. She was so distraught he wondered if she wanted to jump in with Erik. *Will this nightmare ever end?*

After the services were over and the house was empty, he returned to the cemetery to yell at his brother for leaving him. As he approached Erik's gravesite, he noticed Alexa sitting on the grass next to the big hole that held his brother's casket.

"Erik," he heard her whisper. Her voice was as soft as summer breeze. "I'm so sorry. I'm sorry that you're here. I'm sorry you were ever mixed up in this. I can't believe you're gone, lying in a wooden box. If I could change that, I would. You deserve to be on a football field calling plays. You deserve to be going to the university in September, playing college ball, getting drafted into the Pros, and falling in love with someone who loves you just as much as you love her. But most of all, I'm sorry I wasn't the one for you. I'm sorry I didn't love you like you loved me. I didn't deserve you as a friend."

Adam watched as she wiped her moist cheeks. Her hair was no longer in a bun. It was hanging down, long, curly, and draped over her face. She sniffed into her black leather glove. "You would be happy to know that Steve will no longer hurt anyone," she continued. "He's gone. And so is his father. I sent your mother a care package with a check for the expenses. It was the least I could do. My father happily obliged. He's sorry too. We all are—even Dro. Erik, I just wanted you to know that you meant more to me than I ever told you. Things didn't happen right with us and that was my fault. I should have never started a relationship with you knowing I could never commit. It wasn't that I didn't care about you though. It was because I loved him—so much. I always have. Thank you for not faulting me for it in the end. Thank you for being such a good friend, even though I didn't deserve your friendship."

She stood up and dropped two white roses into the hole. She sucked in a breath. "I'll miss you," she sighed. "May you rest in peace."

Adam was so entranced in her words that he didn't see

her turn around until she was staring at him. He decided to break the ice. "Hi. Uh..." He didn't know what to say.

She offered him a small smile. "How are you, Adam?"

"I'm fine," he lied. "How are you? I didn't mean to intrude on your moment with my brother. I didn't mean to listen."

She stuffed her hands into her coat pockets. "I just came to pay my final respects to Erik. He was a really good guy. I'll miss him."

"How was he? You know, before he died? I know he was with you earlier in the day."

It was common knowledge that Erik and Alexa were in some sort of relationship and had recently broke up. Erik had told him that he was hoping to win her back.

She swayed on her feet. "When I saw him, he was fine —a little tense, but fine."

"Do you know why Steve would want to hurt him?"

She hunched her shoulders. "Your guess is as good as mine."

Even though she seemed sincere, he presumed she knew more than she was saying. He was no dummy. He had heard all the rumors. The town was buzzing about a cover up. Not to mention, he knew her family was very powerful. "Well, I guess we'll never know." He walked past her to the spot she had vacated.

"I'm sorry about your brother, Adam."

He bowed his head. "Me, too."

She didn't offer anything else and when he turned to ask her the question he had been dying to ask her, she was gone.

NOVEMBER 5, 2011, Misti's Coney Island:

182

. . .

ADAM WONDERED, as he faced Alexa now, if he would get to ask her that question.

Her cold, dark eyes bore into his. "What's wrong, Adam? Not happy to see me?"

He moved to stand up from his seat and paused when he felt the tip of a gun press into the back of his head.

"Sit back down, Mr. Neal," Dro commanded calmly. "We need to have a talk."

Adam sunk back into the booth. "What's going on?"

Alexa set her gun on the table, keeping one hand on it. "You've come a long way, Adam. I wonder what Erik would say if he saw you now, working with Melissa and whoever else to terrorize my family."

"I wouldn't know because Erik isn't alive to say anything. And you know why he isn't alive? You and your family. I'd say turnabout is fair play, right?"

"What makes you think I had anything to do with Erik's death?"

He straightened his back. "I heard you. I heard you at the cemetery after the funeral. I saw your face when you apologized to him."

Her eyes flickered to Dro then back at Adam. "I don't think you've ever heard me say I was involved in your brother's death. Your brother meant a lot to me. I never wanted to see him dead. I warned him to stay away from me. Not a day goes by that I don't regret my choices when it comes to him. But I didn't kill him. Steve did. If anything, I tried to protect Erik."

"Protect?" Adam howled. "You tried to protect him? You lied to him for months. You led him on. You pulled him into the vendetta between Steve's family and yours."

Her brow creased. "Once again, you're wrong. I didn't

drag Erik into anything. He jumped into it with his eyes wide open. I dumped Erik because I didn't want him to be involved. I didn't want him to get hurt. Steve pulled Erik into his vendetta with my family."

Adam didn't want to believe it. Yet as he stared into her eyes, he saw truth in them. He had thought he saw it back then in the church and at the cemetery, but there were too many people in his head—too many rumors around town. And then there was Janine.

Janine had told him it was Alexa's fault Erik was dead. Janine told him Alexa made sure she was left alone the night Aaron raped her. But as he gazed at Alexa, he knew that Janine had lied to him all these years. It was too late to turn back, though. He was in up to his eyeballs and Janine was, too.

He knew this could very likely be his last day on earth. But he still wanted to ask her the question. "Did you love Erik?" he asked.

She sucked in a breath and looked behind him at Dro. He craned his neck to look at Dro, too. Adam saw the torment in Dro's eyes as he waited for Alexa's answer.

"Yes," she whispered.

Chapter Twenty-One

MAY 10, 1998:

ALEXA BARGED into Erik's room one evening. They had been talking again, and it felt good to have her friend back.

"What are you doing here?" he asked, smiling at her.

She sat next to him on the bed. "Erik, you still have time to get out of this. You don't have to get involved."

"I won't back down." He placed a hand on her knee. "Steve is crazy. I need to make sure he can't hurt anybody I care about. It's not just about you anymore. He's been my friend. He knows my family. He could hurt my mother or my brother. He could hurt Janine. And he could hurt you. He will if he gets the chance."

She squeezed his hand. "It's not your battle. I talked to my father. Let him send you and your family away, Erik."

"I'm not leaving. I won't run away."

"You don't know how dangerous this is. You're worried about your family, but I'm worried about you."

Steve and his family had stepped up their game. Over

the last couple of weeks, there had been numerous public fights. Steve and some of his father's goons cornered Kendrick at a bar and a fight ensued. Kendrick ended up in jail for nearly killing one of the men. Luckily, Pop and Enrique had connections in the District Attorney's office. The charges against Kendrick were soon dropped.

Dro and Chase were involved in a car chase one night on their way home from college. The car was riddled with bullet holes. It was lucky the only injury was a flesh wound to Dro's shoulder.

The same night Aaron, Steve's little brother, trapped Janine as she was leaving her part-time job. Kendrick wasn't there with her because he was busy rushing to Dro and Chase's aid after the car chase. Aaron brutally raped Janine that night and left her to die.

Lei had sent another guard to pick Janine up that night, but he arrived too late. Janine was lying by a dumpster in an alley behind the restaurant. The guard rushed her to the hospital.

Enrique was enraged after Dro was injured and finally gave the order to eliminate the threat. Everything was going down that night. Chase was directed to place a homemade bomb on Steve's father's limo. Chase dabbled in explosives, and he didn't mess up. Alexa was worried that Erik would be caught in the crossfire. She didn't want him to be involved.

She pleaded with him again. "I'm not supposed to be here right now, but there is something going down tonight. I want you as far away from Steve as possible."

"I wish I could say I would, but they invited me to dinner tonight. I accepted in order to get more information on their plans."

She paced across the room. "Don't go anywhere with them, Erik. You need to stay here."

"Why? I want to help."

"We don't need your help. Don't you get it? We're taking care of the problem tonight." She slapped her hand over her mouth. She'd already taken a chance coming there. Dro would kill her if he found out where she was. Now she had let it slip that they were taking care of the problem. "Damn."

"What do you mean taking care of the problem? What are you doing?"

"Don't worry about it. Just stay away from Steve."

"Alexa—"

"Erik, just stay away." She squeezed his hand. "Please?" Then she hurried out.

INSTEAD OF LISTENING TO HER, Erik had gone to dinner with Steve. Alexa watched as Erik walked into the restaurant where Steve and his father were having dinner. She listened as Dro and Kendrick cursed Erik to hell for not following instructions, but all she could feel was fear for Erik's life. They had warned Erik to lay low. But she knew Erik. He was a standup guy and would never let someone he cared about face an enemy alone. That's why she had tried to make one last appeal for him to stay away. And he still hadn't listened.

Once Steve and his party left the restaurant, Steve hopped in Erik's car. Steve's father and Aaron rode in the limo. When the bomb went off, she prayed Erik's car was far enough from the blast to not be affected. She raced to the scene with Dro to make sure everything went off without a hitch. She felt overwhelming relief when she noticed that Erik's car was unscathed.

She scanned the area looking for Erik, yelling at Dro to

stop the truck when she spotted Erik and Steve arguing near the side of the road. Before she could jump out of the car, Steve pulled a knife from his pocket and stabbed Erik multiple times. Erik dropped to the ground like a rag doll.

She screamed as she raced toward Erik. Before she could pull her own gun, Dro fired on Steve, dropping him with a bullet to his chest.

She dropped to her knees next to Erik. "Erik?"

He slowly opened his eyes. "Alexa," he whispered.

She placed her hands on the biggest wound she saw. "Hang on. We're going to get you some help, okay?"

He gripped her hand, holding it against his chest. "I can't. Alexa, I want you to know—"

"Don't say anything. You'll be able to tell me when you get better."

He traced her jaw with his blood stained hand. "I'm not getting better."

"Yes, you are." His eyes drifted shut. She shook him. "Erik?" His eyes fluttered open for a brief second before closing again.

Dro placed a hand on her shoulder. "Alexa, we have to go."

Erik opened his eyes again. "Go," he agreed. "Dro, give me that gun."

She knew what Erik was going to do and she hated the idea, although, she realized he was doing this for her. She gazed at him, tears filling her eyes. "Erik, I'm so sorry. I didn't mean—"

"Stop. I don't blame you. You have to get out of here. Go with Dro."

She reluctantly grabbed Dro's outstretched hand and he helped her to her feet. Then, she slowly backed away from Erik as the sirens in the wind came closer. "Goodbye, Erik."

She jumped in the truck and Dro sped off into the night.

NOVEMBER 5, 2011, Misti's Coney Island:

ALEXA'S EYES flashed to Dro, who was watching her curiously. She cleared her throat. "Yes, Adam, I loved your brother." She bowed her head and tapped her fingers against the table. "But not like he wanted me to love him. I loved him because he was my friend—one of my very best friends. I didn't want him to die. But I wasn't *in* love with him. I've only ever been in love with one person."

"I don't know what to say," Adam sighed.

"Your brother loved his family," she continued. "He was a good guy. He wanted to protect everyone he cared about. That's why he was there that night. Everyone, including me, warned him against hanging with Steve. He wouldn't hear us. And now he's dead."

"My mom never recovered from his death." Adam's voice was so soft she could barely hear him. "She drank herself into her own grave after Erik died. She was inconsolable. And I was only fifteen. I wanted revenge on the people I thought were responsible for my pain."

Alexa wondered if Adam ever really had a chance to live a normal life after everything that happened to him. Most of all, she understood the concept of loyalty to parents and siblings. She couldn't say she wouldn't do the same thing if Lei was gunned down. In fact, she knew she would.

She was raised to draw the first sword. That is how she always lived her life—never scared, never worried, and always in control. Her father told her to never let a vengeful act go unpunished. That's why she knew she would have done the same thing Adam did.

She composed herself, dashing wet tears from her face. "You look so much like him. You caught me off guard at first. Not many people can say that about me." She stood up. "Janine did you a disservice. Unfortunately, you can't take back what you've done."

Adam rested on his feet. "Where's Janine? We have a baby girl."

A tear dropped from her eye. "I know, and your daughter is safe. I can't say the same about you. Do you know who Melissa's partner is?"

He shook his head.

"Well, then..." She looked into his eyes—Erik's eyes. "We don't need you anymore."

Two guards entered the dining area with Kendrick. Kendrick picked Melissa up and slung her over his shoulder. Alexa and Dro followed Kendrick toward the back of the restaurant.

As she entered the diner's kitchen she paused, hand on the wall. When she heard the sound of the muffled shot, she swallowed the lump in her throat, and walked out.

Chapter Twenty-Two

MAY 10, 1998, Pop's house:

DRO WATCHED Alexa as she slept. Nightmares seemed to plague her throughout the night and he guessed it was expected. She had just seen her friend murdered in cold blood that night. As cold and calculating as she could be, Dro couldn't help but appreciate those times when she was vulnerable. It made him want to take care of her all the more.

Pulling a pair of pajama pants out of his dresser, he slipped them on. He knew it was time to wake her up. He didn't want to take a chance that Pop or Ma would come to his room and catch her sleeping with him. At the same time, though, he wanted to wake up next to her. When he climbed into bed, she rolled over. Her eyes red and puffy.

"You're up?" he asked.

She rubbed her eyes and ran a hand through her wild curls. "I had a bad dream."

"I know." He opened his arms and she burrowed into his embrace, snuggling against his side.

"Was I screaming or something?" she asked.

He kissed her forehead. "No. But you were tossing and turning in your sleep, fighting something."

"Wow, I fight in my sleep?"

"Yes, you do. I have to take cover sometimes."

She giggled and he thought it was the prettiest sound he ever heard. "Stop lying, Dro." She smacked his chest playfully. "I would never hit you."

"Yeah, right." He chuckled and pinched her chin gently. "Are you going to be okay? I know you cared about Erik." He hated admitting she cared about any man to the point his death was causing her nightmares.

"I feel so bad, Dro. I don't think I've ever lost anyone I really cared about—except for your mother."

Alexa and his mother had been close. "Well, death is a natural part of life. It's just unfortunate Erik had to die the way he did."

"You mean that?" She kissed his shoulder. "You do feel bad?"

"I'm not heartless. I may not have liked him, but I didn't want him to die."

She picked at his arm, squeezing his biceps. "Me either. Thanks for this."

"No need to thank me. I like having you here, sleeping next to me."

"You better watch out, Dro," she teased. "You're going to be in love soon."

Dro smirked. "Whatever. Go to sleep."

She relaxed in his arms. And just when he thought she'd fallen back asleep, she mumbled, "I love you, Dro."

When he heard her soft snores, he was finally able to

admit it to her sleeping form and to himself. He kissed her forehead. "I love you, too."

NOVEMBER 5, 2011:

DRO STUDIED HIS WIFE. Although she wasn't overtly upset, he could read the disappointment in all of her features. He often wondered how things would end for them. Would they get to ride off into the sunset? He doubted they would. His mother used to say "*Adorar es de vivir*," to live is to love. She always told him that life was all about love. And that love makes people better.

He frowned as he thought about his mother. She wasn't the best role model. She committed suicide, after all. But when he fell in love with Alexa, he finally realized what his mother had been trying to tell him. It was something special to love someone more than your own life. He understood why people searched for the one person that would complete them.

Alexa had been telling him for a long time now that she wanted out. She was tired of the adventure, the danger. She just wanted a quiet life with her family—a life without violence and shady business.

He knew she loved him, but would that love be enough?

He glanced at her out the corner of his eye. "You with me, baby?"

"Yes."

"You don't look like you're here with me. You're off in another place." They were speeding toward a remote safe house in his truck. This house was more like an abandoned shack. "Are you going to continue pretending you're here with me?"

"I'm just thinking, Dro. I miss the kids. I just want them home. This not knowing anything bullshit is really draining me. Every time I go to pray, I stop myself. How can I pray for God to show me mercy when I have never shown mercy to anyone? But then I pray anyway because I don't know what else to do."

He felt her eyes on him and his gaze flashed to hers for a minute before forcing his attention back to the road ahead. "I don't know how to respond to that. I wonder the same thing, though."

She sniffed and he glanced at her again just as she wiped a tear from her face. He pulled into a long, unpaved driveway. Once they reached the house, he put the truck in park. Turning to her, he observed her, taking in her bowed head and slumped shoulders. "You're going to leave me," he said softly. It wasn't a question. It was a statement. After all, he did know her better than anyone. "When the kids are back, you're going to leave me."

She swept another tear from under her eye. "I would never leave you, Dro."

"Not emotionally, physically."

"I have to. I can't live like this anymore. But you don't have to think of it as leaving you. You can come with me."

"I can't just leave, Alexa. I have obligations here. I have a company to run—"

"I keep thinking about the kids. Do you want Kyleigh to grow up like I did under constant guard, learning how to shoot a gun at the age of ten? Forced to marry someone we know is trustworthy? What about Alex? Do you want him to take over a company that has brought him more money than he could imagine, but no freedom to be the man he wants to be? What if he wants to be a doctor, or a mechanical engineer, or even a chef? Don't you want them to be happy doing what they want to do?"

"Of course, I want all those things for our children. But you're making it seem like this Martinez Organization is the same one my father ran. I've worked hard to legitimize this company. We do none of the old illegal activities. For the first time in three generations, Martinez's sole income is from legitimate business. Look at your parents—look at us. Even though our fathers arranged this marriage, I love you more than I love myself. Our life isn't that bad, Lex."

"I know," she admitted. "And I love you the same way. Sure, it worked out for us. What about Lei? It didn't work out that great for him. He loves Ari and will never be with her because of this business. Ari was forced to marry Jackson even though she didn't love him. And don't you think Makayla knows where Lei's heart really is? Look at Chase? He's never been happy in love."

"That's because he's in love with you," Dro muttered under his breath.

She sighed. "We're the exception, not the rule. Even though our lives weren't necessarily bad, we can never escape the past. No matter how much you try, we still need guards, we still need B5's, and we still need guns in every room, explosives, bullet proof glass in our houses or on our cars. For Christ's sake, Dro, our kids can't even open a window without me worrying that some faceless enemy is going to pick that moment to exact some revenge."

He bowed his head and rested it on the steering wheel. He felt the cool tips of her fingers skimming the nape of his neck.

"You know how much I love you," she said. "There are times when I think I'll suffocate if I can't be with you. But I'm a mother. I need my children to live better than I did. I know we can give them all the advantages in life, but we can't give them the freedom they deserve. If I can give them a chance to be free, I will."

Dro averted his gaze. He did want to give their kids freedom. He wanted them to have the life she was talking about. He needed to give her that life, too.

A knock at the driver's side window jarred him from his thoughts. Dro lifted a finger signaling Lei to wait a minute. "I don't know, baby," he said, turning back to her. "I don't know if that's possible. I want to tell you it is, but I just don't know. I do know I can't live without being able to look into your eyes." He lifted his right hand and skimmed her earlobe with his thumb. She leaned into his touch. "I can't let you go," he murmured.

"Let's go together," she pleaded.

He shook his head and ran his thumb over her mouth, down her chin.

"Don't say you can't leave," she told him. "I know you have obligations here, but you're the boss. You can make up the rules. You don't have to follow some invisible path. You can make the path." Then she hopped out of the truck and hurried into the house.

"What's going on?" Lei asked when Dro slid out of the truck. "She okay?"

"Not really," Dro replied. "But she will be as soon as this is over."

Chapter Twenty-Three

MAY 29, 1998, Pop's house:

LEI SAT in the kitchen at the breakfast bar eating a sandwich when Dro walked in. It had been pretty quiet since Erik was killed and the "Steve situation," as they called it, was finished. In fact, this was the first time he'd seen Dro since he went back to school.

Dro sat next to him. "What's good?"

Lei shrugged. "Shit. How long are you in town?"

Dro took half of Lei's sandwich, and bit into it. "Not sure. It depends on if I can get any work done while I'm here." Dro had chosen to take a class spring semester.

Lei nodded. "I hear that. It's hard to concentrate sometimes. I started looking into law schools this week. And I scheduled a LSAT preparatory class."

"I just signed up for the GMAT class myself."

Lei drank from his can of soda. They had all decided early on to go into careers that would take them far away from the "business". None of them wanted to end up working for the Martinez Organization as it was. Their main goal was to legitimize it.

"Did Alexa tell you she was going to major in business administration, too?" Lei asked.

"Yeah, I knew she was leaning toward it. She's eyeing the hotel business. I'm kind of glad she chose that major. It's better than psychology. She would've been trying to shrink all of us."

They both laughed.

Lei opened his bag of chips. "Did she tell you she was trying to go to Duke?"

Dro froze. "She conveniently left that part out. That's...different."

"Yeah, Pop isn't happy. He feels like she needs to stay close. He supposedly has big plans for her."

"I bet she's not happy about that."

"You said it," Lei agreed. "She was furious at him last night. It all came to a head at dinner."

Dro snickered. "Where is she?"

"At the pool with Jon." Lei popped a chip in his mouth.

"Who's Jon?" Dro dropped his half of the sandwich back on Lei's plate.

Lei grumbled a curse. Dro and Alexa were doing something he thought they'd never be able to return from. And it worked for them because their parents had already decided it would be best for them to marry and procreate. That rarely happened in their world. He didn't need examples because he was living proof.

Lei was in love with Ari. He thought they would be able to be happy together, but Enrique was an ogre and a control freak. Now that Ari was pregnant with Jackson's baby, he knew that he would never be able to be with her the way he wanted to. And to make matters worse, he couldn't even count on Pop to try and make a way. Pop agreed with Enrique. Pop thought Ari should marry Jackson.

But what Pop and Enrique didn't know was that Jackson was an ass. He was definitely not going to be good for Ari. He already didn't want Ari to go to medical school. Jackson wanted Ari to change her major to education or something.

Shaking himself out of his thoughts Lei looked at Dro, who was watching him. "What?"

"Where did you go?" Dro asked.

"Nowhere," he grumbled.

"Who's Jon?"

"Jon is some guy she's been hanging out with over the past couple of weeks. She brought him home one day and I met him. He seems okay. He's completely different from Erik."

"Different how?"

"Well, let's just say he's definitely not the athletic type. He looks more like he could be in the chess club or some-thing." Lei chuckled, amused with himself. When he glanced at Dro, though, the frown on his face made it clear he was not amused.

"Why are they at the pool this late in the day?"

"I don't know. Why don't you go to the pool and ask her?" Lei got a kick out of Dro being all jealous, and didn't bother to hide it.

"You're enjoying this too much." Dro rolled his eyes. "I don't get that girl. I mean, Erik just died and she's already taking someone else to the pool?"

Lei choked on the pop he just swallowed. "Why do I get the feeling you're not really talking about swimming? And besides, Alexa and Erik hadn't gone to the pool for months before he died."

Dro glared at Lei. "Shut up, Lei. I'm just saying... Have you had this Jon checked out? Who is he really?"

"He's Jon. Why are you so upset? As far as I knew, Alexa could see other people. Is this a problem for you?"

"Hell yeah, it's a problem for me," Dro admitted. "I don't want her taking anyone else to the pool."

Lei was stunned silent for a minute. Dro was really upset. This was so unlike Dro that Lei had to laugh out loud.

Dro stood up, nearly tipping the barstool over. "What the hell are you laughing at, Lei?"

"You. I wish you could hear yourself right now. You sound like the jealous boyfriend from hell, and you're not even her boyfriend."

"Who said I wasn't her boyfriend? Hell yeah, I'm her boyfriend. What do you think we've been doing?"

"Keeping it light. That's what you said," he reminded Dro.

"I can't stand you sometimes."

"Hey, I just call it like it is. Those are the facts, brother. You laid those rules down, and now you can't take it."

Dro folded his arms over his chest. "Maybe it's time to change the rules."

"You better hope she's fine with that," Lei told him, cracking up. "But welcome to the club." Lei had always sensed it, but Dro had inadvertently confirmed it. Dro was in love with his sister.

"Being in love with your sister doesn't automatically mean we're in some sort of club."

Lei smacked Dro on the back. "Well you gave me hell about being in love with Ari. I felt like I should return the favor."

"Go to hell, Lei."

Lei laughed out loud as Dro stalked out of the kitchen.

NOVEMBER 5, 2011:

LEI ENTERED the safe house behind Dro. Kendrick was standing against the wall talking to Alexa as she took off the rest of her costume. Dro was on a phone call. Lei wondered what Alexa and Dro had been talking about in the truck. Things seemed pretty heated. In his mind, Lei knew she was tired of this life. And the kids being in danger just cemented that in her. And if he was being truthful with himself, he couldn't blame her. He had thought about it many times as well.

He rubbed the back of his neck and cracked his knuckles. It was hell trying not to think about where their family was. The only thing he could do was hope for the best. He knew Pop would die to protect them, but he was only one man. He couldn't be expected to protect everyone. And as he thought about that, he thought about his life.

Lei had spent an extreme amount of time doing what everyone expected him to do. Hell, he didn't even marry the woman he loved because it wasn't expected. Instead, he married one of his best friends in the name of loyalty and honor. Love really didn't have anything to do with it. Sure, he loved Makayla, but not the way he loved Ari. He wondered if Makayla knew that. He felt that she did, but it didn't matter anyway.

Lei would honor his vows because that's the type of person he was. He'd never slept with Ari again once he married, although he dreamed of being with her in that way. The rare kisses they'd shared through the years, when they were alone, never seemed to be enough.

He wondered if his wife and the love of his life were

safe. He couldn't help but wonder if he would continue to live the same way once they were back. A part of him hated to hurt Makayla, but the strongest part of him longed to be with Ari and his daughter. And that part was ready to make the most important choice of his life.

Kendrick approached Lei. "I just got the word that Marnie was picked up by Janine's younger sister, Janet, when Janine and Adam didn't show up to pick her up. I did a check on her. She works a good job as a nurse. And she's married with one child. When they never show up again, I'm sure she'll take responsibility for Marnie."

Lei nodded, hating the fact that the child would grow up without her parents. That was just one of the downsides to this life. They took parents away from children too many times to count. He knew Alexa was thinking about that as well, with her own children being gone. That's why he had a feeling that she wouldn't be around much longer. "Did you tell Alexa?"

"Yeah," Kendrick confirmed. "She wanted to know as soon as I got word. I wish...never mind."

Dro stomped over to them. "What the hell was that drug that you gave Melissa, Kendrick? She's still out cold."

Kendrick shrugged. "It was a simple horse tranquilizer. She should come to any minute."

Dro pinched the bridge of his nose. "Who thinks of that? A horse tranquilizer? The woman weighs one hundred and five pounds wet. She could be out the whole night."

Kendrick sat at the table. "I didn't give her that much. I do know what I'm doing. She should come to in a few hours."

Lei parked in a seat next to Kendrick. "Great, I'm going to try some more of Pop's contacts again to see if he has surfaced." He picked up his phone and punched in a number.

Alexa walked over to the table. "I know we said we were going to stay together, but can someone get us some food? I'm starving."

As if on cue, Chase barreled into the safe house holding bags of food. "I stopped at the store and bought food. I saw Kendrick give Melissa the horse tranquilizer, and figured we would be here for a while."

She smiled and rifled through the bags. "Thank goodness for you, Chase." She pulled a burger out of the bag and sat down next to Kendrick.

Chase smiled. "No problem. I'm going to tell the guards that there is food here."

Lei slammed his phone on the table. "Damn. I had our contact in the police department look in the trucks to see if Pop left any hints. He just told me there was blood on one of the seats."

Alexa gasped. "Was it a lot of blood?"

Lei knew she couldn't take much more of this situation. She already broke down once, which still haunted him. "He said the amount of bloodshed could indicate anything from a bloody nose to a small stab wound."

"Well, which truck was the blood in?" Kendrick asked.

Lei paused, glancing at Alexa. "It was the truck Pop was driving, the gray Navigator."

"Oh, my God." She dropped her burger on the table. "Daddy was driving the kids."

Chapter Twenty-Four

NOVEMBER 6, 2011:

CHASE LOWERED HIS HEAD. "Ari and Makayla had Kendrick's wife and kids. Pop and Ma had our kids." He sat in the chair closest to him. His son, CJ, was in the car with Pop. He felt Kendrick come up behind him and place his hand on his shoulder. Then he looked over at Alexa, who was sitting oddly calm while Dro massaged her shoulders.

Chase had never married. It wasn't because he didn't want to marry though. It was quite the opposite. When he met CJ's mother, he thought he'd found someone he could build a life with. But she was killed in a car accident after CJ was born and he had never found anyone that made him feel that way again.

After she died, he poured that love into his son, choosing little league and cub scouts over bars and women. The only time he didn't have CJ was when the boy was with his grandparents. Chase was really good about letting

CJ's maternal grandparents spend time with him every year. That's why he had gone to pick him up from the airport. CJ had just spent four weeks at his grandparents' house and now he was caught up in this mess.

All along Chase had tried to remain calm. When he was separated from Pop, he kept telling himself that everything was going to be okay. Now, as much as he wanted to maintain that positive attitude, it was getting harder by the minute.

"Well, we don't know whose blood it is," Kendrick reassured them. "Let's not jump to any conclusions."

Chase looked at his younger brother. Kendrick was the "down for anything, and cool under pressure" brother while Chase was always considered the calm, dependable brother. Kendrick could be shot and still remain composed. He guessed they both got their unruffled demeanor from their father.

MAY 29, 1998, Pop's house:

CHASE WATCHED as Alexa and Dro argued outside of the pool house. His friend had just found out Alexa was entertaining another guy at the pool. Dro was livid, but Chase couldn't understand why. Everyone knew that Alexa was in love with Dro even though she never voiced it out loud. He could see it in her eyes when she looked at Dro. And he hoped to find someone who'd look at him the same way, the same way his mother had always looked at his father.

Of course, Chase had messed around with a lot of women. None of them made him feel like he wanted to fight someone. And Dro looked downright murderous in that moment. He almost felt sorry for the fool in the pool house.

Chase, Dro, and Lei had been partners in crime since they were toddlers. They'd spent countless time playing RISK, Dungeons and Dragons, hunting, and other things little boys did. He trusted them more than he trusted his own brother sometimes. And that bond only grew stronger as the years flew by.

Only as they got older, they stopped playing with toys, started following Enrique's orders, and sometimes ended up in adjoining jail cells for the night.

Yet, even though they all were loyal to Martinez, they all shared the same vision for the future. They all wanted to take Martinez in a different direction once they were able to control it. They didn't want to run the same business as their parents. Chase wanted to be like his father though. His father was the president of Martinez Construction and very good friends with Pop and Enrique.

He always knew, though, that he wanted to take his education one step further than his father. He wanted an architecture degree. He wanted to design, not just build. And although he could do both, choosing to major in construction management and architecture, he loved the challenge of design. In fact, he was currently working on his biggest project yet—underground lairs. He wanted to design a complete underground city if he could.

He was jarred from his thoughts when Alexa nearly mowed him down on her way back into the pool house. She turned to him. "I'm sorry, Chase. Your friend just pissed me off." She glanced back at Dro. "Last time I checked my dad's name was Leiland Sr.," she yelled loud enough for Dro to hear.

"It's okay," Chase assured her, unable to hide his smile. "What's going on?"

She crossed her arms in front of her breasts, tapping her foot on the cement. "Dro comes and pulls me out of the pool house, to cut the fool on me for daring to have company."

"Why?" Of course, he knew why—Dro was jealous. He wasn't going to out his friend, though.

"How the hell should I know, Chase? Why don't you ask him— somewhere else? My friend is waiting for me."

Dro stalked toward them, fury etched in his face. "All I want to do is meet Jon."

"See," she shouted, placing her hands on her hips. She glared at Dro. "Why do you need to meet Jon? He goes to my school and he's a good guy."

Dro looked at her incredulously. "He may not be as good as you think. I think it's important that we know who you're hanging out with."

She threw up her hands. "Why? I'm not marrying the guy. He's just a friend."

Chase interjected, "I think Dro just wants to know what kind of friend this Jon is." He wanted to know, too.

She scowled at Chase. "Do you think that gives him the right to come out here acting all deranged?"

Is this a trick question? "No?" Chase answered and asked at the same time.

"See!" Alexa shouted at Dro.

They were all rendered speechless, however, when Jon picked this moment to step out of the pool house. Chase was floored at the sight of him. Jon was pretty ordinary. He was short, skinny, and...white. And he looked like the president of the math club or something, with his Steve Urkel suspenders and glasses. Chase looked over at the shocked expression on Dro's face and couldn't help it—he laughed out loud.

Alexa turned to Jon. "I'm sorry, Jon. Don't mind them. They're just being assholes." She grabbed Jon's hand. "Let's get back to work on this project."

"Project?" Dro stopped her from moving past him. "You're working on a project? Why didn't you just say that?"

She shoved Dro. "Because I don't owe you an explanation. I hate to keep stating the obvious, but you're not my man. Even if Jon and I were going to have hot sex by the pool all afternoon, it would still be none of your business. And you know why? Cause you're not my boyfriend."

"What is wrong with you and Lei?" Dro asked. "Who do you think I am to you?"

"Not my boyfriend," she repeated.

"Would you say I was her boyfriend?" Dro asked Chase.

Chase shrugged. "Sort of. I mean, you act like you are."

"See," she stated. "The key word is 'act'. You act like you're my boyfriend. But that doesn't make it a fact, right Chase?"

Chase threw his hands up in frustration. "Actually, I don't care. What difference does it make anyway?"

"I need to talk to Alexa alone?" Dro glared at Jon, who quickly scurried back into the pool house. "Chase, give me a minute."

"No, Chase, don't leave," she said, giving Dro the evil eye. "Dro may be *jefe*, but he's not the boss of you or me."

Dro cursed. "Listen, I'm not going to argue about this anymore. You're my girlfriend, okay? I don't want you seeing anyone else at all. I thought we already went over this?"

"Like hell we did. We agreed that neither of us would see anyone else when you were in town or vice versa. We never agreed that I couldn't see anyone at all. And why don't you just clock me over the head and drag me to your room by my hair?"

Dro stepped closer to her. "Ha Ha. I guess I'm just having a hard time understanding why this is even a problem. You told me you didn't particularly want to see anyone else. Why are you so mad?"

"Why do you want to change things now?"

Dro rolled his eyes and let out some sort of growl before he pulled her in for a kiss. She flung her arms around his neck. When Dro pulled away, he rested his forehead on hers.

"Because I love you and the thought of another guy experiencing you the way I do makes me want to kill somebody."

She stepped back. "What?"

"You heard me. I'm in love with you, and I need to know that you're with me. I don't want to see anyone else, and I don't want you to see anyone else."

"Oh my God!" she squealed. "You're in love with me? I knew that."

She kissed him.

"I bet you did. You should have said something and put me out of my misery."

She burst out in a fit of giggles. "Nope, it was yours to tell. Now I'm going to have to get rid of Jon."

"I'm thinking that's a pretty good idea."

"Give me five minutes," she said, holding up her hand. Turning on her heel, she bolted toward the pool house.

Chase watched her sprint to the pool house and sighed. One day he'd have that. Until then, there was work to do.

NOVEMBER 6, 2011, *the safe house*:

CHASE ADDRESSED THE GROUP. "Lei, have you had any luck with Pop's contacts?"

"No." Lei plopped down on the old, dingy couch. "There's no information on Pop anywhere."

Chase slammed a fist on the table. "Well, we just continue like we have been. End this and then focus on finding them."

"He's right," Kendrick agreed. "We don't even know whose blood it is. We can't assume it's one of us."

Melissa moaned from the other room.

Alexa pulled her gun out of her holster. "Well, let's break this bitch so I can find my kids."

Chase followed Alexa and the others into the bedroom.

Melissa peered up at them through hooded eyes. Her eyes widened and she sat up. She opened her mouth to say something. Too late. Alexa backhanded her.

"You better start talking, bitch," she warned. "I'm not in a good mood."

Chase wrapped a piece of Melissa's hair around his fist. "And she's not the only one in a bad mood."

Chapter Twenty-Five

MAY 2, 1999:

THE PARTY WAS in full swing. Melissa felt on top of the world. It was graduation and she was ready to start her life. Dro had rented out the entire club on Fifth Street and thrown a graduation party on campus instead of in his home town. It was the event that everyone was dying to get to.

Melissa had put on her slinkiest dress. It was a halter dress, no straps, and it fell an inch above her knee. She was hoping to lure Dro into her bed. Melissa wasn't fazed by Dro's "girlfriend". She knew that she had more sex appeal in her pinky finger than Alexa had in her whole body. Dro would be begging for her company before she was done.

She breezed into the party feeling cool and sexy. The base in the music was pumping, and the dance floor was packed as Juvenile's "Back That Ass Up" started playing. The VIP section was above the dance floor. It was crowded with those closest to Dro and Chase. Although, she wasn't invited to the VIP, she was going up anyway because one of her girls was cool with Chase.

As they walked up the stairs, she was excited. She could feel it. This was going to be her night.

Chase greeted Melissa's friend with a hug. "Licia, glad you could come. I saved you a table over by the bar." Licia and Chase had been kicking it for a few weeks. Licia nodded and Chase led them over to their table.

Melissa waved. "Hi, Chase."

He looked her up and down, his dislike of her obvious. "What's up, Melissa? I didn't think you were coming."

She didn't care that he didn't like her. She wasn't going to let anyone ruin her mood. "I graduated, too. Can't I get out and party like everyone else?"

"Don't start anything," he warned. "I want a peaceful night. The best thing you can do is stay away from Dro."

"Where is Dro?" Licia asked.

He tilted his head in the direction of the VIP dance floor. "Over there on the floor."

Melissa looked on the dance floor and narrowed her eyes at the sight of Dro and Alexa. They were dancing very intimately. She was in front of him, and his hands were wrapped around her from the back. The worst part was that it appeared he only had eyes for her.

When the song ended, an old school slow jam oozed from the speakers. Melissa watched Alexa turn around and wrapped her arms around Dro's neck. He slid his arms around her waist, resting his hands on her butt. She saw him bend lower and kiss her, slowly and thoroughly, as if there was no one else in the room. A pang of jealousy shot through Melissa's entire body.

For the first time ever, she felt like a second class citizen in her town. That fact infuriated her. She was raised like a princess. Her father told her he ran this town, and everyone would have to show her respect. That was the reason why she had so many friends. That was the reason why everyone knew not to cross her. Yet Dro and his family didn't seem to care about her family's reputation. By the time the song ended, she was downright livid. Before she could talk herself out of it, she stalked over to them.

Dro must have seen her coming because he stopped dancing and stepped in front of Alexa. Melissa looked around and realized others had stopped as well.

Dro's graphite eyes bore into her. "Melissa, don't start."

She heard Licia beside her begging her to return to the table, but she wasn't budging. She just knew she couldn't sit there any longer, watching the happy couple fall all over each other. She wanted to let it be known that she thought this whole thing was bullshit. "I'm not starting anything. I just want to talk to her."

Dro opened his mouth to speak, but Alexa peeked around him. "How can I help you?" she asked stepping out from behind him.

He placed a hand on Alexa's shoulder and Melissa's irritation rose to new heights. "I can't stand you, little girl."

"Really?" Alexa asked, sarcasm evident. "Thanks for sharing." And then she turned her back on Melissa and pulled Dro back to their table.

As the music played on, the other people started dancing again. But Melissa could barely control her anger. She stalked back over to her table, picked up her cell phone, and placed a call.

About an hour later, after witnessing countless dances, Melissa perked up at the sight of her cousins strolling into VIP. The Calvary had arrived, and Alexa was going to stop disrespecting her in *her* town. She stood up and pointed her family in the direction of Alexa and Dro on the dance floor. She instructed her cousins to follow her lead and led them over to where they were. Once again, activity on the dance floor ground to a halt. Dro must have spotted her again because he was flanked by his family before Melissa made it over to them.

She stopped in front of them and wondered if she had just brought her family into a bad situation.

Alexa arched a brow at her, obviously not paying attention to Melissa's posse. "Are you here to tell me that you can't stand me again?"

"No, I'm here to kick your ass. You think you're so tough, but like I told you before, this is my town. You're not going to come here and disrespect me like this."

Alexa placed a hand on her hips. "I wouldn't have to disrespect you if you didn't keep coming all up in my face. Why are you here?" She eyed Melissa's entourage. "What? Did you bring your posse to handle me?"

"I wanted you to see who runs this town."

"I don't need to see shit. It doesn't matter anyway. You're at my boyfriend's party acting like a spoiled, petulant child. Are you so desperate that you still want to fight me over *my* man?"

"This isn't even about Dro," Melissa argued. "This is about your smug attitude."

"My smug attitude?" Alexa asked, bringing a hand to her chest. "You brought your family here to intimidate me. I was simply trying to enjoy my boyfriend's graduation party. I could go all night and not even look at you. Yet I bet you were watching me the whole time. It really is unhealthy."

"Ugh," Melissa growled. "I can't stand you. I can't wait to kick your ass out of my town."

"You're going to be waiting forever. I don't fight girls."

"What the hell is that supposed to mean?"

"It means I don't fight girls. I train daily and I'm not

214

going to waste my efforts fighting you or any other girl. Besides, it really isn't a fair fight. I could mop the floor with your messed up weave and not even break a sweat. That's why I don't fight girls. I beat bitch ass men down—like your boy behind you—not stupid, insecure bitches. Why don't you take your family and get the hell out of here? I'm tired of embarrassing you in *your* town."

Melissa took swing at her, and missed, almost falling back. She advanced again. Alexa sidestepped her and somehow Melissa's hair ended up in Alexa's fist. She screamed as Alexa ripped her hair out by the roots and shoved her to the ground.

"I don't know what Melissa has told you," Alexa told the posse. "But unless you want some serious problems, I suggest you get the hell out of this party and take your girl with you." She dropped the hair to the ground. "Aren't you tired of trying to play me, Melissa? When are you going to learn that I don't take shit from anyone? Next time, you may end up with something else missing besides your hair."

And with that, Alexa walked away from Melissa and her family.

NOVEMBER 6, 2011, the safe house:

MELISSA WAS FACING five angry killers and she was all alone. She wanted to scream, but she doubted she would be able to get it out before Chase snapped her neck or Alexa slit her throat.

The Martinez clan was dangerous. After countless run-ins with Alexa in the past, Melissa knew she was a very cold individual. Melissa didn't care, though, because she was dangerous in her own right. And she was chomping at the bit to get even.

Dro stepped into view. "Melissa, it looks like you've been busy planning elaborate revenge schemes."

Melissa noted that Dro still looked good. "Where am I? If you don't let me go, you're going to regret it."

"No," Alexa said. "You're going to regret ever meeting me in about five minutes if you don't tell me what I want to know. So far I know you hired clueless Tommy and others to infiltrate the safe house where I was staying. Before that, you and Janine conspired to get her into Martinez, using her connection to Nicholas to get her past security. In speaking to Tommy, Janine, and Adam, we know that you are working with someone. Who is it?"

"Do you think I'm just going to tell you who that is?"

"Oh I know you're going to tell me. See, I have a few surprises of my own for you—Tommy, Janine, and Adam are no longer in the land of the living. What's to stop me from making you join them?" Alexa held up a cell phone.

"What is that for?" Melissa asked, afraid of the answer.

"Well my buddy, Chase, gave this to me. You see, if I push this button, your Daddy's house will become a bonfire —with him and your mother in it."

A chill ran up Melissa's spine. "You wouldn't?"

"Really? You want to try me?"

Melissa thought about it for a minute. If she didn't give Alexa what she wanted, her parents would be killed. And if she did, she would be killed. Melissa decided to bargain. "You give me that thing and we'll talk," she offered, pointing at the cell phone in Alexa's hand.

Kendrick snatched the phone from Alexa. "I don't think you get it. You don't call any of the shots. The way I see it you have two choices. You either tell us what we want to know and die by yourself, or you don't tell us what we want to know and die with your parents. You pick?"

She poked her chest out and lifted her chin. "If you kill me you'll never find out where your family is."

"Nice try," Kendrick said. "But I know where my family is. Do you know where yours is? I do. They're at home chillin'. They don't know there's a bomb in their crawl space that can go off at any minute. In fact, I think they might even be having people over for dinner according to the maid. So make your choice."

Melissa swallowed past a lump in her throat. At this point, she knew there was no way out. They had the upper hand. When she had been recruited into this, the plan seemed unflappable. They were supposed to ambush the family at the safe house, but only one truck showed up. The only casualties were her men and Nicholas.

Kendrick glanced at his watch. "You're wasting time. In two minutes, I'll make the decision for you."

"Okay. Just please don't hurt my family."

Kendrick pulled up a chair and sat down on it. "Talk. You have five minutes to tell me something good. Don't play me and don't lie to me. Or you can see your parents on the other side."

Chapter Twenty-Six

NOVEMBER 6, 2011, the safe house:

KENDRICK WAITED for Melissa to respond. Of course, she was an idiot, but she was the idiot that was going to help them end all of this once and for all. He scanned the room and then focused on Alexa. She was, for all intents and purposes, the most important person in his life. Sure, he loved his wife and children more, but his bond with Alexa could never be diminished. And the place she had in his life could never be surpassed.

He narrowed his eyes at Melissa. She seemed to be considering her options, which was good for them. He was good at a lot of things, but he was best at reading people. Religious people called it discernment, but he called it power. He could look at someone and tell when they were being genuine or fake. That gift had never failed him. Of course, he didn't know where his family was. Melissa didn't know that, though. In fact, she told him a lot about the situation just by her response.

She gave herself away. At least, he knew that she didn't know where his family was, which gave him hope that they were safe with Pop. And when he met Alexa's gaze across the room, he knew that she felt the same way. Alexa could read people almost as well as he could, but she could read him best of all.

"You have three minutes," Kendrick warned, tapping his foot against the wood floor.

"Uh—I—" Melissa said, obviously stalling.

Kendrick rolled his eyes. She was on the edge of his last nerve. This whole thing was tiring, and that was the understatement of the year. "Two minutes," he informed her, looking at his watch.

"I had an affair with him," she whispered. "We were lovers for about nine months when he told me his true intentions. By then I already loved him. He lit the fire under me when he began talking about your family, especially Alexa's father. I guess he knew him from way back. He had some sort of revenge scheme in mind and played on my distaste for Alexa. He told me who might be open for some revenge. We came up with a plan to use Tommy, Janine, and Adam to help destroy Martinez Organization."

"Did this man ever say why he had it out for Alexa's father?" Kendrick asked.

She sniffed, as tears streamed down her face. "No, and I asked him numerous times. But he keeps everything close to the vest. The only thing I could get out of him was that he went way back with him. They grew up together, or served in the military, or something like that."

"What's his name?" Alexa asked.

Melissa bowed her head.

"What is his name?" Alexa repeated.

"He'll kill me if I say anything," Melissa said.

"You don't have to worry, Melissa," Alexa assured her. "You're going to die anyway, so you might as well tell us."

Melissa choked back a sob. "He's very powerful. His name is Senator Clive Owens."

Kendrick stood abruptly. "You just bought your family some time, Melissa. You can breathe a little easier." He rushed out of the room. The others followed him to the safe house's small living area.

OCTOBER 21, 2000:

KENDRICK AND ALEXA walked into the restaurant holding hands. She was leaning against his side seductively, and he had to keep reminding her to chill out. They were in a public place, and he didn't want to draw unnecessary attention to them.

"Hello, welcome to The Diamond Club," the mai tre'd said in greeting.

"Hello," Kendrick said. "We have a reservation under Guess." They had made their reservation under a fake name so that no one would know they were there.

"Yes Mr. Guess. I'll show you to your table."

As they followed the man to their table, Kendrick placed his hand on the small of Alexa's back. He did a quick scan around the room, checking for people that would know them. Then, his attention was drawn to a large party in the middle of the restaurant—high rollers. The men were all dressed in expensive suits, their wives in fancy dresses. He wondered who they were.

"Kendrick," Alexa whispered in his ear once they reached the table. "Stop looking around."

He pulled her chair out and waited for her to take her seat. The maitre d' ran off a list of wines.

A waiter arrived at the table and introduced himself. As Alexa ordered wine, Kendrick watched her. She was gorgeous from head to toe on a regular day, but she was stunning that night. Her dress was a dark, crimson red. It was floor length, with a slit that ran to just above her knee. More than one of the gentlemen in the huge ballroom couldn't keep their eyes off of her. Her hair was styled in an up-do with curls dangling from the edges. She wore smoky eye shadow and bright red lipstick. His gaze dropped to the dazzling diamond necklace gracing her feminine throat.

Kendrick had always tried to think of Alexa as a sister, but that didn't always work for him. She was a very attractive woman, but most times, he was immune to her charms.

Then there were times like tonight where he was reminded that his best friend was indeed a woman. And he was definitely a man. But he respected her more than anything. She was his equal, and he definitely appreciated that when he needed someone to have his back. She had been there every time he was caught in a less than ideal situation. And he had been there for her the same way.

There was one thing that he knew and embraced— they had a sort of soul tie. He wasn't going to say they were soul mates, but there was something that inherently connected them. Over the years, that connection had caused problems with Dro. And Kendrick understood where the other man was coming from. Dro was in love with Alexa and always had been, in Kendrick's opinion. Dro liked being the man in her life and didn't appreciate the fact that she relied on another man to help her through any problems. It caused many arguments for Dro and

Alexa as well as Kendrick and Dro. But he had let Dro know early on that he had no intentions of coming between them. He also let Dro know that she loved them both in different ways and Dro should respect that and not interfere.

Of course, Kendrick fought for his life after that comment, but he didn't regret speaking his mind. Deep down, he knew that Dro respected him for it.

Kendrick cleared his throat after his eyes traveled down to the low cut "V" in Alexa's dress. If Dro knew what he was thinking right then, he would be killed. But he couldn't say he cared all that much at that moment. After all, he was only human. When he met her eyes, she was staring at him. He shifted in his seat. "Sorry."

She arched a brow. "Penny for your thoughts?"

"I think I'll keep those to myself."

Her light and airy laugh floated to his ears. "You don't have to hide anything from me," she whispered, leaning forward. "Besides, I can tell that your thoughts were less than pure."

He laughed. "Well, then you know some things are better left unsaid."

Her attention was drawn away from Kendrick when a loud boisterous laugh erupted from the 'big party' table. "I wonder what he's laughing about?"

He gently picked up her hand and placed a soft kiss to her palm. "Let's dance."

"Sure."

He stood up and held out his hand to her. As they walked onto the dance floor, an older couple from the big table stepped on the floor as well. Kendrick wrapped his arms around Alexa and pulled her closer. "You do look nice tonight."

She smirked. "Nice? I thought I looked damn good."

"Okay, you look damn good."

They both laughed. He pulled her closer and kissed her bare shoulder. The soft music played as he took in her scent. She had on just the right amount of perfume. He closed his eyes as he buried his head in her neck. He slid his hands down her back and rested them just above her ass.

She pulled back, smiling seductively. "Move your hand one inch lower and I'll cut your dick off."

He snapped out of his thoughts and tried to play it off with a chuckle. "Whatever. You're supposed to be watching our target, not flirting with every man in the restaurant including me."

A loving smile spread across her face. "We're supposed to pretend we're a loving couple. I'm supposed to be flirtatious tonight."

He dipped her. "Just keep an eye on her and we can get out of here."

"I would if I didn't have to worry about you groping my ass."

He spun her away from him and then back. "Hey, I'm a man."

She laughed softly as she wrapped her hands around his neck. "Yeah, I can tell. But don't get brand new on me."

Kendrick smiled at her, keeping up the charade. "Look, I'm not getting brand new on you. I just got caught up for a minute. But the threat of a knife to my important parts has cured me of that."

They continued to dance. To everyone in the room, they looked like a couple in love and they even inspired some others to get out on the floor.

The older couple slowly walked off the dance floor when the song changed. Eventually, Alexa and Kendrick headed back to their table to sit down. When Clive Owens and his party left the restaurant, Kendrick and Alexa followed.

Chapter Twenty-Seven

NOVEMBER 6, 2011, the safe house:

KENDRICK PACED BACK and forth in the living room. "Clive Owens was the senator who hired us to kidnap his wife."

Alexa's eyes widened. "You're right. This is about Daddy."

"It looks that way," Kendrick agreed. "If it is Senator Owens, this is bigger than we thought."

"We need to focus our energy on finding Pop," Dro surmised. "We can't assume he's okay anymore."

"Pop doesn't know this is about him either," Lei added. "We need to hurry."

"Have you heard anything from any of his contacts?" Kendrick asked.

Lei picked up his cell phone and began punching in a number. "It's like he dropped off the face of the earth."

Kendrick grabbed his laptop, tapping furiously on the keys. "We have to do something."

"So what are we going to do with Melissa?" Chase asked.

"Keep her alive until we don't need her anymore," Kendrick replied, glaring at Lei. "We may have to use her to get a line to Senator Owens."

"What happened with Owens?" Dro asked.

Kendrick looked at Alexa. They'd done a couple of jobs for Pop that the others didn't know about. Pop was very secretive, and his policy was that everyone knew only what they needed to know.

When it came to Senator Owens and his wife, no one had needed to know anything. Until now.

Kendrick nodded at Alexa.

"It was supposed to be a simple kidnapping," she explained. "We were to snatch his wife publicly and take her to a safe house, which we did. Daddy switched the plan. I guess Senator Owens wanted her dead, but—" she paused. "Daddy faked her death."

Dro frowned. "Why? What's his connection to her?"

She shrugged. "I don't know. He never told us. I always just assumed that he knew her. Or maybe they were having an affair. He told us to bring her to the safe house and then he excused us."

"So he handled it from there?" Lei asked.

She shook her head. "A week later he called us back and asked us to help him set it up to look like she was killed."

Kendrick stopped typing for a second. "He made it seem like her kidnappers eliminated her, which was what Senator Owens wanted."

"How did he do that?" Chase asked.

Kendrick struggled to remember the details. "I want to say he drugged her with Propofol to knock her out and dumped her in a public park. He told us to watch her.

When she was spotted in the park by a runner, the police were called. She was taken to the hospital via ambulance. He ordered us to go to the hospital and wait."

"Daddy called in a favor to one of the doctors at the hospital. They pronounced her dead then we waited until Senator Owens identified her," Alexa said, taking up the story. "Kendrick and I broke into the morgue, removed her, and took her to a different safe house."

"And he never told you why he was doing this, Alexa?" Lei questioned.

"Daddy must have paid off the funeral home because we were able to sneak her back in so she could play dead for the funeral. Then Daddy took her away himself. We never heard anything else about her again." Alexa eyed her brother. "Lei, I couldn't think of another explanation. Why would Daddy save someone who meant nothing to him?"

"That still doesn't mean he had an affair with her," Lei said. "I mean, I know why you would think that. But this whole thing is unlike him. There has to be more to this."

"It doesn't sit right with me either," Dro added. "There has to be another explanation. Don't go thinking he carried on an affair with this woman. He wouldn't do that to Ma."

Pop and Ma had the respect and admiration of all of them. They were happily married, which was a rarity in this business. Pop loved Veronica more than life it seemed. They married before he shipped off to war. Since they were both teenagers, everyone predicted it wouldn't last. They beat all the odds, though. Veronica had waited for him while he served his country. And when he returned, they began their life together. She stuck by him through everything—his business and the danger it brought to their family. It was hard to believe Pop would violate that trust by having an affair, but why would he risk so much to help that woman?

Kendrick plugged away on his keyboard. "Pop asked me to make her disappear, and set her up with a new identity. I saved it in an encrypted file. If we find her, we may find him."

Alexa ran her fingers through her curls. "That would mean he's been keeping tabs on her this whole time. That's not like him, right Lei?"

"No, but Kendrick is right. We can't find him anywhere else. We need to try her."

"I found it," Kendrick announced, after a few moments of tense silence. "She's now known as Aaliyah Hernandez. And she's in—" He tapped another button on the keyboard. "Puerto Rico?"

"He hid her in Puerto Rico?" Dro asked. "That's too obvious. Why would he hide her there?"

"So he could get to her if he needed to without suspicion," Lei surmised.

"He's hiding her in plain sight so he can ensure her protection," Alexa added.

Dro rubbed the stubble on his face. "But he wouldn't take the kids there. It's too obvious. Everyone knows we have a connection to Puerto Rico." Although Martinez conducted most business in the States, there were still active Martinez businesses in Puerto Rico.

"Hold on," Kendrick said, focusing on the computer screen. "It looks like there's recent credit card activity."

"Where at?" Chase asked.

Kendrick sighed. "Pop must have been in contact with her. She's on the island."

Everyone was silent. Enrique had purchased a private island off the coast of Puerto Rico. It was a protected haven for the family. As children, they were shipped off to it when things were too hot in the States. The only people allowed on the island were family members.

"We need to go there," Dro said. "Pop has been in touch with her. Why else would she be on the island? Lei, call and get the plane ready. We need to be out of here within the hour."

Lei's phone blared. He hit the talk button and turned the speaker on. "This is Lei."

"Lei?" Pop's voice carried through the receiver.

"Pop?" Lei asked. "Where are you?"

"Tell Kendrick to stop looking for her. I'm in B5. You need to come here now. I'll explain everything."

ALEXA and the others followed Dro into B5. They hurried through the kitchen into the living room where Pop was sitting on the couch.

She flung herself into his arms when he stood. "Daddy! Thank God you're okay."

He rubbed her hair. "I'm fine, ladybug."

Alexa reluctantly let her father go and moved aside so the others could greet him. "Where are my children?" she asked. "Where is everybody?"

Pop picked up a glass of amber colored liquid off one of the coffee tables and took a small sip. "I know you all have questions, and I want to answer them."

"Pop—" Dro started.

Pop held up his hand. "Dro—son, let me talk before you ask any questions."

Dro nodded, taking a seat at the dining room table and pulling Alexa into his lap.

"When Chase informed me that someone was following us to the safe house," Pop explained. "I decided to change plans. I had to assume the enemy knew all of the safe house locations, so I made a few calls, and arranged for the family to be hidden where no one would think to find them."

"On the island?" Lei asked. "Why would you take them there?"

"They're not on the island, Lei." Pop took another sip from his glass. He joined Dro and Alexa at the table. "That was too dangerous for them. I knew someone in Martinez was leaking information about the safe houses, so I figured the same person could've leaked information about the island."

"So where are they?" Alexa asked.

"They're safe," Pop answered. "Well protected."

"Pop, you know I respect your opinion, but I need to know where my family is," Dro insisted. "We got a report there was blood in the truck you were driving. Was someone hurt?"

Pop shook his head. "CJ had a bloody nose. Some of his blood must have ended up on the seat. Everyone is fine."

Dro frowned. "Where are they? I need to know."

"I understand that," Pop said, tracing the rim of his glass. "And believe me, I would feel the same way in your shoes. Do you trust me?"

Dro nodded without hesitation. "Of course, I trust you."

"Then trust me on this. The children are safe and protected. So is everyone else."

Dro's jaw ticked. "Fine," he sighed. "I'll accept that for now. But you need to tell us what's going on."

Alexa turned to Dro, her eyes wide. No one ever talked to her father like that. Everyone knew Dro was *Jefe*, but he'd always respected Pop's position in the family and his history with Martinez. Dro never asserted his power over Pop.

"And I'll tell you everything you want to know, son," Pop said, crossing his legs.

"Daddy, how did you know we were looking for Mrs. Owens?" Alexa asked.

"I did some checking around," Pop admitted. "I called in a few favors. I figured out Senator Clive Owens was behind this attack. I knew you and Kendrick would remember that job I assigned all those years ago. Once you remembered, it was only a matter of time before Kendrick started looking for her."

"She's been in Puerto Rico this entire time?" Kendrick asked.

"I needed to keep her safe," Pop said with a shrug.

"Why?" Alexa demanded. "Why did you need to keep her safe? Why have you gone to so much trouble for her, Daddy? Are you having an affair?"

"I can't even believe you would ask me that, ladybug. I would never cheat on your mother."

Alexa jumped to her feet. "I'm sorry, Daddy, but you have to tell me more. This isn't some secret operation, and I'm not a child," she yelled. "You can't just tell me to do something because you say so anymore. Why did you fake her death? Who is she?"

Pop met her gaze, and she swallowed. She had never disrespected him before. "Alexa..." His tone left no doubt as to whom the parent was in this conversation.

She couldn't believe he called her by her given name. Even at her wedding, he called her ladybug and it was a formal event. She averted her gaze from him. "Daddy, I don't mean to yell. But I need more."

"She's right, Pop," Lei added. "We need more."

Alexa smiled at Lei, thankful he stepped in to diffuse the situation.

"When we were young, Enrique and I grew up in the same neighborhood with Senator Owens," Pop began. "Once he was old enough, he decided to distance himself from us because of our illegal activities. He knew he was going into politics. He married, moved away, and never spoke to us again."

"So why would he hire you to eliminate his wife?" Kendrick asked, finally taking a seat at the table.

"He didn't, and I wouldn't." Pop tapped his forefinger on the table.

"So, how did you get involved?" Dro asked.

Pop chuckled. "If I didn't feel like I was on the spot, I could embrace the pride I have for you all. You all grew into very strong, capable people. We always taught you to protect each other. I'm glad that lesson stuck, even if you're protecting each other against me. That's all Enrique and I could have asked for."

When they glared at him, he sighed and continued. "The idea to start a business came from a conversation I had with Enrique. A friend of mine, a CIA operative, sought me out to complete an assassination job. Enrique thought it would be good for me to branch off and concentrate on my own thing. Although Enrique hated to lose my presence on a daily basis, he told me he wanted his 'brother' to be happy.

"I used my connections to start a security business that was a front for contract work with the CIA. Officials with the CIA contacted me when they wanted certain jobs done, more specifically eliminating threats to national security." Pop was the point of contact and he assigned tasks to the group. They were instructed to use whatever means necessary to carry out these "hard tasks".

"I spent many years working for Enrique," Pop continued. "Although, I wanted you all to work on the legitimate side of the business, sometimes the lines were blurred. This was one of those times."

Pop rubbed his graying beard. "I heard from a close business associate that Senator Owens had put the word to the ground that he needed his wife taken care of so I arranged for one of my employees to accept the job."

"Why, Daddy?" Alexa asked. "Why would you intercept this job?"

"I would never let Owens eliminate his wife and he knew that. That's why he tried to keep his plans from me."

"I still don't get it," Dro said. "Owens obviously didn't want to get you involved. But you got involved anyway. Was this some sort of revenge for something that happened when you were younger?"

"No, but I wasn't going to sit back and let Owens have my sister killed."

Alexa gasped. "What?"

"You heard me. Owens was married to my sister. I couldn't let him kill her."

Chapter Twenty-Eight

THE ROOM WAS SILENT. Alexa could hardly believe the huge bombshell Pop had just dropped on all of them. Owens' wife was his sister? They'd grown up believing he didn't have any family, except for them.

Pop finished his drink and set the glass on the table. "When we were younger, Clive and my sister were in love. When Clive opted to leave the neighborhood for greener pastures, he took my sister with him. I fought to keep her from leaving. I knew once he got her away, I would never see her again. She was determined, though. We lost touch, but I still kept tabs on her."

"Why didn't you tell us you had a sister, Daddy?" Alexa asked, feeling betrayed.

"When she left, I told her she was dead to me. It hurt me that she fell for Clive's lies and turned her back on me. So, I—I turned my back on her. I didn't speak about her again."

"So, this friend, the one who told you about Clive hiring a hit man...who was it?" Lei asked.

Pop sighed. "Over the years, I let my emotions rule me when it came to my sister. Ultimately, I just couldn't let her go completely. I hired someone to work for Clive and watch out for her. He would report back to me monthly. Apparently, he was the one that Clive ordered to find a hit man. I always knew Clive was unfaithful to her, but she would never believe me. He was also verbally and physically abusive. Yet, I never thought he would try to kill her. I couldn't let that happen."

Alexa rubbed her temple, feeling a headache coming on. "So, you did all of this to save your sister. Why lie to us?"

"I didn't lie, ladybug," Pop argued. "I just didn't tell you everything. It didn't matter anyway."

"Why wouldn't it matter?" she asked incredulously.

"I knew I had to make her disappear. No one was to know she was still alive, or she would have been in danger."

She let out of humorless snicker. "But we're the ones you asked to do this job. You couldn't tell us? You couldn't even tell me that I was saving my aunt?"

"Ladybug, you know there are things that have to remain a secret."

"This is not one of them," she shouted. "You know what? I'm tired of this life. I'm tired of this 'need to know' shit. At some point, you thought it wise to train us to work with you. You asked us to help you. I have killed people for you, Daddy. I've slaughtered people because you gave me the word. And for some strange reason, you felt you couldn't even trust me enough to tell me I was saving my own aunt. I'm tired of this life and all these unwritten rules of conduct. You owed me the truth, Daddy. And whether you want to believe that or not, it doesn't change how I feel about this."

Pop's eyes flashed to her. "Alexa, I'm still your father." His voice was low and controlled. "You will respect me."

"The question is do you respect me, Daddy?" she cried. "Do you respect me as a woman and a part of this team?"

Dro gripped her hand and tried to pull her back on his lap. "Alexa, calm down."

She ripped her hand from his and backed away from the table. "I'm fine." She crossed her arms. "So, Daddy, tell me what we're going to do now? The sooner we do it, the sooner this is over."

Dro cleared his throat. "Pop, why did you send her to the island? It's not safe."

"It is for her," Pop insisted. "No one knows who she is. She doesn't even look the same anymore. She's a different person. And she's protected."

Alexa turned her back on Pop when he tried to meet her gaze. It was the first time she had ever done that to him and her heart ached.

"We need to figure out the next move," Lei said, standing by Alexa. "I want this over too."

Alexa was happy that Lei had chosen her side. She couldn't help but resent her father.

It felt like some sort of betrayal to be finding out about this now, after so many years. Everything happening now stemmed from that one event. Now all of their lives were in upheaval.

"I agree," Pop stated firmly.

"We left Melissa at the old safe house," Kendrick said to Pop. He glanced at Dro. "Do you want me to make the call?"

"There's no need to keep her around," Dro ordered.

"Don't get rid of her body," Pop interjected, drawing all of their attention. "I want it found out in the open."

"That's not how we do things," Alexa argued. "We don't want anything traced back to us."

"Would I tell you to do something that traces back to you?" Pop asked. "I do have a plan, ladybug. Melissa's body will send the right message to Owens."

"You want her found in the park?" Kendrick asked. "Just like Owens' wife. I mean, your sister?"

"Exactly. This time Melissa will be dead, and Owens will know that I'm on to him."

Alexa rolled her eyes. She still couldn't believe her father had kept so much hidden from them. She scowled at the man she had admired above all else. "I spoke to her. I helped her. Did she know who I was?"

"We talked about you and Lei," Pop said softly. "She knows you're married to Dro and that you have two children. That's really all that she knows. We're not close. I saved her, yes, but some things are never forgotten."

She snorted. That was just like her father. He was old school. He never forgot betrayal. His sister would probably feel the effects of betraying him for the rest of her life.

"I want to meet her formally," she said to Pop.

"You can meet her once we take care of Owens."

"Why didn't you take care of this back then?" Alexa asked, feeling her anger rising. "It's not like you to leave stuff open."

Pop rose from his seat and approached her.

At this point, Alexa didn't want to have anything to do with him. She was angry and she wanted him to know that he hurt her.

"Ladybug, I'm not a perfect man." He placed his hands on her shoulders. "You know this. I had my reasons for leaving Clive alive. I'm not going to explain them now. The only thing you need to know is that now I want him dead. He's caused me and my family too much trouble. He came after my children and my grandchildren. Now, he'll pay with his life."

———

OCTOBER 10, 1999, *Pop's house*:

POP WAS WAITING in the kitchen, when Alexa and Dro walked through the side door. The lights were dimmed, and he was sipping on a cup of coffee.

Alexa gave him a slight smile. "Daddy, you didn't have to wait up."

Pop noted her red, glassy eyes. She'd been crying. "I wanted to see how things went."

"She did a good job," Dro said. "It was a clean kill. The cleanup crew went in right after we left."

Pop reached out to rub her face. "You've been crying."

She sniffed and bobbed her head.

"Why?" Pop asked.

She sucked in a deep breath and met his gaze, lifting her chin. "It was hard. I cried for his life—his family. But the job is done."

He kissed her forehead. "Sometimes we have to put aside our emotions to get the job done. And you have done a great job of that. That's why I trust you to be a part of this, ladybug."

"Thank you for trusting me," she said. "I just want to make you proud, Daddy."

He cradled his daughter's face in his hands. "You never have to worry about whether I'm proud of you, ladybug. I've always been proud of you, even when you were drooling on all my ties."

She wrapped her arms around his neck and embraced

him. He glanced at Dro. "Can you leave us alone for a minute, son?"

When Dro left the kitchen, Alexa dropped her bag on the floor and sat down on a barstool. Pop opened the freezer, and pulled out a bowl of ice cream. He set the bowl in front of her. "This is for us to share," he said, pointing to two spoons on the counter.

"Daddy, you hate peanut butter and chocolate ice cream." She dipped her spoon into the treat.

He watched her take a few bites then dipped his spoon into the bowl. "I love you. And if you love peanut butter and chocolate ice cream I guess I can love it too. I wanted to talk to you, and I figured we could eat and talk?"

"What do you want to talk about?" she asked, spooning up another bite.

He hesitated and then cleared his throat. "Some people would wonder why I raised you to be a killer." She stilled and her eyes flew to his. "Sometimes I wonder the same thing. I feel like I should at least share with you my thought process."

She bowed her head again and continued eating.

He followed suit, grimacing after he swallowed the ice cream. He really didn't like this shit. He set his spoon down on a napkin. "When you were born, I realized I loved you more than my own life. I had already felt that type of love for your mother, but this was different. A father's love for his children knows no bounds, just like a mother's love for her children. You were my princess—the cutest little piece of happiness I'd ever known. You and your brother are the reason why I strive to be better."

A tear fell from her eyes and onto the counter.

He handed her a Kleenex, grateful Veronica always kept a box in every room. "When I realized that, I also realized my choices in life would ultimately affect your safety. You and your brother were my greatest vulnerability. I figured the best way to ensure your protection would be to train you to defend yourself, by any means necessary. It was pretty unheard of for girls to be trained as equals to men. I took the risk and it paid off. You have exceeded all of my expectations, ladybug. Don't tell your brother, but you're the best of them all. And if or when one of my enemies chooses to exact revenge against me by using my children, I know you can take care of yourself. The truth is it might have been the most cowardly act I've ever committed."

"You're not a coward, Daddy."

"I am. I couldn't bear the thought of you or your brother being hurt because of my line of work. That's why I trained you and Lei to be able to kill, legally. You know the old saying, 'kill or be killed?' That's what I was thinking. And that—that makes me a coward. You may not understand now, but I hope you will one day."

"Daddy, you're not a coward. You're the bravest man I know. You had to make choices for me and Lei. I don't fault you for that. You did what you thought was right for your circumstances. I know that when I'm a mother, I'll do the same thing."

He tilted his head and studied his marvelous daughter. She never ceased to amaze him. "You're very profound for your young age, ladybug." He picked up his spoon again.

She touched her spoon to his and he chuckled. She grinned at him. "I love you, Daddy." She stood up and held out her arms. They embraced each other tightly. When she finally backed away and went back to her ice cream, he watched her eat.

"So, you and Dro?" he asked.

A blush crept up her face. "Why do you ask?" she said, avoiding eye contact.

"Well, I noticed something different between you after your birthday party at the hotel." And he'd found the damning evidence of a tryst in the gym after she'd worked out with Dro a few days earlier. "Are you two an item?"

She swirled her spoon around in the bowl. He wondered if she was trying to come up with a suitable explanation for the condom he found. As much as he loved Dro, he still had the overwhelming urge to throttle him.

"Well, we're not officially an item. But well, you know..."

Pop decided not to push her. His heart wouldn't be able to handle any real details. He was tempted to demand she stay celibate forever. "Ladybug, you know you can tell me anything?" But he secretly hoped she wouldn't tell him anything about her sex life.

"Daddy, there really isn't much to tell. I know you would like us to get married, so we decided to see each other casually. There's no commitment or anything. I'm too young for that."

He was impressed with her level of maturity about the whole marriage issue. His fear for her safety had prompted him to agree to Enrique's request that their two children marry and join their families together. "That's true. I do want you to experience life, ladybug. I just don't want you to be doing things that will prevent that from happening."

"Things like what?" she asked.

Now it was his turn avoid eye contact. "You know, sex and things like that. I don't want any grandkids now."

She giggled. "No grandbabies here, Daddy. You definitely don't have to worry about that."

He sighed with relief. He didn't want to have to maim Dro. "Good. And I want you to date other men before you settle down."

"I do date other boys, Daddy."

"Good." He stood up and kissed her forehead. "I'm going to head up to bed. Your mother is probably wondering where I am."

She peered up at him with big, doe eyes. "Don't worry, Daddy. I'll be okay."

Pop instantly pictured her at four, calling his name over and over. He smiled at the memory. "Well, you should know I always worry. But I have a feeling you will be just fine, ladybug. When you see Dro, tell him I need to talk to him in the morning. And..." He paused. "No sex in the house."

She choked on the bite of ice cream she'd just placed in her mouth, spraying the cold concoction on the clean countertop.

NOVEMBER 6, 2011, B5:

"I NEED A MINUTE." Alexa ran toward her bedroom.

Lei placed a hand on Dro's arm. "I got this, Dro. Give us a minute." Lei glared at Pop and followed Alexa.

Deciding it was time to speak to his children alone, Pop went after them. He caught up to Lei in the hallway. Lei pushed the door open and stepped in first.

Alexa was sitting on her bed, running her feet over the carpet. Lei placed a hand on her shoulder. "Alexa, it's okay. It could've been worse. He could've been cheating on Mom."

"I would never do that," Pop said. He sucked in a breath when Alexa's bloodshot eyes flew to his. He hated to hurt her, but it was plain to see that he had. His heart ached at the sadness and anger in her eyes. He never wanted her to look at him like that.

"I feel like you didn't trust us with this information and it hurts," she said. "It makes me question my trust in you.

"It's not that I didn't trust you."

"Then, what was it?" Lei demanded, sitting next to Alexa. "You can't tell me that you don't understand why we're upset."

"I do understand. The only thing I can say is that I thought it was best at that time to keep it quiet. I don't regret many things, but I do regret that. Her name is Alexi Lei Richardson." Alexa gasped. "She's my younger sister by three years. When our parents died, I took it upon myself to take care of her even though I was only nineteen. When she started dating Clive, I forbade it. I thought he was too old for her. Not to mention, he was studying to be a cop. She rebelled. She continued to see him behind my back. When he left, she ran away with him. She believed Clive when he told her that Enrique and I were nothing but trouble, even though I gave up so much for her. Clive moved to D.C. and they married. I didn't talk to her again until you kidnapped her."

"You named me after her?" Alexa asked, tears standing in her eyes.

"I love her, ladybug. She's my sister. I just couldn't forget what she had turned into when she married Clive. He wanted to be in politics and he was constantly acting like we were scum. Even though we were close growing up, he distanced himself from anything that had to do with us and the old neighborhood. I felt like she turned her back on me when I had given her everything. But when you were born, you looked so much like her. I couldn't help but name you after her."

"How did she react when you told her who I was?" she asked.

"She cried," he confessed softly. "She was happy I still had space for her in my heart."

"So why wouldn't you let us have space for her in ours?" Lei asked, his voice cracking. "You always told us family first. Why doesn't that apply to her?"

"I don't know, son. I'm sorry. I guess I was stuck in the old way. Betrayal is unforgivable. It can mean death. But you're right. She's still my family. And that's why I couldn't let Owens have her killed."

Alexa sighed deeply. "I'm glad you protected her. And there's still time in life to correct this. I want my children to know her. I want you to have a relationship with her. We need to get to work." She walked out and left the two men in her bedroom.

Chapter Twenty-Nine

NOVEMBER 7, 2011:

A MORNING JOGGER discovered Melissa's dead body lying in the park. Alexa and Kendrick watched from a window of an adjacent building as the cops scoured the park looking for clues. The news reporters were lined outside the yellow tape trying to get a story for the eleven o'clock news.

"Déjà vu, huh?" Kendrick sighed.

"Pretty much," Alexa agreed. "I hope Daddy knows what he is doing."

"Do you have any doubt?"

"I want to say no, but everything about this makes me uneasy. I'm used to getting rid of bodies, not leaving them around to be discovered." Although they were careful to use gloves when handling Melissa, anything could have been left on the body or on her clothes. "I'm done after this," she said after a few minutes.

"I know."

"I just can't do it anymore, Kendrick. I guess I'm getting soft in my old age."

He nudged her with his shoulder. "I guess you are. You're not the only one."

She studied him. "You are too?"

"It just doesn't give me the same thrill that it used to. I used to get a rush of adrenaline, but now? I don't know. I miss my wife and my kids. And if you leave..."

"You can't live without me, huh?" she joked.

He rolled his eyes. "No comment." He wrapped an arm around her neck and she dropped her head on his shoulder. "What about Dro?"

Alexa wished Dro would come with her, but knew he wouldn't. One of the things she loved about him was his loyalty to Martinez. She doubted he would leave when he felt he was obligated to stay. "I don't know. But it doesn't change anything. I have to leave for the kids."

"Stop trying to act all brave. I know you, remember. You're going to be a wreck without him."

"I won't be without him," she replied, staring at a crack in the ceiling. "He's always going to own my heart, Kendrick. I'll never be with anyone else. I just can't be with him here."

DRO GRIPPED the steering wheel as he sped toward the Martinez offices. Pop was riding shotgun. They had ridden most of the way in silence and Dro preferred it that way. He had a lot on his mind.

"How are you and Alexa?" Pop asked, breaking the silence.

The question threw Dro for a loop. "Why?"

"I get the feeling there's some sort of disconnect between you."

"We're fine," Dro lied. "We're both tense people, especially when we feel threatened."

"And you're both very driven and extremely loyal."

"Pop, Alexa is probably going to leave me when this is over."

"What?" Pop seemed surprised. "You just told me you were fine."

"We are fine. But she doesn't want to raise the kids here." He shrugged and tried to focus on the road ahead. "I can't say I blame her. I mean, I'm going to try to keep her here, but we all know how that's going to work out. Eventually, she will resent me and then what? I love her. I want her to be happy."

"What about your happiness? Would it make you happy?" Pop asked. "Listen, I've watched you and my daughter build a life together for a long time. I know you would be miserable without her."

Dro knew it too. He wouldn't be able to let her go, and he wouldn't be able to go with her. How was he going to deal with this? Deciding to push that question to the rear, he changed the subject. "With all due respect, I don't feel like talking about this right now. I need to focus on the plan." He turned the volume up on the stereo and continued toward their destination.

LEI ENTERED THE SECURITY ROOM, where Chase was tweaking a special project for Dro. He dropped a folder on the desk. "Are you ready, Chase?"

"Just one more—there. All done."

Lei slid another folder into his briefcase. "We need to

meet Pop and Dro over at Martinez. Kendrick and Alexa should be there once they wrap up at the park."

Chase grabbed his hat. "What time does the flight leave?"

"Five o'clock. That should give us enough time to take care of loose ends. Are you sure you don't want one of us to go with you?"

"I have everything under control on my end, Lei. And you all have everything under control on yours. I just have to brief Kendrick on a few things before I leave. I talked to my father. They are staying put in Canada."

"Good." Lei extracted an extra gun out of the weapons cabinet. "We're all set then."

WHEN ALEXA ARRIVED at Martinez with Kendrick, everyone was there.

"The cops are handling the scene at the park," Kendrick told the group. "The news has been reported and our contact at the hospital morgue touched base with us. It's a waiting game now."

Alexa eyed Dro, who was busy typing on the computer. "Everything looked eerily similar to Alexi's faked death," she added. "Owens should take the bait." She wrapped her arms around Dro from the back.

"Did you leave the surprise?" Pop asked.

"Yes," Kendrick and Alexa replied simultaneously.

"They shouldn't miss it," Kendrick added. "It will trace right back to him."

Lei handed Pop a manila envelope. He opened it and skimmed the contents. "Then, we wait," he said.

"What are you doing, babe?" Alexa opened one of

Dro's desk drawers and pulled out a bowl filled with star-burst candies.

Dro kept his eyes on the computer. "Taking care of some business. No telling when I'll be able to get back to the office."

She popped one of the candies in her mouth and ran her fingers through his hair.

He stopped typing and sighed deeply. "What's up?" he asked.

"Nothing."

Since he was being so secretive, she didn't care if he knew she was lying. She wanted to discuss leaving town with him, but the time wasn't right. She watched as he worked. Eventually, she headed over to the sofa and plopped down next to Kendrick.

When three o'clock arrived, Alexa noticed Chase and Dro huddled by the desk. She wondered what they were talking about and what Dro was thinking. He was ignoring her and hadn't even looked at her since she arrived.

Chase gathered his bags. "I guess I better head to the airport."

Kendrick closed his laptop. "Okay, bruh." He turned to her. "You want to roll?"

She wasn't doing anything else. "Okay."

Chase said his goodbyes to everyone and they left.

ONCE ALEXA, Kendrick, and Chase were gone, Lei gave Dro a stack of papers. "This is everything you wanted. Also, Kendrick switched the flight itinerary so that no one will be able to trace Chase."

Dro examined the documents. "Have you heard from our contact at the hospital?"

Lei nodded. "Owens had someone sneak him into the morgue to view the body about an hour ago."

"Apparently Owens took Melissa's death rather hard according to my contact," Pop chimed in. "He insisted on going to view the body. Because Melissa's family has its own money, police are doubling their efforts to find the killer."

"And our hospital employee made sure that there were cameras on Owens when he arrived even though he thought they were turned off," Lei added.

"That's good." Dro leaned back in his chair. "This will all be over soon, then."

Chapter Thirty

NOVEMBER 7, 2011:

KENDRICK HOPPED on the freeway after leaving the airport. He felt antsy, but he couldn't figure out why. Everything was happening too quickly and it felt off to him. He glanced at Alexa, who was staring out the window. "Alexa, what's up? What's on your mind?"

"I don't know. Something just doesn't seem right about this. It's too easy. I mean, Daddy's idea was good. We set Owens up for Melissa's murder and then he goes to jail. But nothing is that easy."

Kendrick arched a brow. "I agree with you, but I trust Pop. He knows Owens so what else can we do?"

She leaned her head against the window. "Nothing. We just let this play out."

He frowned when he spotted a black GMC Envoy driving on his ass. The windows were tented, making it difficult to see who the driver was. "I think we have company." He picked up speed. The car behind them sped up as well, riding the bumper.

Alexa craned her head to look back. "Can they be any less obvious?"

"You have a present in the back."

She climbed into the back seat, while he kept his eyes on the road. In the rear view mirror, he saw her remove the double barrel shotgun from its leather case and load it.

He pressed down on the gas again. "They're not making any sort of move yet, but they will soon."

"Well, I won't move until they do," she said.

He turned and caught her climbing to the third-row seat. Kendrick rolled down the deserted stretch of highway. The car switched lanes and he swerved into the lane in front of them. He gripped the handle of his gun. "Alexa, you're up."

The truck tried to pass on the other side and Kendrick blocked it. He tapped a button on the dashboard. The bottom of the rear window lifted slowly.

ALEXA KNEW the exact moment the occupants of the truck realized that her shotgun was trained on them. The passenger immediately opened fire on them. Kendrick swerved back and forth. Since the truck was outfitted with bullet proof material, her only concern was a stray bullet hitting her through the open window.

Lifting herself up on her knees, she pulled the trigger and blew out the front left tire. The truck swerved. She guessed the driver was trying to keep it on the road. From the front seat, she heard Kendrick curse.

"Alexa," he yelled. "We have more company."

She promptly blasted the front right tire, causing the

truck behind them to flip over and roll off the road into a corn field.

She closed the rear window and hopped into the middle row of seats. Noticing a black car coming their way from the opposite direction, she reached up and pushed the sunroof button. Bullets pinged against the exterior of their truck and she heard Kendrick's gun fire in retaliation. The other car bumped the side of their truck, knocking her back onto the seat.

She regained her footing, stood up through the open sunroof window, and fired on the car. Ducking down, she reloaded the gun then she jumped up and fired again, hitting the back tire. A backseat passenger shot at her. She fired, striking the man. From the passenger seat of the sedan, another guy opened fire on her.

"Shit," she screamed, falling down onto the seat. "Damn-it, I'm hit."

"Alexa," Kendrick shouted from the front seat.

"Fuck!" A sharp pain radiated through her left arm. Bullets continued to hit the truck and she faintly heard Kendrick firing back. She couldn't move her left arm. Extracting her pistol from its holster, she stood up and fired again at the car. The front passenger slumped over. She unloaded the clip at the car, finally hitting the driver. The car flipped over and burst into flames.

Plopping down heavily onto the seat, she shouted, "Let's get out of here."

———

KENDRICK EYED Alexa through the rearview mirror. She tugged her leather jacket off. He tried to focus on the road, but he was concerned. "The first aid kit is in the third row," he shouted.

He saw her reach back and pull the white box from its place. Turning back to the road, he jerked the steering wheel sharply to the left. She moaned from the back seat and he glanced through rear view mirror. She had fallen onto her side.

"Kendrick, keep your eyes on the road," she growled.

When they arrived in the garage at Martinez, Kendrick stopped the car and hopped out. He rushed to the back door and opened it.

Alexa's skin was pale and clammy. She was hit worse than either of them thought. Bright red blood seeped through her shirt and he figured she was hit in the chest. "Alexa, we need to go to the hospital." He placed a hand on her forehead.

She smacked his hand away. "We don't. I'm fine. I'm just hot—and cold." She tried to climb out of the truck, but when her feet hit the ground, she collapsed.

Kendrick caught her before she hit the ground. "Alexa, you're hit worse than you think. You're losing a lot of blood. We need to go to the hospital."

She struggled against him, but his grip was firm. "We can't go to the hospital, Kendrick. It's too dangerous. Just take me in."

A wave of panic descended on him when her legs buckled again. Scooping her up in his arms, he dashed to the private elevator.

———

DRO'S HEART dropped into his stomach as Kendrick burst into the door holding an extremely pale Alexa. "We need help here," he shouted, laying her down on the sofa. "Call a doctor."

Dro raced across the office to Alexa. Dropping to his knees, he picked up her wrist to feel for a pulse.

"What happened to her?" Pop asked.

"Kendrick, where was she hit?" Lei asked.

Dro couldn't form a question if he wanted to. His focus was on Alexa. When he glanced up at Kendrick waiting for the answer, he noticed the other man's eyes were glued to her too. Dro placed his hand under her head. "Alexa? Baby?"

She opened her eyes slightly and coughed. "I'm fine, Dro." Her voice was weak. "I'm just a little lightheaded. Call the doctor so he can patch me up."

"You're not just lightheaded." He wiped a bead of sweat from her brow. She was burning up. "We need to get you to the hospital."

"I can't go to the hospital, Dro," she groaned. "It's not safe. The police have to be alerted for every gunshot wound and we can't afford that right now."

"Do you think I care? I don't care about what's safe." Deciding he wasn't going to argue with her, he picked her up, cradling her in his arms. "Call Dr. Lambert," he ordered Lei. "Tell him to meet us at the hospital."

Lei dialed the doctor, while they rushed to the private elevator. Luckily Chase had designed a second, private garage with an elevator that only went to the floor that housed their private offices. No one was allowed to use that garage or elevator.

"Dro," Alexa argued.

"No," he snapped. "This is not up for discussion. We're going. Now." And they needed to get there soon—before it's too late.

DR. LAMBERT WAS on staff with the hospital and a colleague of Ari's. He had worked with them on many occasions and was willing to bend the rules to help.

Once they arrived at the hospital, they were immediately escorted to a private room by an orderly. Dr. Lambert met them there and went to work on Alexa. Although they were in the hospital, the doctor fudged the medical records. Alexa was admitted with severe pain in the abdomen, suspected internal bleeding. The staff was hand-picked by Dr. Lambert to assist in her care, so that the true nature of her injury would remain hidden.

Dro was worried that she might need surgery. On the way to the hospital, they all had listened as Kendrick explained to them what happened on their return from the airport. Even though Kendrick was relaying the details, Dro barely heard him. His mind was with his wife and how tiny and frail she seemed in his arms—how precious she'd always been to him. He'd always considered her a strong woman, but even the strongest woman could succumb to a bullet.

Lei contacted Chase and told him to stay alert. They weren't worried about the men figuring out where Chase was going because Kendrick had already changed the flight plans. They just wanted him to be aware of the situation.

Pop called one of his contacts to check on the family. He still hadn't disclosed their whereabouts. He also checked for an update on Owens. According to his contact, Owens was questioned by the police after they discovered his pendant in Melissa's hand. They hadn't made an arrest yet.

Kendrick hacked into the police department's computer and found out a warrant was in the works for Owens' mansion. When the warrant was executed, the police would find a few conveniently placed items that belonged to Melissa, including the fur coat she was wearing when she went missing.

Dro paced back and forth in the hallway outside of Alexa's room. It had been hours since they arrived. He couldn't get the image of her limp body out of his mind. He hadn't wanted to say it then, but he saw the life draining from her eyes. It scared him. She wasn't light-headed, she was dying.

Chapter Thirty-One

NOVEMBER 8, 2011, *the hospital*:

DRO SAT at Alexa's bedside, his head on her belly. The bullet punctured a lung and damaged blood vessels, which caused the severe loss of blood. The doctor managed to remove the bullet that was lodged in the lung cavity. Dr. Lambert also ordered a blood transfusion. Now they just had to wait.

"Baby, come on now," he murmured. "Wake up for me. Let me see your beautiful eyes." He willed her eyes to open. There was no movement. He ran an index finger over her hand then gripped it in his and brushed his lips over her palm. "I need you, baby. The kids need you. I told you my life doesn't make sense without you."

Silence.

As a tear dropped from his eye onto her hand, he watched it drizzle down her pale arm. He ran his thumb over the wet streak and placed a tender kiss to the same spot.

He was startled by a hand on his shoulder, but he didn't acknowledge the person who walked into the room.

"Son?" Pop whispered.

Dro rested his head against her belly again.

"Alejandro?" Pop called again.

The fact that Pop addressed him by his full name would normally make him pay attention, but he couldn't bring himself to look at him. Nothing mattered to him now —nobody except his wife. Instead of answering Pop, he whispered to Alexa, "*Despertar, mi amor*. Wake up, baby. I promise I'll take you away from here and make your dreams a reality. I'll do whatever it takes to make you happy."

IN ALL THE years Pop had known Dro, he'd never seen him so desperate or heartbroken. He couldn't help but feel for him. Sure, he had his own issues to deal with. Alexa was his daughter, his beautiful baby girl. The pain they both felt was real, palpable. He squeezed Dro's shoulder. "Son, everything will be okay. You just have to believe."

"*Te quiero, cariño*. I promise to take care of you. *Por favor, abre tus ojos bonitos*," Dro continued. "Please, open your eyes for me."

The raw emotion seeping out of Dro as he begged Alexa to open her eyes got to Pop. "I'll wait outside." Finally giving up on getting through to Dro, he backed away.

Dro talked to Alexa in hushed tones as if Pop wasn't in the room. "*Vivir y morir, cariño*. We promised to live and die together. Our children are waiting for us. I can't do this without you. Wake up. *Despertarse*."

Pop shuffled to the door and turned back to Dro, who

was still whispering to his daughter in a language she loved and understood almost as well as he did.

———————

DRO HEARD the door open again and stopped talking. He studied Alexa's still form. He listened as the footsteps got closer to him.

"Dro, you need to take a break." Lei's voice echoed in the tiny, cold room.

Ignoring Lei, he kept his eyes on his wife. He didn't want to leave her. *What if she wakes up?* He wanted to be the first thing she saw when she regained consciousness.

"We need to talk, Dro," Lei persisted. "And the doctor needs to examine her again."

The door opened again and the light flickered on. "Alejandro, I need to look at her again," Dr. Lambert announced as he stepped in the room.

"Why? Why do you need to look at her again?" Dro could feel his temper rising. *Why can't they just leave him alone?* He wanted to throttle the doctor for interrupting him. He wanted to kill Lei for insisting they talk about business when his wife was lying in a hospital bed. He glared at the doctor. "Can't you see her? She's not moving. She's barely breathing. Why do you need to look at her again?"

Dr. Lambert stepped back. "I need to..." He swallowed visibly. "I need to check her vitals."

"Dro, let the man do his job," Lei said. "We need to talk anyway."

Dro gave Lei a dirty look. "I'm not leaving her. What the hell is wrong with you, Lei?" Glaring at Dr. Lambert, he ordered, "Check her and then leave."

Dro stood by the door while the doctor hurried

through the short exam, jotting notes on a piece of paper. When he was done, the doctor quietly left the room.

Lei sighed, running his hand over his bald head. "Dro, you're not doing Alexa any good by sitting here like this, snapping at her doctors."

Dro ignored Lei and returned to his seat. He clutched her hand and laid his head back down against her stomach.

"Owens has been arrested," Lei updated. "There's a bail hearing set for five o'clock. The prosecutor is going for no bail, but it looks as though the Judge will grant it."

"Handle it, Lei," Dro growled. "Do you need me to hold your hand or something? You know what to do."

"We really should talk about this," Lei insisted.

Dro whirled around to face Lei. "I said handle it."

"I understand you're upset. But you're not the only one who's loves Alexa. She's my sister, in case you forgot." Lei shook his head and left the room.

OUTSIDE THE ROOM, Kendrick, Pop, and Lei were huddled in a corner.

"We're going to have to handle this ourselves," Lei said. "Dro is not going to do anything as long as she's here."

Kendrick bowed his head. "Well, we need to deal with this sooner than later."

Lei raised his arms. "Don't you think I know that?" he hissed. "But Dro isn't budging. He told me to handle it."

"Well, then we will handle it," Pop said simply. "We go forth."

Before they could disperse, Dro opened the door. "Lei, you're right. We need to talk. So, let's talk."

OWENS WAS DENIED bail after Pop placed a call to one of his contacts. The senator was ordered to be transferred to a protected cell in the county jail.

Pop entered the long hallway leading to Owens' cell, after paying off one of the guards.

"What are you doing here?" Clive asked when Pop stopped in front of his cell.

Pop surveyed Owens, choosing not to answer his question. The years hadn't been kind to the Senator. Owens' salt and pepper hair was wiry and unkempt and he looked tired.

Owens pointed away from the cell. "Leiland, you need to leave."

"I was just taking a moment to enjoy watching you behind bars."

Owens smirked. "I won't be here long. Don't worry. What you need to be worried about is who really killed Melissa and framed me for it."

"I don't know what you're talking about," Pop said innocently. "The only thing I know is you abused my sister for years and she finally died from that abuse."

Owens gripped the cell bars. "Now, we both know your sister is not dead," he sneered.

Pop pushed his glasses up. "Do we? As far as I know, my sister's lifeless body was discovered in a park. And I know who made that happen."

Owens snickered and pushed away from the bars. He paced around the cell like a caged animal. "Give it up, Leiland. I know what you did, old friend."

Pop crossed his arms over his chest. "I'm not your friend, Clive."

Owens strolled back to the bars. "Oh, I know. The way

I see it, you're going to wish I was your friend. You are going down, Leiland. I can't wait to see it. As for your sister, I'll save that for when I see her again."

"The only way that will happen is if you die. Trust me, nothing would make me happier."

"You've always been a little too cocky—you and Enrique. But you know where he is, right? Most likely burning in hell. And I believe you'll never truly hurt until you lose something important to you, like your daughter."

"Well, Clive, I know you tried to kill my daughter. But understand this; you will never hurt a hair on her head..." Pop knew he couldn't speak as freely as he wanted at the jail, but that didn't stop him from coming to see Clive. After all these years, he wanted Clive to see his face. He wanted his face to be the last face the senator saw, but that was all in due time. He snickered and stepped back from the cell. "I'll see you in hell first."

"Get out," Owens growled. "You'll regret the day you ever decided to mess with me, Leiland."

"I don't regret anything, Clive." Pop started down the long hallway. "Make sure you sleep with one eye open. You never know what could happen to you in prison."

"Guard," Owens shouted.

Pop smiled, turned, and tipped his head at the livid prisoner. Owens could yell for a guard all he wanted, but no one was coming. He'd paid the guard handsomely to disappear for a couple of hours. He whistled as he inched away from Owens.

OVER THE NEXT FEW HOURS, Alexa remained unconscious. Lei had finally convinced Dro to leave her bedside to eat, but he didn't go too far, only as far as it took to get something to eat from the cafeteria. When he was done, he continued his vigil.

Seeing Alexa, lying so still in her bed, Dro couldn't wait until this was all over—until he could put all of this mess behind them.

The shrill sound of one of the monitors filled the room. Before he could call Kendrick, the hospital room was flooded with medical personnel. Lei and Pop stormed in behind Kendrick. They watched helplessly as the doctors shouted orders and prodded Alexa with medical equipment.

"You all need to wait outside," Dr. Lambert instructed.

"I'm not leaving," Dro said.

"Alejandro, you need to wait outside," the doctor pressed.

"Dro, come on. The doctors have to work on her." Lei grabbed his arm and pulled him toward the door.

Outside of the room, Dro paced back and forth. He was going crazy. The doctors had been in there for thirty minutes and he was worried sick. The hospital door creaked open and Dr. Lambert stepped out of the room. They all surrounded him.

"What's going on?" Lei asked. "Is she okay?"

Dr. Lambert swallowed. "I'm sorry."

"What are you talking about?" Pop bellowed. "What are you sorry for?"

Kendrick cursed. "Right, what are you sorry for?"

"Lambert, what's wrong with my wife?" Dro growled.

"We tried to..." The doctor's voice was grainy. "I'm sorry, Dro. She's gone."

Chapter Thirty-Two

AUGUST 13, 2002:

DRO PEEKED into the hospital room and was greeted by a smiling Alexa. He grinned at her. "Hi, baby."

"Hey." Her voice was scratchy. She cleared her throat.

He looked down at his wife and his newborn baby girl, Alejandra Kyleigh Martinez. Kyleigh was wrapped in a pink blanket and Alexa was holding her against her bosom.

"That's my baby girl?" His eyes filled with tears of joy as he looked at his daughter's plump, red cheeks. He shook his head in awe. He'd never seen anything so precious.

"Yes, it's her."

He bent lower and kissed Alexa gently on her forehead. Then he looked at the tiny Kyleigh and rubbed her full head of jet black hair. "She's so small," he whispered. "So beautiful."

"I know. She's perfect."

"I'm sorry I wasn't here."

"Shhh. No need to be sorry. Kendrick was here.

Although, I'm sure he was scarred for life from the images."

Her soft laugh caressed his ears. "I wanted to be here," he told her, his voice shaky. "You know I did."

"I know you had business. The important thing is you're here now."

He swallowed roughly and reached for his daughter. She placed a squirming Kyleigh in his arms. Kyleigh opened her eyes and he gasped. "She has my eyes."

Alexa beamed. "Yeah, they're beautiful like her Papa's."

He cradled his daughter in his arms and rocked her. "She's so beautiful. I can't believe I'm a father. I'm your Papa," he whispered to Kyleigh. "*Soy su Papá, la nena.*" He picked up Kyleigh's little hand and swept a finger across her soft skin.

"Did you take care of your business?" Alexa asked.

He bounced Kyleigh in his arms. "Everything is taken care of. Lei is outside. He can't wait to see his niece. He's adamant that you named her for him."

"He would think that. I just liked the name." They had decided to name their first born after him, whether it was a boy or a girl. Alejandra meant "defender/helper." Alexa wanted to call her by her middle name, Kyleigh, which was fine with him.

His daughter cooed in his arms and he felt his heart open up. "I just can't believe it." He glanced at Alexa. "Tell me about the birth. How are you? Are you sore?"

"You have no idea. But I'm good. My water broke at noon, and Kendrick just happened to be with me." Alexa had been on bed rest since Paul attacked her. "I'm just glad she is finally here. Getting her here, though, was very painful. It was worse than getting shot."

She scooted over to clear a spot for him. He climbed in

the bed next to her and she nuzzled into his side. "I kind of wanted to shoot the nurse, though," she continued. "She kept telling me to breathe, and I didn't want to breathe. I threatened them with bodily harm if they didn't just pull the baby out. Of course, they wouldn't." She giggled at her own recounting of the story.

He chuckled and kissed her on her forehead. "I was worried. Kendrick called screaming you had gone into labor and threatened to kick my ass for leaving him with you."

Her light, airy laugh filled the room. "He couldn't take it, especially when I broke his finger."

It was his turn to laugh as he imagined Alexa snapping Kendrick's finger. "That's why he had that brace on his finger? That's funny."

"Well, he didn't think it was that funny."

He kissed Kyleigh's forehead. "Thank you, baby."

"What are you thanking me for?"

"For my life. You and Kyleigh are my life. I never thought I would feel like this. I really didn't want to. I can't imagine things any different. I love you so much. Thank you for giving me my life."

She wiped a stray tear that fell from her eyes. "I didn't do anything. I just love you."

"I know. You love me through everything."

She reached out and rubbed Kyleigh's hand. "You do the same for me. But next time I decide to go into labor with your child, be here."

"No doubt."

She rubbed the top of Kyleigh's head. "I want to give her everything I have. And some things I didn't have. I never want to fail her. I never want her to feel fear."

He wrapped his arms around Alexa and held both of his girls in his arms. "I know the feeling." And he did because that's how he felt about her—and now Kyleigh. Dro and his two girls settled into the bed. Eventually, they all fell asleep.

NOVEMBER 20, 2011:

DRO CLOSED his eyes and clenched his fists. He opened his eyes slowly, but it was still there—Alexa's casket.

He sucked in a deep breath and willed himself not to lose it in the middle of the funeral. As the Pastor spoke, none of his words registered, going in one ear and out the other. But that was what he expected anyway. The Pastor, although he'd met her, did not know Alexa. There were certain things the Pastor could say, but he wouldn't be able to capture her spirit. He wouldn't be able to describe her smile or the way her hair fell like waterfalls down her back when she wore it curly. The Pastor wouldn't be able to describe how her voice coated his insides and stilled his fears. Closing his eyes again, he sighed.

Dro never thought this was something he would have to do. He felt his hand being squeezed and looked to his left. Veronica was gripping his hand. Pop flew her, Ari, and Makayla in for the funeral. He didn't want the kids there, though. He couldn't stand seeing their crying faces or swollen eyes. The eulogy seemed to go on for hours and Dro wanted to stand up and order it to be done. He was "The Boss" after all. He could have things his way if he wanted. He knew this needed to be done, though, so others could say goodbye to his wife. His love. They needed closure, even though he just wanted it to be over.

He swallowed as he stared at the picture of Alexa

standing next to the casket. It was a beautiful picture of her, but it still didn't do her justice. She was even more beautiful in person. He longed to see her, to wrap his arms around her tight and never let go. He couldn't.

"Dro, they are wheeling the casket out," Lei whispered in his ear. "We need to go."

Dro rose to his feet and then followed the casket down the long aisle, with Ma on one side and Pop on the other.

At the cemetery, Dro watched as they lowered the casket into the ground and heard the soft cries of the mourners. He felt numb. He saw Chase kneel down by the grave and toss a rose in the hole. Kendrick had chosen to skip the funeral and Dro couldn't blame him. He would have skipped it, if he could have gotten away with it.

Pop stood beside Dro in silence for a few minutes.

"Son, it's time to go," he whispered.

Dro scanned the area. The cemetery had cleared out. The only people still there were those closest to him.

Ari squeezed his hand. "Let's go, big brother."

He nodded and let her lead him away.

In the limo, they sat in silence as the car drove them to their destination. "The plane is ready, Dro," Lei said, closing his cell phone.

"Did you take care of everything else?" Dro asked.

"Everything is good. Are you sure you want to do this?"

Dro peered out of the window. "I need to do this for her and for the kids."

When the limo arrived at the private air strip, the car emptied. Ari and Makayla entered the jet after saying their goodbyes to Veronica and Pop. Chase said his goodbyes next.

Lei kissed his mother's brow. "Bye, Ma." He embraced his father. "Talk to you soon, Pop."

Tears gathered in the corner of Pop's eyes as he patted Lei's back. "Bye, son. Take care. I'll be seeing you." Lei climbed the stairs into the jet.

Dro turned to his in-laws—his real parents. They were there for him more than his own. "I'll be in touch."

Veronica caressed his jaw. "Bye, Dro."

Pop embraced Dro. "Don't worry about things here. I'll take care of everything. Then, I'll see you again."

"I know," Dro said. "You've always taken care of everything, Pop. I can't thank you enough. I love you both. Thank you."

Chapter Thirty-Three

NOVEMBER 21, 2011:

FOR ANYONE curious enough to view their flight plan, it would seem like they were headed to Puerto Rico. Instead, they landed in Alicante, Spain—off Costa Blanca.

Since Kendrick hadn't gone to the funeral, he'd flown to pick up the kids and his wife from Pop's private compound in San Jose. It had surprised all of them when Pop revealed their location. Pop had managed to build a little haven no one knew about. They were all greatly relieved that the children were safe.

The limo pulled into the circular driveway of a massive estate in the mountains. When Kyleigh was born, Pop had secured the property and charged Chase with renovating it. Chase had spent nearly a year and a half in Spain, modifying the land and putting his own special touch on it.

When they exited the limo, the other passengers stood in awe. The house was just one of five on the ten acres of land purchased in the hills of Alicante. For security reasons, Dro bought all of the homes in the vicinity.

Ari had chosen to stay in Dro's villa, in a separate wing. After Alexa died, Ari informed Dro that she was tired of working and was ready to move on. The others pretty much followed suit.

Dro liquidated the Martinez Organization, choosing to leave that part of his life behind. He transferred ownership of Martinez Construction over to Chase. The construction business headquarters were relocated to Spain. Since Chase had practically lived in Spain for over a year, he had already made plenty of contacts and lined up other jobs.

Although Dro sold most of Martinez's holdings, he chose to maintain ownership of the Martinez hotels, including the one in their home town. Over the years, they'd acquired hotels in various places, including Florida, Las Vegas, Brazil, and Madrid. Alexa had a passion for the hotels and insisted he expand that business. Kendrick agreed to help him run the hotels. The hotel in Canada was transferred to Chase and Kendrick's parents, The Wilsons, because that's where they wanted to relocate.

Pop purchased Martinez Security from Dro with the provision that he would change the name of the company. Dro didn't want to be associated with it anymore. Pop also took over the business interests in Puerto Rico, including the casino and resort.

Pop stayed behind to tie up some loose ends for Dro. Then he and Veronica planned to go to their villa in San Jose, even though Dro wanted them to come to Spain. Pop promised to visit as often as possible.

Lei chose to remain on as legal counsel for all the businesses, but he would live in Spain with the others.

Dro stared at the sprawling, luxury villa sitting in front of him. The home was beautiful and, by far, Chase's best work. Dro was impressed by the modern architecture. There were large glass windows and all rooms had views of the sea. There was a small gym, which was attached to an indoor pool on the lower level. There was an infinity pool outdoors as well, and a large garden on the grounds. The beach was less than two miles away from the house, and he was looking forward to taking the children as much as possible. He smiled as they walked through their home. He remembered how he and Alexa dreamed of making love on the beach. After he took a tour of the front of the house, he walked back into the main living area. Most of the windows were retractable and offered an intermingling of indoors and outdoors. They were open now, and he could feel the soft gentle breeze.

He'd just sat down on one of the plush couches in the living area when he heard the children's innocent laughter. He smiled as Ky and Alex bounded toward him. He chuckled as they pummeled into him.

"Papa," they both screamed.

Kendrick was close behind with the other children. "Hey," he said, leaning against the arm of the couch. His hand was clutching his chest, like he was out of breath. "I need to work out. This is the third time they beat me in a race."

Dro greeted Kendrick with a hug. "What's up? You look comfortable."

"I am. Feel that breeze?"

Dro had never seen his friend look this relaxed, especially in light of everything that happened. From the looks of it, Kendrick had already benefitted from the nice, mild weather in Spain. He was dressed in khaki colored linen pants and matching shirt. He wore no shoes.

"How is the family?" Dro asked. "Are they adjusting well?"

"Good, considering everything that happened. They love Spain, though."

"It is beautiful," Dro agreed. "Chase really outdid himself on this."

"I know," Kendrick said. "All of the homes are beautiful."

Dro gazed at his two children. He rubbed Ky's hair and looked into her matching steely eyes. "I missed you, baby girl." He smoothed a hand over Alex's hair. "You too, hijo."

Ky squeezed his waist. "I missed you too, Papa. We were gone for a long time."

"When are we going home?" Alex asked.

He embraced his children again. He never wanted to let them go. "We are home. This is our new home. You like it, don't you?" They bobbed their heads. Dro opted not to explain what happened yet. He needed a moment. "I'm going to put my things in my room and then I'll come down and we can talk, okay?"

The children cheered and then bolted out of the room. They screamed with laughter as Kendrick chased them through the house.

Dro climbed the massive staircase to the second level, which housed the bedrooms. The master suite was situated on the south end of the house.

As he entered the room, he felt the sea breeze whip across his face. The glass windows leading to his private terrace were open, allowing the air to flow through the room.

The huge en suite bathroom was separated from the rest of the room by French doors. The bathroom had a fireplace against the wall and a giant whirlpool tub.

As he took in the ceramic tile on the floors and the

walls, he thought about all the changes that were about the take place.

For once, he was looking forward to living life on his terms without the shadow of Martinez looming behind him.

After he explored the walk-in closets and sitting room attached to the bedroom, he sat down on the edge of the bed and enjoyed the breeze. He rested his elbows on his knees and lowered his head.

He felt the cool tips of small fingers on the nape of his neck, lifted his head, and gazed into the smiling eyes of his wife.

NOVEMBER 8, 2011, Alexa's hospital room:

DRO GLARED AT LEI, his eyes like a raging thunderstorm. "I said handle it." Lei rolled his eyes and left the room quietly.

When Dro turned back to Alexa, her eyes were open. "Why are you being so nasty?" she asked with a scratchy voice.

"You're awake." He picked up a cup of ice water off the table and held it out for her to take a sip.

She coughed lightly. "I told you not to bring me to the hospital."

He kissed her chapped lips and skimmed her face with his hand. "You scared me half to death. The bullet hit a vein. You were bleeding to death."

"Really?" She tried to sit up in the bed and winced in pain.

Dro could hardly believe he was talking to his wife. "I was going out of mind. I was ready to kill everyone."

"I can tell." She coughed again and he gave her another sip of water. "You really should try being a little nicer."

He kissed her again, trailing his fingers across her face. When he backed away, she tried to sit up again. She cursed and held her hand over her chest.

"Maybe you should stop moving, baby?" he suggested. "You're all bandaged up. They had to pull the bullet out, so it's going to be tender. Luckily, Dr. Lambert was able to do the surgery without getting more staff involved."

She grunted as she shifted in the bed. "We need to talk. Go get the others."

He hesitated, wanting to keep her to himself for a little while. He wanted her happy, though, so he walked to the door. As he opened it, he looked at Lei, Pop, and Kendrick. "Lei, you're right. We need to talk. So, let's do it."

The men followed him back into the room.

"Why are y'all looking like someone died?" Alexa asked, covering her mouth as she coughed.

Dro watched a gamut of emotions play across each of their faces.

Pop rushed over to her and held her until she begged for mercy. Once Pop let her go, he moved aside to let Lei and Kendrick greet her.

Kendrick mussed her hair. "Don't you ever do that to me again!"

She smiled at Kendrick. "I promise, which leads me to my point." Glancing at Dro, she reached for his hand. "I'm tired, baby. It's time. I can't do this anymore."

"I know," Dro sighed. "I'm going to make it happen. I've already been working out some things. You're right, Alexa."

He caressed her face and tucked a strand of hair behind her ear. "I'm the boss, and I promised to always make you happy. I understand you want something different for our children. I want the same thing. So, here is the plan."

NOVEMBER 21, 2011, Alicante, Spain:

DRO FACED HIS WIFE. When she opened her mouth to speak, he planted a searing kiss on her lips. Pulling back after a couple of minutes, he drank her in. "I missed you, *novio*."

"I missed you too," she breathed, beaming at him.

Dro had laid out the whole plan to the group that evening in the hospital room. Chase had already gone ahead to the house in Spain to get it ready for them. Dro explained to her that the surest way to make sure she wasn't sucked back into the life was to "kill" her. Of course, the fact that she really did get shot made it easy.

Dro would work with Lei to give Alexa a new identity. To the world, she would be known as Lena Ky Hernandez. They'd had to pull Dr. Lambert into the plan, but he helped them make sure everything worked out in the hospital.

Once Dro had decided to make her disappear, Pop had suggested they use the same drug he used on his sister to knock Alexa out. Kendrick rigged the monitors to go off as if she was in code blue. When they injected her, Dro panicked. The drug would take fifteen to thirty minutes to work. The monitors went off as planned and he immedi-

277

ately wanted to abort the whole thing. But he knew this was the only way.

Dr. Lambert pronounced her dead, and Kendrick whisked her away from the morgue that night. The antidote was administered by Dr. Lambert at a deserted safe house. When Alexa came to, Dro had sighed with relief.

Pop suggested they hold a memorial for her within two weeks which would give Alexa time to heal from her gunshot wound. It would also give her and Kendrick the time they needed to pick up the children from Pop's villa in San Jose and fly to Spain. Dro agreed because he wanted her out of the country before the memorial service.

Time passed by quickly, as he tied up loose ends at Martinez and played the grieving husband. But there was a large part of him that wasn't acting. The thought of Alexa really being in that casket had forced him to go through a real grieving period. It was probably the combination of everything that had happened, along with the fact that he was ending a major part of his life.

When it was time for the funeral, Kendrick was already in Spain and decided not to come back. It was too close to home for him since Alexa had almost died. It was too real to all of them, and because of that, Dro knew he was making the right decision by letting Martinez go.

When everything was said and done, the decision to leave life as he knew it wasn't hard. It was the execution of everything that caused the doubt. There were so many uncertainties, so many things to do.

Fortunately, Owens was no longer a threat. He was found hanging in his cell a couple of days before the memorial. When they received the news, Dro remembered the smirk that crept across Pop's face.

Dro snapped out of his thoughts and stared at Alexa standing before him. She lifted herself up on the tips of her toes to place a kiss on his mouth. He cradled her face in his hands and poured his soul into that kiss. He wanted her. He wanted to make love to his wife. It had been so long.

Just when he started luring her to the bed, there was a soft knock on the door. He reluctantly pulled back from her. "Come in."

Ky and Alex burst into the room. "Papa! Mama!"

The kids ran into both of them. Dro didn't think it could get any better than this. He picked Alex up in his arms. "Hijo, you're getting so big. Both of you are."

Ky squeezed his waist. "Are you happy to see Mama?"

Dro slid his hand up Alexa's back and into her hair. Pulling her closer to him, he grazed his lips against hers. "Very," he murmured against her lips.

Alexa blushed as Dro raked his eyes over her. She was a vision to him, dressed in a white linen, floor length sundress. Her skin was kissed by the Spanish sun, and he noted she dyed her hair a warm brown, which brought out her eyes and her golden skin tone. And the best part? She hadn't straightened her hair. It was just the way he liked it, wavy and flowing down her back. She was glowing. He couldn't help but stare.

"Ugh, Papa," Alex groaned. "You opened your mouth when you kissed Mama. That's gross."

Alexa giggled and Dro let the sound wash over him. He grinned at his son. "You won't think so in a few years."

"*Sí*, Alex," Ky told her little brother. "That's just what adults do when they're in love."

Dro raised his eyebrows. His daughter was growing up so fast. He patted her head affectionately. "Right, that's what adults do. You have a long time before you can do that, Ky."

Alexa smacked Dro's shoulder playfully. "Papa has a

double standard, Ky. He's right, though. You need to wait for the right person first."

"Unlike her Mama," he whispered against her ear. Even after all these years, he still hated the fact that Kendrick gave Alexa her first kiss.

Dro kissed Alexa again and Alex buried his head in his papa's shoulder.

"Stop, Papa! Nasty," Alex screeched.

He barked out a laugh at his son's antics. He ran a thumb over Alexa's plump lips. "Okay okay. Let's go downstairs. I'm sure Mama told you some of the things that are going on. I want to make sure you're both all right with everything. There are going to be some important changes in our lives. Everyone should be downstairs by now and we're going to have a big family dinner." Dro set Alex on the floor and both kids bolted out of the room. He looked at Alexa again. "I love you."

She wrapped her arms around his neck and kissed his chin. "I love you, too."

Epilogue

DECEMBER 2, 2012:

IT WAS the Christmas holiday and everyone was gathering in Spain.

Alexa spent an enormous amount of time getting the house ready. Her parents were flying in from San Jose. Chase and Kendrick's parents were flying in from Canada. Everything had to be perfect.

The weather in Spain during the month of December was mild, but it was too rainy and cold for the children to play outside. So she had a house full of stir crazy children running around.

The hoard of kids traipsed through her living room, screaming at the top of their lungs. Kendrick's kids were there, playing while they went shopping. CJ was there as well. "Go down to the gym, children. You're making me nervous," she yelled, wishing she hadn't given Sara the afternoon off.

A chorus of 'Okays' sounded as the children ran to the

gym on the lower level. She shook her head and smiled to herself. The children had flourished since the move. It wasn't hard for them to catch on in school because they already knew the language. Spanish was a requirement in the Martinez household. And they had each other for a support system. The kids reminded her of Chase, Kendrick, Lei, Dro, Ari, Makayla, and herself while they were growing up. When they were young children, they had promised to always stick by each other. They kept that promise as they grew into adults.

She sighed as she focused on the mounds of Christmas decorations piled up in the living area. There was still much to do around the house. She had managed to talk Dro into helping her put the nine-foot Christmas tree up the night before, but he disappeared when it was time to put all the decorations on it. She reached into the box of ornaments she insisted on bringing with her when they flew to Spain. Dro wanted to start over on everything, but she couldn't bear leaving her special ornaments—ones given to her throughout the years by the people nearest to her heart like her daddy and Dro's mother, Laila. Even Enrique had given her a couple ornaments before he died.

She thought of Laila and Enrique often. She wondered if Laila would've been happy Dro found a way to distance himself from the life that suffocated her. She convinced herself that even Enrique would be proud of the business acumen his son had.

Dro was a totally different person away from the pressures of the Martinez legacy. He didn't have to dress in suits anymore when he went to work at the hotels and he made it a point to spend more time with the children every night. In fact, she was furious with him when he insisted on being the one to teach the children how to swim. He claimed her breaststroke was a little off. Of course, after he took her on a little private walk on the beach, she forgave him. Alexa blushed when she thought about their dream of making love on the beach being realized, not that they'd never made love on a beach before. This time, though, they made love on a beach without guns hiding in the sand next to them.

She had even convinced Dro to go to church with her and the children. She never expected forgiveness for all of her actions, but she still felt a peace when she entered the cathedral with her whole family. She was thankful to God for their new life.

She busied herself putting the ornaments on the tree. "Baby," Dro called. "Baby, come here. I have surprises for you."

Knowing the surprise in store, she bolted into the foyer, and straight into her father's arms. He lifted her up off the ground. "Daddy, I'm so glad you're here."

When Pop set Alexa down, she hurried into her mother's waiting arms. "Ma, I'm so happy to see you. I missed you too."

Veronica embraced her daughter. "I missed you too, baby."

"Ladybug," Pop said, folding Alexa into his arms again. "Fall on my neck again."

"The kids are going to be so excited," Alexa chirped. "I didn't tell them you were coming. I wanted to keep it a surprise." In all the excitement, she hadn't realized there was another person in the house. When she turned her attention to the woman standing next to her father, she gasped. Staring into the older woman's eyes was like looking into a mirror.

Realizing who it was, she wrapped her arms around her aunt, Alexi. They held on to each other, rocking back and forth. Alexa finally pulled away. "I'm so glad to meet you. I wish it was under different circumstances." She had hoped to meet her aunt sooner, but it never worked out. She was happy to hear that Pop moved her from Puerto Rico to his villa in San Jose. They were slowly rebuilding their relationship.

Tears gathered in her aunt's eyes. "I'm so glad to be here. I thank you for everything you did to help me out of my situation. I cannot wait to know you."

Tears welled in Pop's eyes when she turned to him. She took in the sight of her entire family. "Come on in. I want the kids to see you all."

Everything was working out so well for them in Spain. Now she would have everyone dear to her heart with her over the holidays.

The family gathered for dinner that evening, and Alexa couldn't stop smiling. She managed to convince her mother to spend the first part of the year with them. When her daddy found out, he insisted on staying too, along with Alexi.

"Why are you smiling so much?" Dro asked, squeezing her hand.

She leaned forward and placed a kiss against his mouth. "No reason—just happy."

"Is that all?"

"Well, there is something else, but you have to wait."

He traced invisible circles on hand. "You know I hate waiting."

We are sitting here together eating dinner," Kendrick said, interrupting their private talk. "No private conversations, Dro."

Dro tossed a dinner roll at Kendrick. "Mind your own business, Kendrick."

"Well, I guess things really are back to normal," Pop mused, hiding his amusement with a hand over his mouth.

"Not quite," Lei added sadly.

Alexa glanced at her brother and her heart broke for him. Makayla passed away in September. What she thought were bad cramps turned out to be ovarian cancer. Her death came swiftly, and she succumbed only six weeks after the diagnosis.

"Yes, we all miss Makayla." Pop dabbed his eyes with a napkin.

"We do," Ari agreed, placing her hand on top of Lei's.

"She would have been so happy to see everyone here," Lei said softly.

Alexa wiped the tears that had streaked down her face.

When Makayla was in the hospital, she had called Ari to her side and confronted her on her ongoing relationship with Lei. Ari apologized and tried to sooth her by telling her they'd never slept together since he married. Makayla had been shocked because she assumed they were. With tears in her eyes, Makayla begged Ari to take care of their guy because he had always taken care of her. Ari promised her she would.

Alexa watched Lei and Ari. She hated that Makayla's death was the reason they were making strides to be together. Lei took Makayla's death hard, as did everyone else. Although Lei was still in love with Ari, he loved Makayla very much. It was hard for him to live without her because they'd been together for so long. Alexa was sure Makayla would want him to be happy in life. She guessed time would heal the rest.

The table was silent for a couple of minutes, each person lost in their own thoughts.

Alexa cleared her throat after a while, capturing everyone's attention. "Since Kendrick can't stand for there to be secrets, I guess it's okay for everyone to know." Everyone turned their attention to her, and she blushed. She squeezed Dro's hand. "Baby, I'm pregnant."

The color drained from Dro's face, and the table erupted in congratulations. As different members of the family got up from their seats and hugged her, she was amused by the blank look on Dro's face.

Kendrick smacked Dro on the back. "Is '*Jefe*' speechless?"

Chase laughed out loud. "It looks that way."

Everyone laughed as Chase and Kendrick teased Dro. Alexa smiled at the carefree look on Chase's face. He was happy. She guessed it might have something to do with the Spanish woman he'd been seeing over the last couple of months.

"Baby, what's wrong?" she asked Dro.

He seemed to finally snap out of his trance. "You're pregnant?"

"With twins," she joked.

The table erupted into fits of laughter when Dro was rendered speechless again. He glared at everyone around the table and all the laughter and giggles screeched to a halt. He leaned closer to Alexa. "Twins?" His voice cracked.

"*Psych*! It's just one." She burst into fit of giggles. Everyone else followed suit.

Dro frowned. "Good one. Ha Ha. I'll get you." He pointed at her teasingly.

The table roared to life again when Kendrick announced that Kara and he were expecting as well. "And Dro, that means you have to be there for your own wife this time." Kendrick teased.

Dro scowled at him. "You're just the comedian today, aren't you Kendrick? When will you stop bringing that up every time the conversation shifts to babies?"

Kendrick winked at Alexa. "Never. My finger is still crooked because of your wife. I'll never stop bringing it up."

She looked at Dro with a mock sad face. Kendrick had never let Dro live down Kyleigh's birth and Dro's absence, even after Dro was present and accounted for at Alex's birth.

After they all enjoyed dessert and drinks by the fireplace, Dro stood in their bedroom staring at the town below them. She wrapped her arms around his waist from the back. "I still can't get over how beautiful Costa Blanca is at night," she breathed.

He placed her hand over his heart. "It is nice."

"What are you thinking about?"

He turned to her, wrapping his arms around her. "Nothing, just life. I still can't believe you're pregnant."

She nuzzled into him. "Well, we weren't exactly protecting against it." He kissed the top of her head and they swayed back and forth to their own music. She ran her fingernails through his hair.

"Are you happy?" he asked.

"Very. I love it here."

He kissed her forehead, her nose, and then her mouth. She fell into the heated kiss and he pulled her closer to him. "*Te amo*," he whispered against her lips.

She smiled brightly. "I love you too."

She placed her forefinger on his mouth when he leaned down for another kiss.

"What's wrong?" he mumbled. "Are you nauseous or something?"

"I just wanted to tell you something."

"It better not be about a multiple birth. One more is enough."

"I'm sorry about that," she giggled. "You were just so silent. It was very funny."

He smacked her behind playfully. "Not that funny." He nipped her, below her ear.

When his gaze met hers again, she ran her finger down the side of his face. "Dro," she said, getting lost in his stormy eyes. "I love you. Thank you for my life."

THE END

About the Author

L. R. (Elle) Wright is a devoted wife of many years. She is the mother of three children who inspire and motivate her to follow her dreams. In addition to writing, Wright loves to plan events for her friends and family.

Join the Elle Wright Reader Group!

Connect with Elle!
www.ellewright.com
info@ellewright.com

Also by Elle Wright

Edge of Scandal Series

The Forbidden Man

His All Night

Her Kind of Man

All He Wants for Christmas

Once Upon a Bridesmaid Series

Beyond Forever

Jacksons of Ann Arbor

It's Always Been You

Wherever You Are

Because Of You

All For You

Wellspring Series

Touched By You

Enticed By You

Pleasured By You

DECADES: A Journey of African American Romance

Made To Hold You (The 80s)

Distinguished Gentlemen Series

The Closing Bid

Women of Park Manor

Her Little Secret

www.ingramcontent.com/pod-product-compliance
Lightning Source LLC
Chambersburg PA
CBHW030532270626
47155CB00024B/2746